The Lies We Tell

Sicilian Mafia Wars
Book 4

Meaghan Pierce

Pierced Soul Publishing

Editing by Comma Sutra Editorial

Cover Design by Books and Moods

For all the girls who didn't know they could hold their own until they had to

Dear Reader,

Please be aware that *The Lies We Tell* contains content that may be triggering for some. For a list of content warnings, please see the next page.

The Lies We Tell contains the following content: domestic abuse and violence

Prologue

He liked the pain. The rush of sensation through his nerve endings when someone landed a blow or he blocked one or his fist connected with its mark. It reminded him that he was alive when he could be—maybe should be—dead.

Anticipating his opponent, Matteo feinted, avoiding the right hook and spinning so he came up behind the man, wrapping his arm around his neck. The satisfaction of getting the upper hand was intoxicating.

The guy struggled against Matteo's hold, but he tightened his grip. Not enough to cut off the guy's air, but enough to remind him what he was capable of. Matteo nearly smiled when he felt the man's muscles bunch, and before the guy could plow an elbow into his stomach, he twisted his body to the side, dragging them both down to the floor and pinning him to the mat.

The man grinned up at him, lips pulled back over a row of even, white teeth.

"Funny, that doesn't look like boxing."

Both men glanced over at the redhead making her way

across the gym floor, tall and slender in jeans and a light sweater the same color as her bright blue eyes.

"Course not, *deirfiúr bheag*. I'm trying to teach the Italian here some new moves so he can stop being pummeled in the ring."

She stopped next to the raised platform, tongue poked into her cheek, and lifted a brow. "Looks like you're the one being pummeled from where I'm standing, brother."

"Callum likes to be on his back," Matteo said with a grin, pushing to his feet and reaching down to offer Callum a hand up.

"Fuck off," Callum snapped, shoving the extended hand away and rising on his own while she laughed. "You fuck off too, Maeve."

Maeve shook her head, a smile still ghosting the corner of her mouth. "You'll have to forgive my brother, Matteo. He's a sore loser."

"I haven't lost anything," Callum grumbled. "I was going easy on him to prove a point. What did you interrupt us for, then?"

Maeve sobered, looking from Matteo to Callum and back. "There's something I just got notified about I think you should see."

"Okay," Matteo replied, curious about the odd tone in her voice.

"Come down, and I'll show you."

With no further explanation, Maeve disappeared down a narrow hallway that led to a small office. The gym wasn't the main base of operations for Dublin's reigning mob boss, but it was frequented by loyal Quinn soldiers, and Maeve often liked to work there.

Matteo ducked through the ropes and used a towel to wipe his face and chest before tugging his shirt over his head and following the hallway to the office at the end. Maeve was seated behind the desk, fingers flying over the old keyboard.

She'd been trying to talk her grandfather into upgrading the tech across their entire base of operations for at least a year. So far, Eoghan Quinn hadn't been interested enough to make the investment.

Callum followed him inside the office, dwarfing the already small space with his large frame. Maeve continued typing until she found what she was looking for, swiveling in her chair and beckoning Matteo around the side of the desk.

He stepped up behind her, bracing one hand on the edge of the desk and the other on the back of her chair to get a better look at the ancient screen. She'd pulled up a newspaper article, but it wasn't local. It was in Italian.

He'd been teaching her Italian for the better part of two years. Almost as soon as he'd arrived in Dublin to seek a meeting with her grandfather about making deeper connections to the drug trade in western Europe, she'd begged for lessons.

She was a fast learner, and it had been nice growing a little piece of home so far away, even if she couldn't shed her pronounced Irish brogue when she spoke it.

He frowned at the headline. **Local Businessman Commits Suicide**. "You need me to translate?"

She glanced back at him and shook her head, pointing to the name in the first paragraph. "Lorenzo Bianchi. Isn't that your da?"

Matteo froze, gripping the edge of the desk as he quickly scanned the article. *Lorenzo Bianchi found dead in the study of his family villa from a single bullet wound to the head. The owner and CEO of some of Sicily's most popular casinos, he is survived by three sons and a daughter. Funeral services are scheduled for…*

Stumbling back from the desk, Matteo crossed his arms over his chest in an effort to ease the building pressure. The room felt constricting, suffocating, and he glanced at the door over Callum's shoulder.

"What happened?" Callum demanded.

"My father is..." He couldn't bring himself to say the word.

"Dead," Maeve finished for him.

Callum let out a low whistle. "We'll go down to the pub and pour one out. But you'll have to tell me if we're celebrating or mourning."

Matteo snorted. That was the question, wasn't it? Celebrating or mourning. He hadn't exactly left Sicily on good terms with his father. In fact, Lorenzo Bianchi had made it quite clear what he expected of his oldest son before Matteo slammed the door of the only home he'd ever known and never looked back.

He'd defied every expectation his father had ever had of him and then some. He'd done things his father refused to even dream of. The relationships he'd forged all over Europe, the money he'd made, the businesses he owned.

His father had never understood the vision, the end goal. And when Matteo tried to make him see, Lorenzo doubled down on the old ways that were killing them. Now he was dead. And by his own hand, no less. It seemed a cleaner death than the son of a bitch deserved.

"Matteo. Are you all right?" Maeve asked in Italian.

"I'm fine," Matteo replied, switching to English at Callum's annoyed huff. "My father's dead. Good fucking riddance."

"That's it?" Maeve said. "There's nothing else you want to say?"

"There's nothing else to say."

Heart squeezing painfully in his chest, Matteo pushed around Callum and rushed to the end of the hall. He needed fresh air in his lungs, even if it was the chilly, gray, misty air of Dublin and not the bright, fresh air of Palermo.

The pavement of the parking lot was still wet with this morning's rain when he slammed through the doors, but the sun was trying to force weak streams through the thick clouds. Wherever it succeeded, the droplets of water sparkled gold.

He imagined the weather at home. The heat and the sun and the breeze and the crisp smell of the sea. He'd traveled all over the world, and nowhere else on earth could compare to Palermo's sights, sounds, and smells in early summer.

But he'd left that island behind a long time ago. Going back had never felt like an option before. That part of his life was closed. Firmly. His father made sure of that. But now his father was dead. What was really stopping him from going home again?

The door opened behind him, and Matteo heard the scrape of several pairs of shoes across the pavement. Maeve stopped at his left elbow, her head barely coming up to his chest, and Callum stopped at his right. They matched in height, but Callum was easily twice Matteo's size, roped with muscle.

Beyond Callum stood Roarke, one of Eoghan Quinn's most ruthless soldiers. Roarke had always reminded Matteo of Alexei, his father's enforcer. Equally ruthless and expertly skilled with a blade.

"Dead, then," Roarke said in his deep, lilting brogue. "And the coward's way out too."

"Jesus, Roarke," Maeve muttered.

"I'm only saying."

"Well, say less, for fuck's sake." Maeve leaned around Matteo's back to glare at her brother's best friend. "You should go back," she said to Matteo.

"Why?" Matteo asked. "What's left for me there?"

"Everything," Maeve assured him. "Palermo is your birthright. You can't just walk away from it when they need you the most."

"They don't need me. They haven't needed me for seven years. They have my brothers, my father's loyal capos." Matteo took a deep breath at the unexpected ache. "I'm sure my father has already named Domenico as his heir. He was next in line. The natural choice."

"And what about your grand plans for Sicily? For doing what your father never could and making them pay, making them bow to you?"

Matteo scrubbed a hand over his face. "What about them? I was drunk on Jameson and whatever the fuck else you were shoving into my hands that night. It was all bullshit."

"In my experience, being drunk makes the words more true, not less," Roarke said.

"Aye, and you would know," Maeve replied, a bite to her voice. "If you don't go, you'll always wonder," she said to Matteo. "Family is important to you. I can tell by the way you talk about them when we practice."

Matteo cut Maeve a sideways glance. She was entirely too perceptive for her own good.

"That's why I should stay away. The damage is already done. Dom can handle it now."

"What utter fucking bullshit."

Matteo clenched his jaw. "It's not bullshit, Callum. I have that big drug deal closing in Scotland next week and the one in Bruges the week after that. I can't just fuck off to Sicily on a whim and leave them hanging."

"We could be persuaded to handle a little business on your behalf," Callum replied, rolling his eyes. "We do have some experience in the drug trade, as you know."

"If you go back, I'll go with you," Maeve said into the long stretch of silence.

"You'll fucking what?" Roarke demanded.

"I've been talking to Grandda about taking a break before he makes me marry someone."

"Now you're getting married?" Roarke snapped.

"Not yet." Maeve sighed, crossing her arms over her chest. "But he wants me to. Soon. I could hold him off a year at least, spend some much-needed time away from Ireland, if I was helping you settle in and carry out your plans for Sicily."

She looked up at him, her eyes sweeping beyond him to Roarke and her brother before settling back on his face. "He would agree if it was to help you. Let me help you, Matteo."

He had plans for Sicily—to bring down the families that had so often tried and failed to wipe out the Bianchi name. Plans that would be impossible to execute without the support of his brothers and sister. And what reason did Dom, Luca, and Carina have to help him? He'd abandoned them.

But he couldn't say the idea didn't appeal to him. To go back, cut the families that had tried to use them and push them out down to size, and sit on Sicily's throne.

He'd been able to do so much on his own these last few years. The opportunities were limitless with the wealth and power the island of Sicily would provide with all five territories under his control.

It was a move his father had always been too weak and too unambitious to take. But the more he thought about it, the more he wanted to do it, the more he wanted to hear people whisper the Bianchi name with reverence instead of disrespect.

"Did the article say when services were being held?"

Maeve gave him a small smile. "Five days. I guess you better start packing. *Il Signore.*"

Chapter One

8 months later

"He's mine to deal with. And I know you have him."

Matteo looked around at the opulent room decorated in dark greens and browns. It felt out of place in the seaside Sicilian villa. A room more suited to a mountain hunting lodge somewhere in Europe.

He'd been in a room like this before, but in Germany. A sprawling mansion in Hesse that could only be called a castle with its spearing towers and winding gardens. The man who owned it wore tweed jackets with leather elbow patches and smoked a pipe.

To this day, the smell of tobacco reminded Matteo of the ten million euro deal he'd closed for drugs and laundered money. They'd shaken on it, and then Matteo had been invited for dinner with the neighbors. Elegant, old-money families who didn't know the man who'd purchased and restored the crumbling eighteenth-century manor was trafficking drugs and women right under their noses.

"Why would I be hiding one of Gallo's men?" Antonetti replied, pulling Matteo back to the present.

"That is an excellent question. If I had to guess, I'd say it's because he's been helping you poke your nose where it doesn't belong. I don't recall you being such a risk taker before. You surprise me."

Salvatore Antonetti remained reclined in his antique desk chair, but his temper was evident in the way he gripped the leather arms with white knuckles. Antonetti might never admit it, but Matteo was getting to him. The realization made Matteo smile.

Of all the Dons on this island, Antonetti required the most effort to take down. He was very well-connected across Europe. He had a lot of contacts ready and willing to back him against a play for power. But so did Matteo.

He'd spent years building up to this moment. His connections were just as strong, his bank accounts just as full. And he wanted this more than Antonetti wanted to keep him from it.

"Nothing about the way you've handled any of this business on the island has surprised me," Antonetti sneered. "You're as inadequate as your father was."

Matteo's laugh was cold and derisive. "I'm not interested in your opinion of me. I only want Gallo's henchman. He's of no use to you anymore. He'll never be able to help you find whatever it is you've been looking for. No matter how much money you throw at him."

"You say that with such confidence," Antonetti replied. "How do you know I don't have what I need already?"

"Because if you did, you wouldn't have agreed to meet with me."

Antonetti's lip curled back over his teeth. He didn't like being outsmarted and definitely not by a man young enough to be his son. Something that gave Matteo great satisfaction.

"I don't know what's more pathetic. That you think

you've got the upper hand or that you think you can take me down."

Matteo's grin was razor-sharp. "Underestimating me was Gallo's mistake too. I'd hate to see you make the same one. We can do this the easy way or the hard way."

The boy standing next to his father's chair snorted softly, and Matteo swept him with an appraising gaze. Tomaso Antonetti was young, barely nineteen if he was a day, and the only male heir Salvatore had managed to produce. Illegitimately, if the rumors were true. Matteo was inclined to believe they were.

Tomaso's hair was bright blond, whereas Salvatore's was black, aside from the peppering of gray at his temples. The kid had his father's nose and mouth, though. And, apparently, his arrogance.

"Did you have something you wanted to add, boy?" Matteo replied, noting the flash of anger in the kid's eyes.

"My time is too valuable to waste on someone as insignificant as you."

The kid's voice was thin and squeaky, like his balls hadn't dropped yet, and Matteo chuckled. "Then why are you here in this meeting? You probably have schoolwork you should be doing."

Luca barely managed to swallow a laugh, and Matteo fought hard to keep the grin from his lips.

"That's enough," Salvatore barked. "I agreed to this meeting as a sign of good faith, but I won't have you come in here and insult me and mine. I don't—"

"Excuse me, Father. Have you… Oh," a female voice said from behind them.

Tessa, Matteo assumed, unless Antonetti had more illegitimate children running around. He very likely did, but Matteo had never heard of him claiming one of the girls as his own.

Salvatore Antonetti made it clear he had no use for girls except to trade them like chattel.

Something he had attempted to do by agreeing to marry his daughter to the youngest Gallo son. Not that she'd make it to the altar since they'd killed him along with the rest of his family two weeks ago. The papers hadn't hesitated to run with the story that the whole thing was a murder-suicide.

Matteo had spent months slowly chipping away at Gallo Industries. It made perfect sense that with everything he'd built crumbling beneath him, Nero Gallo would shoot every member of his family while they slept and then put a gun to his own temple. The papers didn't need to know it had been Gallo's niece who'd pulled the trigger.

She deserved her revenge just as Matteo deserved to sit on Sicily's throne. And he would, as soon as he got rid of Salvatore Antonetti.

"I'm in the middle of a meeting, Tessa," Antonetti replied, voice dripping with disdain.

Matteo bristled at the tone. It was one he knew all too well from his own father.

"I see that," Tessa replied. Her soft, lyrical voice had an edge of forced sweetness that made Matteo want to grin. "I didn't mean to interrupt. The caterer wanted to know if you had a chance to look over the final menu for the New Year's Eve party."

Antonetti shot Matteo a look, and the scowl deepening his features smoothed into a smug smile. "I haven't yet. Do you have a copy?"

Matteo shared a glance with Luca as Tessa moved into the room behind them. Another power play from Antonetti. Making them sit here and wait while he handled this mundane business for a party they weren't invited to.

Turning back to Antonetti, Matteo's heart stuttered in his chest. Tessa was rounding the edge of the desk and setting a piece of paper in front of her father. Everything he'd ever heard about Antonetti's only daughter had been unkind. Obviously all of those assholes were blind.

She was stunning, with thick black hair hanging in loose waves down to her waist. A waist that flared out into very generous hips, making Matteo's mouth water at the sight of them. The image he was conjuring up of running his hands and then his lips and then his tongue over the curve of her thighs and swell of her hips and stomach made his pulse pound.

She was wearing a pair of loosely tailored slacks and an oversized cable-knit sweater. He wouldn't mind the opportunity to peel it off her and pay homage the curves that were surely underneath. A woman with a body like a goddess deserved to be worshipped like one.

When Matteo caught her eye, she raised a single challenging brow. It only served to make his cock painfully hard.

Antonetti made a few quick notes on the paper and slapped his pen on the desk, drawing Matteo's attention again. He held eye contact while he handed the paper back to Tessa and dismissed her.

"Tessa," he said once she'd reached the door. "Don't interrupt us again."

"Yes, Father."

The door closed with a soft click, and the room was silent again, save for the ticking of the grandfather clock against the far wall.

"My apologies," Antonetti said at last. "Parties have so many moving parts. Where were we?"

"You were explaining to me why you are wasting your time hiding a man who is ultimately useless to you." Matteo cocked his head while Antonetti's jaw tensed. "It's a little odd. Isn't it a little odd, Luca?"

"It's very odd," his brother agreed.

"So tell me," Matteo said, turning to face Antonetti again. "Where is Drago?"

"I'm done playing these games with you," Antonetti snapped. "Drago is under my protection. He works for me now."

"You're making a mistake," Matteo warned.

"The only one making mistakes here is you. And you've been making them since the summer. Since your weak father put a bullet in his brain and you descended on this island like a plague. You should have let your family's name die out. This last gasp for power will not be remembered kindly by history."

"The victors write history. And I think we'll do just fine. I've taken down three of you already. What's one more?"

Antonetti waved a dismissive hand, eyes alight with anger. "You really think these little games you've been playing make you a victor? Romano and Varda were already so weak they were practically asking for it. And Gallo didn't know how to make sure his own mess was cleaned up. I have no such weaknesses. I have nothing but time and money and power."

"Gallo said much the same, and look how he ended up." Flashing a smile and pushing to his feet, Matteo slowly buttoned his suit jacket. "I always get what I want, Salvatore. Deliver Drago to me by Friday at five, or I'll be back to take him by force."

"Are you threatening me?" Antonetti growled, reaching out a hand to stop his son from advancing.

"No. I'm telling you exactly what's coming. You can hand him over now, or you can test my patience and my word. It's up to you."

Neither Antonetti nor any of his men stopped them as they made their way to the door and back through the winding maze of Antonetti's villa. Matteo didn't really want to come all the way back to Syracuse in a few days' time, but he had a mess that needed cleaning up.

"You really think that was wise?" Luca said, matching his pace to their SUV parked at the edge of the driveway. "Telling him we plan to come back here and raid the damn place?"

They had to dodge around white panel vans unloading linens and place settings and crates of Prosecco and wine. When they finally reached their waiting car, Matteo nodded to the driver, who held the door open for him, and climbed into the backseat. He twisted his watch around his wrist while he waited for Luca to get in the opposite side.

"Considering we wouldn't be here at all if you hadn't let Drago slip through your fingers, I hardly think you should be questioning my judgment on how we get him back."

Luca's jaw flexed, and Matteo sighed, rubbing his temple with two fingers. His campaign to take Sicily over the last eight months had mostly gone according to plan, but none of it had felt easy.

The first family to fall, the Romanos, were quick to topple. Granted, he could have handled it better with his sister Carina. But he never seemed to be able to do right by her, even before he left.

Varda fell soon after the Romanos were ushered under the Bianchi banner. He'd butted heads with his brother Dom a few times waging that war, but what the fuck else was new? He and Dom had been at odds their entire life.

Gallo had been the messy, complicated one. His money and political connections had hardly paved the way for an easy takeover. And as much as he was still wary of trusting her, Matteo had to admit they would probably still be taking swipes at Gallo if not for the help of his niece, Sienna.

Still, losing Drago had been a complication he had not appreciated. Especially when the man had proven to be relentless in pursuit of information about Matteo that was none of his damn business. Information Matteo hadn't even shared with his own family.

"Antonetti underestimates us. He always has. I imagine he thinks I'm bluffing," Matteo explained. "Let him find out the hard way I'm not. Was Sienna able to get anywhere with hacking his security system?"

Luca fired off a quick message and tucked his phone into the breast pocket of his suit jacket. "She and Maeve have been working on it all day. She said they should have an update for us by the time we get home."

"Good. If I have to come all the way back to this side of the island again, I don't want to walk away empty-handed."

Chapter Two

Why did everything always seem to go to hell all at once? Nothing in her life ever managed to go right for long. There was always a bump in the road, a complication, a six-foot-two wrench in her goddamn plans.

Her father stood across the room with his hands tucked casually into his pockets but an evil glint in his eye. The one that said her actions had consequences and now the payment had come due.

He took a step forward, and she took one back. She would not cower, but that didn't mean she'd forgotten the last time he stepped into her room uninvited with that look.

Not that he ever really waited for an invitation. Or asked for one. She had no rights here. No privacy, no respect, no expectation of human fucking decency.

Things had at least been marginally better before her mother disappeared. Not that her father had put much effort into finding his missing wife. She remembered only a single visit from the police and a handful of stories in the paper.

That was it. Then everyone just moved on as if Eliana Antonetti had never existed at all.

That was almost eight years ago now. Eight years of being at her father's mercy, of dodging his blows and his temper, of fighting not to let him break her. She didn't know how she'd managed to hold on this long. Sheer stubbornness, no doubt.

"Father, I—"

His gaze snapped to hers, anger sparking in eyes so dark they looked black, and she clamped her mouth shut. He wasn't ready for interruptions. Even though he hadn't said anything for several minutes, she'd spoken without permission. Again.

Normally she wouldn't take quite so much care not to rile him. She'd learned to handle the blows and the barbs. But when he looked at her like that, self-preservation kicked in. That and the memory of the time he broke her ribs.

"I spent a considerable amount of time and money planning your wedding to Dante Gallo. And I spent years before that making matches for you that would benefit us both."

She bit the inside of her cheek to keep from snorting in disagreement. He definitely wouldn't like that. But it was a joke to think he'd ever arranged a single marriage that did anything but benefit him and him alone.

Dante Gallo was the first man her father selected under the age of forty. And he'd had a target on his back.

"Somehow, you managed to run them all into the ground. Even the ones that didn't care about appearances."

He raked her with a look from head to toe, and she fought every instinct she had to shield herself from his disapproving gaze. She'd long since stopped caring what he thought about her body or her weight or the shape of her face or the many other things he delighted in criticizing. But that didn't mean she enjoyed being appraised like a piece of meat.

Her father had been trying to get rid of her since she was

sixteen, making matches with whoever would agree to take her off his hands in exchange for more money or more power or whatever deals he made in his office.

Sometimes she ruined them on purpose—who the fuck wanted to be married to a seventy-year-old man?—and sometimes all she had to do was step into the room.

"And now here we are. Another one ruined."

"You say that like I'm the one who killed him," she mumbled, unable to help herself.

Stumbling back when her father advanced, she tripped over the edge of the carpet and rammed her elbow against the wall. The blinding pain distracted her long enough for her father to get his hand around her throat and shove her against the cool surface.

"I am tired of dealing with you, Tessa. I am just as eager for you to become someone else's problem as I am to get what I need to take down that Bianchi bastard. Which is why you will do what I ask and be the definition of perfect at this party I now have to salvage. And you will do it without complaint. Do you understand me?"

She met his gaze head-on, refusing to cower or bow and scrape. Her stubborn streak really was going to be her undoing. He mistook her silence for agreement, releasing her and taking a step away.

But she was tired. Tired of being seen as a pawn to arrange in whatever way would offer him the most benefit. Tired of being treated as worthless simply because she hadn't been born with a dick swinging between her legs. Tired of being shoved aside for the boy whose mother was just a nameless slut her father had been fucking while her mother miscarried three sons.

"And if I don't?"

He froze in the middle of her bedroom, and her gaze

dropped to his side, where she watched his large hand curl into a fist. "Excuse me?"

His voice was low, deadly. A warning if she'd ever heard one. And still, she couldn't bring herself to back down. What he was asking of her was a death sentence as surely as if he threw her out the window at her back and onto the stone patio below.

"What if I refuse to do as you say, to follow your orders?"

"I wasn't aware I gave you a choice, Tessa."

"I'm not interested in playing your games anymore, Father. Find another chess piece to move."

He spun, his hand connecting with her cheek before she could anticipate the blow. It snapped her head back so violently she crashed into the wall and sagged against it. Something warm and wet trickled down her face, and she swiped at it with her fingertips.

Blood. She stared at it, numb. Still better than broken ribs.

"Watch how you speak to me, you little bitch," her father snarled. "You have been a burden since you drew your first breath, and if you aren't careful, if you continue to disappoint me, I will do what I should have done years ago. Rid myself of you. Permanently."

Tessa laughed then. She couldn't help it. After everything she'd been through in the last eight years, hell, in all twenty-one of them, he thought threatening her with death would motivate her? She was already dead. A shell of a person in a body with a beating heart.

"Kill me then. What's the difference? Now or later. I'm dead either way."

He took a step toward her, pausing when she didn't even flinch and cocking his head to study her. She met his steely stare with her own. If he was going to kill her, she wouldn't make it easy for him. Not that she imagined her father had any qualms about murdering people. Least of all the daughter he'd never wanted.

Swallowing when he reached up to wrap his fingers around her throat, she dug her fingernails into the palms of her hands. She wouldn't give him the satisfaction of emotion. Detached, cold, unfeeling. That's all he would get from her.

His fingers tightened, squeezing until her throat constricted and it became harder and harder to pull in enough air. He watched her with a curious intensity, like he was studying her death, committing it to memory so he could relive it later. The sick fuck.

When her vision dimmed at the edges and her fingers began tingling before going numb one by one, she had to fight against her body's basic survival instinct. He'd enjoy it too much if she fought back. If she was going to die today, she'd do it with some fucking dignity.

"You are committed, aren't you?" her father said, his voice muffled under the sound of the blood rushing through her ears. "I guess you need better motivation."

His grip loosened enough for the feeling to rush back to her hands, the sensation like needles pricking her skin from the inside out. Her throat burned, and the extra oxygen made her sway on her feet.

"If you won't do it for yourself, do it for your mother."

She jerked against his hold, her stomach flip-flopping at the sadistic gleam in his eye. "Why? She's dead."

"Are you absolutely certain about that?"

Of course she was. Wasn't she? If her mother had been alive all this time, she would have reached out. There's no way Eliana would leave her only daughter to suffer at the hands of her husband. She knew what a monster he could be. No. If she was going to stay away this long, it could only be for one reason. She wasn't able to come back.

"I don't believe you."

Salvatore sighed, releasing her throat to reach into his pocket for his phone. She swallowed, wincing at the rawness as his thumb tracked across the screen searching for…whatever the hell he was searching for.

Then he paused, a grin that could almost pass for triumphant if it wasn't stretched so wide, spreading across his lips. He turned the phone in her direction. On it was a photo of a woman staring out through the window of a small villa.

Tessa reached for the phone and then yanked her hand back, looking up at him. He dangled it in front of her, a taunt as much as proof. Taking it from him, she brought the image close to her face.

Using her fingers, she zoomed in on the figure, and her breath caught in the back of her throat. Mama. They had the same thick, dark hair, the same sloped nose, the same high cheekbones. People used to ask if they were sisters rather than mother and daughter.

She'd spent so many years praying for her mother to come home. Down on her knees, rosary clicking between her fingers, asking God and the Virgin Mary and all the saints to bring her mother back safely.

Eventually, she'd given up on the fantasy that her mother would come back or that she was even still alive at all. It was more likely her father had killed her and not batted an eye. He hadn't even pretended to look for her, and two weeks later, he was moving his bastard son into the house. The boy he'd always wanted.

But the timing was too convenient. And if Eliana really was alive, where the hell had she been all this time? Why had she never come back to rescue her daughter from this nightmare?

"How do I know it's really her?"

Salvatore sighed, plucking the phone from her fingers and

clearing the screen. "Your mother didn't want to accept her shortcomings at not producing a living heir. She didn't want to treat my son as her own in this house. When I told her she didn't have a say in the matter, she threatened to take you and leave."

"What did you do?" Tessa breathed, heart hammering in her chest.

He tapped the phone against his palm. "You think I would let her just walk out on me? Let her take you when I needed you to secure a good match with a useful alliance? Of course not. So for the last eight years, she has been my…guest. When she behaves, I even let her go outside."

The idea of her mother being a prisoner all these years made her sick to her stomach. Then again, was it very different from her own captivity? Locked behind the walls of her father's compound unless he felt like letting her out to keep up appearances.

Tilting his head, he pinned her with an expectant look. "Now you have a decision to make. Your defiance or your mother's life. You choose."

She dropped her eyes to her father's phone, capturing her bottom lip between her teeth. He could be lying. Trying to manipulate her into doing his bidding. But if he wasn't. If her mother was alive and Tessa had the power to save her, to be reunited with her… Did she really want to take the chance and refuse?

Of course she didn't.

"And if I choose to do what you say? What happens?"

"When everything is finalized, I'll give your mother back to you." He turned for the door, pausing with his hand on the knob. "But Tessa? If you disappoint me, the only way you'll ever see your mother again is in pieces."

He closed the door quietly behind him, and her legs wobbled as the threat settled in. Gripping the back of the chair in front of the vanity to stay upright, she squeezed her eyes shut. What if she went through with all of this for her father when she could find freedom in death, and he was doing nothing but stringing her along?

But what if he was telling the truth? What if her mother really was alive? Held captive by her father in much the same way Tessa had been these last eight years. Both of them existing in a prison they had no way to escape from.

Either way, she had to know for sure. Which meant she'd do exactly what her father wanted. But she'd hardly be a willing accomplice. Once he moved her into a position he thought would benefit him, she would do everything in her power to beat him at his own game.

And this time, she was going to make sure she came out on top.

Chapter Three

Matteo had the printed pages of the layout of the Antonetti villa spread out on the conference table. Between his assistant's tech skills and Sienna's advanced hacking abilities, the two of them had sourced blueprints from Antonetti's most recent remodel.

Sienna was still working on getting eyes and ears inside the compound by cracking into the surveillance system, but it was advanced, and she wanted to be sure she didn't trip any hidden alarms that would shut them out. Matteo wanted to be sure that didn't happen too.

They still had two days before Antonetti's deadline to deliver Drago to them. Matteo knew he wouldn't. He had men sitting on Antonetti, following him across the Syracuse territory. It was business as usual.

No one had spotted Drago, but that wasn't surprising. The villa was massive, with at least a dozen bedrooms and outbuildings for staff. Antonetti generations were usually much bigger than the meager showings they'd had the last few rounds. Salvatore was one of only three sons, the other two already dead, and he had his own problems fathering a male heir.

It delighted Matteo to know Antonetti had been forced to recognize a bastard. If only because he knew how much it bothered the asshole. The Antonetti name was as old as Bianchi on this island. They'd been allies once, long before Sicily had been swallowed up within Italy's borders.

There'd been some falling out Matteo couldn't remember, though he was sure his father had told him the story once. Hard to say how accurate it was, being filtered through so many generations. In any case, it hardly mattered now. Before the spring, the Antonetti name would be finished for good.

Once Antonetti fell and Matteo had control of his hotels and the ports in his territory, the whole of Sicily would be at his command. Everything he'd set out to achieve would be done. Well, almost everything.

Unifying this Bianchi generation so their children and their children's children would grow up allies instead of adversaries didn't seem to be going as well. No matter how much he accomplished or how well he proved himself, his brothers and sister were eager to push back at every turn.

His singular focus since returning to Sicily had been to claw his way up from the bottom of the heap and put them comfortably on top. They didn't need to know the shit he'd waded through to get them to this place, the favors he had to pull, the people he had to sell his soul to.

He didn't see the need to drag them into the mud he was struggling so hard to get out of himself. When Sicily was his —theirs—maybe he would explain. But not before. What was the point? They just needed to trust him to get them where they wanted to go.

He was already doing it. They only needed to be patient a little while longer. Everything was falling into place.

The heavy glass door opened, and Matteo glanced up to

see Maeve enter, carrying a cup of coffee in one hand and a small bag from his favorite bakery in the other. She set both on the table in front of him and moved to stand at his side.

"It's a pretty straightforward layout. Not as twisted in on itself as I was expecting," she said, gesturing at the wing Antonetti had added on a few years ago. "You figure it out yet?"

"I'm getting there," Matteo replied, picking up the latte and taking a sip. Perfect, as it always was. "Are the others on their way?"

"I just sent out the reminder ping. Dom responded first with his usual chipper greeting."

Matteo sighed. "I'm sorry."

She waved a hand at him. "Don't be. You've met Roarke."

Taking another sip, Matteo chuckled, then sobered. "I wish Antonetti would make this easy on me and just give the fucker up."

"Where's the fun in that?"

Matteo snorted. "What's he going to accomplish by protecting Drago still? He can't really think he'll get the information he wants now that I know he's looking."

"He's probably just trying to buy himself enough time to work another angle. You'll get Drago yourself and cut him off at the knees."

"Yeah," Matteo replied quietly.

He glanced out at the sea of empty cubicles stretching to the elevators. He'd purchased this office building for the express purpose of renting out most of the other floors and using this one as a hub for his newly formed Bianchi Corporation.

The goal was to absorb Gallo Industries under the Bianchi banner and rebuild their reputation within Italy and beyond under new management. Owning the freight company would make transporting drugs to and from the island and across

Europe much easier. A far smoother operation than how he was currently doing business.

Closing drug deals from afar was hardly ideal, and he knew he couldn't lean on Callum and Roarke to cover his ass forever. The plan would come together eventually. The sale of Gallo Industries from Sienna to him would be final in the new year.

Once that was done, he would push ahead with his strategy to weaken and eliminate Antonetti. Then it would be nothing but growth and money and power.

"I hope you didn't start without us," Luca said, pushing into the conference room with Sienna on his heels.

Sienna shot him a tentative smile, and Maeve a genuine one, before following Luca around the opposite side of the table and taking a seat. She set a laptop in front of her and opened the lid.

In the last few weeks, Sienna had gone to a salon and let them work magic to dye her hair back to its natural shade of brown. Matteo had to admit it looked better than the ashy blond she'd shown up on their doorstep with.

"You okay with the two of them?" Matteo asked Maeve under his breath.

Maeve looked at Luca and then Matteo and smiled. "Of course. You kept warning him off me anyway. He probably only would have slept with me out of spite."

"I'm only trying to—"

"I know. You'll start to sound like Callum in a minute. Protecting my virtue and all."

Carina and Alexei pushed in before Matteo could reply, and he spotted Dom winding through the maze of empty cubicles through the glass.

"Can I get anyone anything to drink?" Maeve asked once they were all seated.

When no one spoke, she turned and shot Matteo an

encouraging look and slipped out, leaving them to their business. Matteo didn't have many secrets from Maeve. Truthfully, she knew more about what he'd been up to the last seven years than the people now staring up at him.

She might be like a sister to him, but the relationship there was wholly different. Easier, less encumbered by the sins and failings of his past decisions.

"Well, I don't have all day," Dom said when Matteo paused too long.

Setting his coffee on the table, Matteo picked up the printed pages. He fixed them to the whiteboard behind him with magnets, fitting them together so they made a single large image. Smoothing the corner of the last page, he turned back to the group.

"Any luck on getting into the security systems?"

Sienna shook her head. "Not yet, but I think I'm close. The security looks very similar to my uncle's systems, with a few tweaks and upgrades. If all goes well, I can get in by dinner."

Nodding, Matteo turned to Dom. "I have some ideas on the best way into the compound, but I'm interested in your thoughts."

Dom raised a single brow but chose not to hurl a retort. Progress, since Dom rarely held his tongue about anything. Matteo needed—no, wanted—Dom on his side the most. And not just because Dom was his second in command and the best general they'd had in decades.

Dom had run this family in Matteo's absence. He put up with all the shit from their father Matteo had skipped out on and kept them from going under while their father mismanaged funds and did his best to run the casinos into the ground. And for that, Matteo was eternally grateful. Even if he could never find the words to say it.

"Any idea where he might be hiding Drago?" Dom asked.

"It's hard to say without being able to see inside. The

place is fucking huge. And very ugly. Antonetti seems to enjoy mixing Italian styles with more central European ones."

Luca shuddered dramatically. "Truly hideous."

"If I had to guess, I'd say he's in the main house where someone can keep an eye on him." Matteo tapped the map with his knuckle. "Easier to keep him out of sight that way too."

"I'd feel better if we had eyes in there," Dom said, sweeping a look at Sienna, who nodded. "The place is probably crawling with people. Vendors from that damn party and guards alike. Antonetti might not have a lot of muscle left with his dwindling family stock, but he's rich enough to hire security."

"There was a lot of it when we were there. I'm sure he'll have more on the day of the party," Luca added, tapping the tip of his pen on the closed notebook in front of him.

"Right." Dom narrowed his calculating gaze on the blueprints and tilted his head. "Without being able to see inside and localize the raid, it would have to be a pretty big hit. A risk with extra people there setting up for a big New Year's Eve bash."

"It could wait until—"

"It couldn't," Matteo insisted, ignoring Carina's scowl at the interruption. "Drago is an asset to Antonetti, and I want him eliminated. Sooner rather than later."

"Never mind the fact that he has something on you," Luca said.

"That's inconsequential." The lie rolled smoothly off his tongue. "This is about weakening Antonetti."

Matteo could tell Luca didn't believe him by the way he snorted and shifted in his seat, but that's all the information Matteo was prepared to share with his family today. They didn't need the details of how Drago poking through his international business dealings put too much at risk. They only needed to focus on getting this done.

"Well, I can build a full-scale assault, but it would be better to do it earlier in the morning when the house is mostly empty and people are still sleeping. We have more wiggle room on timing with eyes inside, but earlier will always be better than later."

"I'll get those eyes for you," Sienna assured them. "I'm very close."

Matteo nodded. "Draw them both up," he said to Dom. "We'll execute whichever one we have to."

"Will do. Franco is still visiting for the holidays. I'll ask him to come by the house and patch in Otto over the phone," Dom said of their top two capos.

They all pushed back from the table, pausing in their retreat to the door when Matteo cleared his throat. "Dom, are Emilia and the twins still here?" Matteo asked of Dom's fiancé and the brother and sister she was raising after their mother had been killed.

Dom raised a single brow, crossing his arms over his chest. "They are. I figured we'd stay until after the raid was done. Why? Are you kicking us out?"

"No, no." Matteo waved a hand in the air, rethinking his offer of a family dinner. They'd likely take it the wrong way anyway, and he had work to do. "Of course not. Sienna, I'll expect an update before the end of the day."

Grabbing his coffee and the bakery bag from the table, he breezed out and disappeared into his office. Closing the door behind him, he dropped the bag on the corner of his desk and crossed to the window overlooking Palermo's business district. It was cloudy today, but on a clear day, the view stretched all the way to the sea.

He'd missed this place and these people every single day he'd been away from them. In seven years, he'd never settled anywhere very long until Dublin. And even Dublin, as vibrant and busy as it was, couldn't hold a candle to Italy. To Sicily.

And yet nothing was as he wanted it to be. Some wounds were too deep to be healed. But if he couldn't give them unity, he would give them strength and power. And getting rid of Drago would bring them one step closer.

Chapter Four

She gave up on sleep in the hour just before dawn, sliding out of bed and pulling a robe on over her pajamas. Stuffing her feet into slippers, she crossed to the balcony doors and threw them open to a blast of frigid air.

Her breath fanned out from her lips in white puffs, and goosebumps pebbled her chest and forearms, but any lingering fogginess dissipated. The sky was just beginning to lighten at the horizon, winking out the stars as it faded to shades of purple and then the vast stretch of inky black that curved overhead.

It was the last day of the year. She'd be getting married today if not for the Bianchis taking out the Gallos only a few weeks ago. She felt a sense of relief that she wouldn't have to be a bride today. Like she'd slipped the hangman's noose for the thousandth time.

But her father still meant to use her. There was only one way to truly be free of that. And death was no longer an option. Not until she was reunited with her mother, anyway.

Salvatore Antonetti was up to something. Because the man Matteo Bianchi threatened to come back and retrieve when he visited the other day was currently sleeping in a bedroom just down the hall. He'd been under heavy guard since he showed up on their doorstep weeks ago, demanding to see her father.

She didn't understand the game at play, but she knew she wanted no part of it beyond getting her mother back. If there was a chance her mother was alive, no matter how small, Tessa would do whatever she could to be reunited with her. It was the first ray of hope she'd had in such a long time. It was all she had left.

Turning to go back inside, she shut out the cold and sank onto the edge of her bed. The sky continued to lighten, shifting from purples to pinks and then the faintest line of blue and gold as the sun's rays peeked over the horizon.

The house began to wake on the other side of the door, the soft shuffle of footsteps drifting through the wood. Slipping out of her pajamas, she pulled on the first outfit she'd been instructed to wear today for breakfast. Her father's parties were never just a party. They were spectacles, and she was meant to be on full display.

Of the outfits that had been chosen for her, she liked this one the best. A pair of tailored white pants with a billowy navy blue blouse trimmed in lace. There was jewelry she was supposed to wear with it. More understated than what had been selected for the party, but still expensive enough to show off her father's wealth.

Pulling the velvet pouch from her jewelry box, she eyed the bridal gown hanging at the far end of the closet. It was nothing but mountains of tulle stacked layer after layer until it looked like a cupcake, even without a body in it.

She hated everything about it, from how heavy it was to how constricting the high neckline felt. Maybe she could get away with burning it now that Dante Gallo was dead.

Fastening the simple sapphire studs in her ears and

twining the bracelet around her wrist, she slid her feet into the flat shoes dyed to perfectly match the top and turned off the closet light. Sidestepping the impossibly large dress, she stood before the full-length mirror and studied herself.

She'd need makeup to cover the bruises on her throat that had gone an ugly purple, but if she styled her hair just right, she could hide the cut on her cheek from where her father had backhanded her. It wouldn't be perfect, but she'd had plenty of practice hiding the marks he'd inflicted over the years.

The door handle rattled, startling her, and she moved to open it. The maids usually knocked instead of just trying to get in without an invitation, but it seemed too early for it to be anyone else. She'd only opened it a fraction of an inch before someone shoved at it from the other side, knocking her back into the room so hard she nearly fell.

Drago. Breathing hard and covered in—was that blood?— he barely spared her a glance before immediately turning and putting his full weight against the door. But someone was on the other side of it, forcing it open.

Tessa backed away, quickly rounding the bed to put distance between her and whoever the hell Drago was fighting with. If she were a stupid romantic, she might assume Drago had come in here to protect her from the person trying to kill him right now. But she knew better. He'd hoped for a convenient place to hide. And now he was probably going to get them both killed.

With one last violent shove, Drago flew back from the door, and the man who stalked in after him made her gasp. Matteo Bianchi. He held a knife low at his side, and his shirt sleeve was ripped open, blood oozing down his arm and onto the carpet.

When Matteo caught sight of her across the room, he halted his advance toward Drago, his eyes widening before he glared, lip curling back over his teeth in a snarl. But the look wasn't for her. It was for Drago.

"You ran to a woman's room to get away from me?"

"To protect her," Drago lied, not even bothering to glance in her direction.

"And who's going to protect you from me?"

Matteo lunged for Drago, swiping the blade across his shoulder and making him cry out. They circled each other, Drago's hand pressed to the gash in his shoulder but unable to contain the blood.

Matteo looked cool, determined, focused, but Drago's eyes darted around the room, looking for the cleanest and best escape. Not through the door, Matteo was blocking that exit for both of them, shifting his broad frame to act as a barrier.

She hadn't climbed down the trellis outside her window since she was a little girl. She doubted the aged wood could hold her weight now, not that she wanted to try. Being stabbed to death seemed better than voluntarily jumping off the balcony. Maybe if she asked nicely, Matteo would kill her quickly.

"Fucking do something," Drago snarled at her. "Don't just stand there. Get me something I can use as a weapon."

Matteo looked at her, a wicked grin crossing his lips as he scanned her from head to toe, not a hint of disdain in his gaze. It was all heat and desire and victory, and despite the knife dripping blood in his hand, it made her shiver.

"You think she's going to come to your rescue? Maybe she'll enjoy watching your death as much as I'll enjoy inflicting it."

Seizing on Matteo's momentary distraction with her, Drago surged forward, but Matteo was faster, pivoting in the nick of time and wrapping his arm around Drago's shoulders to hold him in place. When Drago squirmed, Matteo pressed two fingers into Drago's wound, and Drago gritted his teeth and went still.

"This is the price you pay for fucking with me," Matteo said.

Eyes never leaving hers, Matteo brought the knife to the side of Drago's neck and shoved it in to the hilt, pulling it out rapidly. Blood splattered both men as Drago's mouth opened in a silent scream. Matteo released him, and Drago sank to his knees, gripping his neck in a useless attempt to stop the bleeding.

When Drago finally collapsed to the floor in a widening pool of blood, Matteo crouched down to make sure he was dead, wiping off the flat of his blade on the back of Drago's shirt. Bringing his eyes up to meet hers again, he raised a finger to his lips to indicate she should be quiet and moved to the door again, preparing to slip out.

"Wait!"

He stilled with his hand on the knob, looking back at her over his shoulder. Her pulse pounded in her ears as she stared at Drago's lifeless body on the floor. This would be her only opportunity.

"Take me with you," Tessa said, unable to keep the tremor from her voice.

Matteo studied her for a long moment, ignoring the crackling of what sounded like a walkie-talkie in his pocket. He didn't move, didn't speak, just watched her with an intensity that sent an unfamiliar tingle racing down her spine.

"I just killed a man."

"I know. I was there."

At the sound of footsteps in the hall, he eased the door shut and again indicated she should be quiet. When the steps receded, he turned toward her, stepping over Drago's body and crossing the room to stand in front of her.

"Please," she said, voice breaking on the word as his eyes

took her in. His gaze caught on the cut on her cheek, and he took a step closer. "I can't stay here," she added when he still didn't speak. "If you don't take me with you, my father will—"

Eyes darkening, he gripped her chin, tilting her head to study the deep purple bruises on her neck from her father's fingers.

"Is that who gave you these?" he demanded, voice dark and deadly.

She nodded, curious about the way her skin warmed under his touch. She needed to focus. He was her escape, not her savior. Finding her mother was the only thing she cared about.

Releasing her chin, he traced a fingertip over the outline of one of the bruises on her neck, pausing when she swallowed at the contact. Inhaling deeply, he took a step back, and her heart sank. He was going to leave her here at her father's mercy.

"You have thirty seconds to pack a bag, and then I'm leaving."

She stood rooted in place, wondering if he was serious or just waiting for her back to be turned to stab her with the knife still in his hand. As if reading her mind, he flipped the blade closed with a flick of his wrist and slipped it into his pocket.

"Twenty-eight seconds," he said, a smile teasing the corner of his mouth. "Better hurry, *piccola*."

Sucking in a sharp breath, Tessa ducked into the closet, grabbing a bag and shoving clothes into it. She barely registered what she tossed in, taking whatever her hand touched next. Just enough to last her a few days. Assuming she lived that long.

Rifling through her jewelry box, she pulled out her mother's pearl necklace and matching earrings, something that had been passed from mother to oldest daughter for generations. Tucking them safely into the outer pocket of her bag and zipping it shut, she stepped back into the bedroom with it slung over her shoulder.

Matteo reached for it, easing it down her arm and ignoring the way she flinched. He took her hand, squeezing it tight when she tried to wrench it from his grip.

"Down the back stairs at the end of this hallway." He quietly pulled the door open and peeked out. "Across the lawn and through the side gate. There are three SUVs parked there. You'll get in the back of the second one." He looked at her sharply over his shoulder. "You do not stop for anyone's command but mine."

She nodded, breath sawing in and out of her lungs as she followed him out of the bedroom and quickly down the hall. There were more bodies littering the floor outside Drago's room. Clearly the Bianchis made quick work of the men ordered to guard him.

The stairs were empty and quiet, and she wondered if her father even knew his walls had been breached yet. His room was in the wing on the opposite end of the compound, but the alarm should have woken him. It should have woken everyone.

Dew clung to her feet as they raced across the back lawn, keeping to the shadows the climbing sun threw over the grass. Matteo felt along the ivy-covered stone wall for the wrought iron gate she knew was just beyond the red flowers her mother had loved so much.

Finding it, he shoved at the latch, and the gate swung open on creaking hinges. He pulled her through behind him, but she stopped short, her hand falling from his. Over a dozen men stood around the SUVs, all of them imposing and deadly. Most of them covered in blood.

"It's about fucking time," a man who could have been

Matteo's twin said. "What took you so lo—" His brow pinched into a frown when he saw her, and he took a menacing step forward.

Matteo stepped into the man's path, shoving his shoulder. "She's mine," he growled. "And she's coming with us."

The word *mine* whispered across her skin and settled in her chest, and Tessa shook her head to clear it. This whole fucking thing was a means to an end. Her mother. She had to do everything in her power to get her mother back.

"We're not in the habit of bringing back souvenirs," the other man snapped.

"And I'm not in the habit of asking for your permission. Get in the fucking car, Dom."

Dom swept her with a look of disgust before turning back to Matteo and drilling two fingers into Matteo's chest. At least those kinds of looks she could handle.

"Of all the times to think with your fucking dick. I hope you know what you're doing, brother."

"Load up," Matteo said in response. "Tessa?" he called over his shoulder, voice softening. "You remember which car?"

Licking her dry lips, she skirted around both men and scrambled into the backseat of the second SUV. The men in the front seat cast her curious glances—until Matteo climbed in behind her and they retrained their eyes on the road in front of them.

When the car rolled forward, slowly navigating the narrow alleyway, she twisted in her seat to stare back at her father's compound, watching it until they turned onto the busy street and it disappeared.

She'd either done everything exactly right or made the biggest mistake of her life. But there was no going back now. The only way through was forward.

Chapter Five

When the SUVs pulled into the driveway of the Bianchi villa, Matteo stepped out of the second while Dom climbed out of the first, glaring daggers at him. Matteo let Dom handle the quick debrief, shouldering Tessa's bag and motioning for her to follow him.

The house was quiet, even though it was almost eleven. Matteo prayed he could get Tessa safely into a guest room before he had to figure out an explanation for the rash and stupid thing he'd done by taking her. What he really needed was a quiet minute to wonder just what in the fuck he'd been thinking.

Long story short, he hadn't been. Not when faced with her long, thick hair and heart-shaped mouth and boundless curves. He hadn't been thinking anything other than *mine* when she looked at him with those big brown eyes full of fear and curiosity and asked him to rescue her.

Which is why he needed to catch a fucking break and get her hidden away so he could come up with a plausible explanation for why he'd kidnapped his enemy's daughter and brought her into his home. He was so close, almost there.

Turning left at the top of the stairs, he followed the long hallway to the end. As he was about to round the corner, Luca's bedroom door opened to his right.

"Oh," Sienna said, curious eyes darting from Tessa's nervous face to Matteo's. "Did…something…happen?" Sienna wondered.

"Baby girl, who are you tal—" Luca stopped short at the sight of Tessa and Matteo standing in the hallway. "What the hell is she doing here?" he demanded.

Matteo looked down at Tessa, who, to her credit, squared her shoulders in the face of Luca's scowl instead of cowering. It made lust punch through him. That's exactly the kind of fire that got him into this mess, and he needed her to cut that shit out so he could think.

"We'll debrief in the study in ten."

Turning on his heel, Matteo strode away from Luca and Sienna's whispered conversation and rounded the corner leading to his room. There were only two rooms in this area of the house. The primary suite on one side of the hallway, and a large guest bedroom on the other.

Matteo suspected the second, slightly smaller room was for wives who wanted to avoid sharing their husband's bed every night. Not entirely uncommon, but a room his own mother had never really used as far as he knew.

Twisting the knob, Matteo pushed the door in and motioned for Tessa to go ahead of him. Eyes wide, she did a slow turn, studying the space. It was bigger than the bedroom he'd found her in, more than twice the size.

He set her bag down on the floor by the bed and shoved his hand into his pocket, taking a deep breath.

"There's a private bathroom through there." He gestured to a door in the far corner. "And if you need anything, use the intercom to call Giulia. She'll bring you whatever you ask for," he said, indicating the black box on the nightstand.

"You should be comfortable here for…the foreseeable future."

She continued staring at him without speaking, and he had to force himself to step back toward the door instead of closer. If he moved any closer, he'd be able to smell the fresh tropical scent of her shampoo. The same scent that had been driving him crazy on the three-hour drive from Syracuse to Palermo.

"Thank you," she said softly when he reached for the knob.

He gave a curt nod. "I'll be back later."

Stepping into the hallway, he heard the echo of the door closing as he turned the corner. Angry voices drifted from the direction of the study as he jogged down the stairs. They were going to hate this.

Dom must have called Carina and Alexei on the drive home because the entire family was gathered, hands waving madly as they discussed their new unwelcome houseguest. Sienna saw him first, brushing a hand down Luca's back to get his attention, and then slowly the room quieted, all eyes turning to Matteo.

In the silence, Matteo crossed to the desk, leaning against it and crossing his arms over his chest. He wanted to wrap this up quickly. He didn't have the answers they wanted, like why Tessa Antonetti was unpacking in one of the guest rooms and what had possessed him to bring her here in the first place.

Plus, he needed a shower. He was still speckled with Drago's blood.

"All in all, it was a perfectly executed raid," he said.

"You've got to be fucking kidding me." Dom snorted. "At what point in our perfectly timed plan did we add kidnap the enemy's daughter? I must have missed it."

"I made a judgment call," Matteo replied.

"A fucking terrible one," Carina added. "You can't just bring the enemy into our home and expect us to be okay with it."

"You live in Marsala now." Matteo bit back a sigh when Carina narrowed her eyes. Definitely the wrong thing to say. "Antonetti was clearly using his daughter as a punching bag. I wasn't just going to leave her there."

Carina softened, leaning back into Alexei when he wrapped an arm around her shoulders. "That doesn't make her less dangerous. We have no idea where her loyalties lie. Or what Antonetti might do to get her back. She could put the entire family in jeopardy."

"We have everything on the line here," Luca added. "If anyone can bring this whole thing crashing down around us and wipe out every bit of the work we've been doing since the summer, it's Antonetti."

Matteo scrubbed a hand over his face. "I know."

"I thought you were the least likely to think with your dick," Luca said.

Pinching the bridge of his nose, Matteo sighed. If he had a good reason, he might actually give it to them. But he didn't, and really, an explanation wasn't needed anyway. He was the one in charge. He was the one who bore the weight of the burden and responsibility for keeping this family afloat, for taking on their enemies, for building an empire that would last long after they were all dead.

He'd never made a single choice that wasn't in the family's best interest. Not before he left, and not since his return. His decision today might have been impulsive, but it had already been made.

He would do his best to make sure Tessa Antonetti wasn't a problem for them. He wouldn't jeopardize everything he was striving to build, not even for a woman he wanted to spend the rest of his life exploring.

"Like I've been doing every day for the last eight months, I will continue to make sure this family's best interests are at the forefront of every decision I make. Whether you agree with it or not."

"Except for this one," Dom pointed out. "You can't tell me you've thought this one all the way through to the end, Matteo. She could be a fucking spy!"

Matteo nodded. "An idea I've considered."

Granted, one he should have considered much sooner than halfway from Syracuse to Palermo. Like before he said yes to her desperate plea to be rescued.

"That's it? You've considered it?" Luca threw up his hands. "All the shit you've been giving me for the last few weeks about Sienna, as if I somehow betrayed this family because I didn't tell you my contact was related to Gallo. As if that fucking mattered," Luca spat. "And you do this?"

"Luca," Sienna said, voice low and soothing.

"No. You were helping. You never did anything but help us. And we cannot say the same for this girl. Can we?"

"It's not as if I plan on keeping her in my confidence and telling her our strategy."

"She's got fucking ears, Matteo," Carina said with a roll of her eyes.

"Then I guess you'll have to stop complaining about meeting at the office. I'm done discussing it," Matteo said firmly, pushing away from the desk and crossing to the door. "I'm going to wash this blood off me. The staff is preparing a nice dinner for New Year's Eve, and you're all welcome to stay if you choose."

"Emilia and I are leaving with the twins," Dom said. "I prefer my family doesn't break bread with hypocrites and traitors."

Matteo clenched his jaw but kept his expression neutral. "That's your choice."

"Sienna and I are going out," Luca replied, voice tight as he wrapped an arm around Sienna's waist.

"We'll stay." Carina shared a meaningful look with Alexei over her shoulder, who nodded. "Carlotta's cotechino and lentils are my favorite."

Inclining his head, Matteo stepped into the hallway. He made it exactly two paces before the arguing started up again.

"This is hands down the most insane thing he's done so far," Luca said, and Matteo couldn't disagree.

He was not a man who made rash decisions. And taking Tessa was as rash a decision as he'd ever made. They wanted an explanation he couldn't give. He had no idea why he'd said yes to her. She was not his to protect, however much he might want her to be.

And that alone was a thought he certainly shouldn't be having. Whatever her reasons for asking to leave with him, he would find them out and then send her on her way. Somewhere safe if she didn't want to stay in Sicily. He had plenty of contacts she could stay with until she found her footing. Even if the idea of shipping her off to the continent twisted sharply in his gut.

But that was his best option. Hers too, he was sure. He wasn't one for relationships, anyway. And certainly not with the daughter of his enemy. It was too messy, too unpredictable, too...fuck. Why was he even thinking about that? It's not like he was actually going to sleep with her.

She was as off-limits today as she had been when he first saw her in her father's office. All that had changed was the location. Right across the hall from his fucking room. Apparently he was a glutton for punishment.

He reached for his bedroom door, pausing when he heard Tessa's open across the hall. Matteo looked over at her framed in the doorway. She'd pulled her hair back in a high ponytail, exposing the bruises on her neck and the cut on the apple of her cheek, but she was still dressed in the same navy top and white pants she'd been wearing before.

"My father won't care that I'm gone. He's been trying to get rid of me for years." She wrapped her arms tight around her middle when he raised a brow. "Sorry. I didn't mean to eavesdrop, but the discussion was very…spirited."

"What do you want? Why did you ask me to take you?"

She lifted her chin, and his eyes dropped to her throat, to the marks her father had left there.

"I want to help."

His gaze snapped to hers. "Help with what?"

"With taking down my father. Whatever I can give you to help you get rid of him, I will."

He tried to find the lie in her words, but with the way she watched him, her arms wrapped tight around her as if to protect herself, he saw only sincerity.

"Why?"

"Because he's a monster. But…"

"But what?" he prompted when she did nothing more than stare at the wall beside him.

"I need to find my mother."

"I thought…"

There'd been something in the paper about Eliana Antonetti right before Matteo left the island. But his mother had just died, and he was too mired in his own grief then. He couldn't bring the details into focus.

He tried again. "What happened to her?"

"She went missing. I thought she was dead, but now I'm not so sure. I have to be sure." Her eyes were big and round and full of tears. "I'll give you whatever you want if you help me find her."

"I'll take that under consideration," Matteo said and watched her slowly deflate.

She nodded, a small, sad smile curving her lips. "Okay."

Slipping into his room, Matteo leaned back against the door and rubbed the heel of his hands against his eyes. He might really be insane for bringing her here, for wanting a taste of that mouth, for wanting a taste of everything else on her body. But at least now he might have something. A use for her beyond the things he wanted to do to her in the dark.

Maeve was decent at finding people, and if Tessa had actionable intel on her father's dealings and associates, this would be a very beneficial partnership. Hopefully one that would shut his brothers up.

Then once her father was dead and she was reunited with her mother, she could be well on her way to living happily ever after, safe from her father's abusive clutches.

All he had to do was make it through a few weeks of not thinking about her living just across the hall. How hard could it be?

Chapter Six

The cool air sent a chill through her as she stepped out of the shower and reached for a towel. The fogged-up mirror blurred her reflection, which was just as well. Any time she caught sight of herself, all she could see were the ugly bruises on her throat and face.

She wished she'd thought to grab makeup in her mad dash to pack as much as possible in Matteo's thirty seconds. It almost made her grateful she'd been allowed to hide away in her room since she'd arrived yesterday. The angry voices drifting up from downstairs were loud enough without her having to be in the thick of it.

She hadn't seen anyone else besides the maids who brought her a covered tray for dinner and came back this morning to collect it and offer her breakfast. But she wouldn't be able to hide out forever. She imagined Matteo's hospitality would only extend as long as her information proved useful.

Her father didn't exactly make a habit out of keeping her in his confidence, but Tomaso had a big mouth, and occasionally she overheard things. She knew enough to give Matteo something useful. She hoped.

At this point, she didn't care who ended up with control over the island. All she wanted was her mother. And as long as she got what she wanted when everything was said and done, the two of them could fight to the death as far as she was concerned.

Wrapping a second towel around her hair, she quickly dried herself off and crossed to the closet. One of the maids, an older woman with hair going gray whose name Tessa couldn't remember, had insisted on unpacking Tessa's small collection of clothes.

Two pairs of jeans, a handful of tops, and some bras were all she'd managed to stuff into her small bag. She was going to have to go shopping for a few things and figure out who was responsible for laundry.

Hopping into a pair of jeans and tugging an emerald green sweater over her head, she unwrapped her damp hair and dropped the towel into the hamper before turning back for the bathroom and running her fingers through it to get out most of the tangles.

Pulling it back in a quick French braid since she didn't have any hair products, she secured it with a tiny elastic she'd found marooned at the bottom of her purse. After brushing her teeth with the toothbrush and toothpaste someone had left in the bathroom, she turned off the light.

The curtains were pulled back on the wide set of double doors, but the sun was hidden behind thick clouds. Wind rustled the trees lining the edge of the property, and she moved closer when she noticed two figures strolling across the back lawn.

If she stepped out onto the narrow balcony, leaned far over the railing, and looked to her left, she could see the Tyrhennian. The sound of the waves crashing against the base of the cliffs was familiar, but the view was better, all green grass and trees instead of the short outbuildings surrounding her father's compound.

Looking out to her right, she saw four cottages sitting neatly side by side and connected by a winding walkway that led to the kitchen. The figures were moving away from the cottages, on their way to work in the house, she imagined.

The closer they got, the easier it was to recognize the old butler, carefully adjusting the lapels of the black suit he wore. He was a tall, lanky figure, head bent, listening to the woman walking next to him and talking with her hands. She was dressed in a pale gray and white pants suit, and Tessa wondered what exactly her role was. Head housekeeper, maybe.

When the figures disappeared from view, she turned away from the window and studied the room. Her bedroom at home was a closet by comparison, half the size at least, with a small uncomfortable bed that was as old as she was and the same pink and green furniture she'd had as a child. It still looked like the room of a little girl.

But this one was richly decorated in shades of pink and gold with pops of crimson. The four-poster bed was draped in a canopy that reminded her of a fairytale. All it needed was curtains to draw between the posts and shut out the light.

The dresser and vanity matched the bed, antique hand-carved pieces polished to a beautiful shine by the army of maids that were no doubt required to maintain a house this size.

Maids who had probably been tasked with tracking her and reporting all her movements back to Matteo. Just like they did at home. At this point in her life, she'd developed a finely honed skill of knowing when she was being watched. Which is probably why when Matteo went to bed last night, she'd felt him on the other side of the door as clearly as if they'd been standing eye to eye.

It was just her instinct kicking in and not the way she remembered his gaze dragging over her when they were alone in her bedroom back home, Drago's body between them. Those dark brown eyes with a ring of amber around the irises taking her in from across the room. Even the memory of it sent unfamiliar sensations rippling through her.

She hardly knew what to do with the attentions of a man. Especially not one who looked like Matteo. He was tall, over six feet if she had to guess, with broad shoulders and a trim waist under those three-piece suits he liked to wear.

His hair was dark but streaked with gold that looked like he spent a lot of time in the sun. She couldn't picture it, though, the ever-serious Bianchi Don having fun at the beach. Her favorite thing about him might be his beard. Neatly trimmed, it gave him a rugged, dangerous look, along with the scar slashing through his right eyebrow.

The man was mysterious. She was going to have to be careful around him.

A knock sounded on the door, and she glanced at the antique gold clock on the nightstand. The maids had come in before she took a shower. Were they back to let her know she wasn't ever going to be allowed out of her room? Just a prisoner in a different villa.

"Coming," she said, reaching for her phone where she'd tossed it on the end of the bed and heading for the door.

Tugging it open, she stopped short. Matteo's eyes were trained on the phone in his hand, brows drawn together over a serious expression as he read whatever was displeasing him.

She watched him read for a bit longer, his mouth moving rapidly, before clearing her throat to get his attention. Finally, he noticed her standing there, his gaze traveling the length of her body before settling on her face. There was that unfamiliar tingle again. She didn't like how unsettled it made her feel.

"Did you need something?"

Locking his phone with a click, he slid it into his pocket and turned to face her fully. "I need your phone."

Expecting him to ask for information about her father, she was thrown off by his demand. "My phone? Why?"

"As a precaution."

Tessa waited for him to elaborate, but when he didn't, she huffed out an irritated breath. "You're going to have to give me more than that."

Matteo raised a single brow. "I don't have to give you anything. You're a guest in my home, and now I want to make sure you're not going to eat my food and sleep under my roof and stab me in the back."

"Well, then dump me at a hotel or a bus stop or something if you don't want my help then because I'm not giving you my phone so I can be both trapped in this room and at your mercy."

When he took a step forward, she took one back, her chin lifting in defiance as she shoved her phone into the back pocket of her jeans. Matteo's eyes darkened, his gaze dropping to her hips and then snapping back to her face.

She had the distinct impression he wouldn't hesitate to put his hands on her to get what he wanted. She also had the distinct impression she wouldn't mind as much as she maybe should.

"You're not trapped in this room. And I'm not leaving you at a hotel or letting you hop a bus to Christ knows where. You'll get yourself murdered."

"One less problem for you to deal with then."

A muscle in Matteo's jaw twitched, and she had to stop herself from reaching up to run her finger over it.

"Your phone, Tessa."

She took another step back and shook her head. "How am I supposed to find my mother if you take my phone?"

"That's not a concern for me." He paused, watching her in a way that heated her blood and made her stomach twist. "Don't make me ask again."

Tessa crossed her arms over her chest and narrowed her eyes. "Don't talk to me like I'm a child. If I want to deal with that, I'll go back home to Syracuse."

Matteo moved forward so quickly she didn't have time to skirt the bed before she was backed against one of the posts and his body was pressed against hers. He kept his eyes trained on hers as he placed his hands on her hips.

The heat from his fingertips seared through her jeans and into her skin like molten lava. What in the fuck was wrong with her? She could not let her guard down around these people, and here she was, panting like a puppy just because he was touching her.

"You're trying my patience, *piccola*," he said, his voice low, breath warm on her cheek. "I need your phone."

"No," she replied, giving his shoulder a half-hearted shove. "I asked you to take me away from my father. Not keep me prisoner here."

"No one's keeping you prisoner," Matteo assured her, skimming his hands along the curve of her hip, fingertips ducking under the hem of her sweater and sliding it up until he brushed bare skin. "You can leave anytime you want."

"But not with my phone."

"For your own safety."

She tried to shift away, but he held her fast, fingers digging into the soft flesh of her hips in a way that made her cheeks heat—from embarrassment or arousal, she wasn't sure. She'd never been close enough to a man to confuse the two sensations.

"What exactly are you trying to keep me safe from?" Tessa swallowed when his eyes dipped to her lips.

"Yourself. Your father. Retaliation." His voice was deep and husky. "Take your pick."

It happened all at once, the tightening of his fingers on her waist, the press of his body, the tilt of his head as he brought his mouth down against hers, the warm wet sweep of his tongue along her lower lip. It was electricity and heat and need all at once, snapping across her skin and sinking into her center.

Her arms hung limply at her sides. She didn't know quite what to do with them, but he didn't seem to care as long as her mouth remained an eager participant, and she was more than willing as his tongue brushed against hers and drew a moan from low in her throat.

He tasted like black coffee and chocolate, and she'd never tasted a more heavenly combination. Pulling her hips closer, he angled her head back, and took full advantage, sinking deeper into the kiss as his hands traveled around the curve of her ass and squeezed roughly.

Her breath caught in her throat, and the sound urged him on. When he fitted his thigh between her legs, she reached out to grip his forearms to steady herself, and he groaned at the contact, squeezing her ass again harder.

She liked when he did that, and she wanted to figure out how to make him do it again. His hands shifted on her ass, and she rocked against his thigh in response, shivering when another groan slid from his lips.

A noise in the hall startled them both, and a moment later, a maid carrying a silver breakfast tray was standing in the doorway, staring at them with wide eyes. But he didn't jerk away looking guilty like she expected him to. Instead, his hands tightened on her, and he pressed his thigh more firmly against her core, a small smile ghosting his lips when she jerked at the pressure.

"We're almost done here, Giulia. Give us a minute."

The older woman bobbed in a quick curtsy and shut the door behind her, sealing them in. Matteo's gaze skimmed her face and neck, catching on the bruises and frowning.

"How's your throat?"

"Fine," she said, though her voice sounded a little raspy to her own ears.

Not from her injury, though. From the memory of his lips on hers and the rough feel of his beard. She wouldn't mind feeling that on other places on her body. At least three of them came immediately to mind.

"Good."

His fingertips danced across her backside, and just as she thought he'd squeeze it again, he plucked her phone out of her pocket and took a quick step away. Searing rage quickly replaced the chill from his absence.

"You asshole!" She ignored his raised brows, stalking forward to drill a finger into his chest. "I'm not a fucking toy you can use to get what you want and then discard. Give me back my phone!"

"I didn't use you." He slipped her phone into his pants pocket and reached into his jacket. "I wanted to kiss you. I wanted my hands on your ass and my tongue in your mouth. The phone being close enough to grab was merely a bonus I capitalized on."

Tessa snorted and gave his shoulder a rough shove. "Yeah, right. Something tells me you don't do anything without a ten-year plan and a to-do list."

He frowned and took two steps back to put distance between them. The cool, indifferent mask he often wore fitted itself into place, and he held a slim black box out to her.

"What is that?"

"It's a phone," he replied, as if it was obvious. "Take it."

She accepted the box and lifted the lid. It was so new it still had the sheer plastic protector over the screen. "Why did you take my phone if you were just going to give me another one?"

"Because this one"—he patted his pants pocket—"isn't secure." He indicated the box with his chin. "That one is. Your father can't track you or listen in on your calls or whatever the hell he could be doing with this one. You're welcome."

Matteo turned for the door, pausing with his hand on the knob. "You're not a prisoner here, Tessa. You're free to wander and find something to do to amuse yourself. If you need anything, you only need to ask the staff."

He didn't give her a chance to respond, tugging open the door and disappearing through it before she could even form words. Slamming the lid back on the box, Tessa tossed it onto the middle of the bed and ran her fingertips over her lips.

She would not—could not—get too close to Matteo Bianchi. She was here for one thing. To find out what the hell had happened to her mother. And too much was at stake for her to get distracted.

Chapter Seven

Matteo stalked down the stairs and slammed out the side door, following the wide stone path around the corner of the house to the upper garage. He typed in the numeric code and shoved his hands deep in his pockets while he waited for the door to slowly climb the tracks.

He surveyed the cars he'd ordered delivered from the private garage where the Bianchi car collection was stored. His father had added to it in Matteo's absence, but these were still his favorite. Well, these and the newest Ferrari Spider.

Each one was polished to a brilliant shine and kept in perfect working order. They were as beautiful today as they had been the day they rolled off the lot. Grabbing the keys for the Lamborghini out of the lockbox, he tore out of the driveway at a dizzying speed, quickly shifting to punch it on the straight stretch.

Go in, exchange her phone, get out. That was all he'd intended to do. One minute she'd opened her mouth to defy him, and the next, he fused his mouth to hers, desperate for a taste of her.

It wasn't like him to lose control like that. He didn't like that it was apparently so easy to do with Tessa Antonetti. He couldn't afford a distraction. He didn't want one. And yet every time she crossed his mind, it was damn near impossible to get her out again.

The more he saw of her, the more he wanted to see, the more he wanted to take her to a quiet room, lock the door, and not let her out again until they were both sweaty and sated. And those thoughts were precisely why he had committed to never being alone with her.

Except for today's unavoidable errand. Swapping out her phone to ensure her father wasn't spying on them through it had been a compromise Matteo made with Luca early this morning. He didn't think Antonetti had those kinds of tech skills at his disposal, not with Drago dead. But anything was possible, and Matteo could agree it was better to be safe than sorry.

Antonetti hadn't reached out about his missing daughter yet, but he wouldn't be able to get to her at the house. Not physically, anyway. Which only left her devices. Now she had a new device that her father couldn't get to. It was both good for the family and good for her.

The farther away she was from her father's abuse, the better to Matteo's mind. And now Luca could take a break from harping on him about how dangerous and stupid this all was. Besides, she wasn't a prisoner. He'd let her leave anytime she wanted. And if he didn't want that to be anytime soon, he wasn't going to examine that too closely.

He pulled into the underground lot beneath his office building and got out just as his phone signaled. Crossing to the elevator, he swiped his access card against the pad and stepped in when the doors opened with a cheerful ding.

Don't forget about my offer, Tessa's message read.

He sent back a quick noncommittal reply and set his

phone to silent. He really needed to purge her from his thoughts for a while. Work would help. It had always been a welcome distraction.

Reviving an empire on the brink of collapse was a time-consuming undertaking. Not to mention he still had so many irons in the fire across Europe. Maeve had been a huge help in monitoring the international dealings and holdings, but he'd lose her by the spring, and even though she'd already begun to talk of training her replacement, he didn't want to think about it.

She glanced up from her desk stationed outside his office when she heard him approaching and smiled in her easy way. Nothing about his friendship with Maeve had ever been complicated. A nice change of pace when he was constantly faced with the tension between his family.

"You're later than usual."

Matteo pursed his lips and reached into his pocket for Tessa's old phone. "Took a little more persuading than I anticipated to swap out her device."

Maeve's brow shot up. "I hope you were at least nice to her. Don't look at me like that. You're very gruff and unforgiving when you want to be."

"I was very nice," he muttered, passing the phone across the desk. "I want you to destroy this."

"You want any information off it first?"

"Yes."

The guilt rose unexpectedly, but he pushed it back down. He had a responsibility to keep his family safe, even from someone as seemingly harmless as Tessa. A deep dive into her phone would set their fears aside when Maeve found nothing of concern.

"Got it," Maeve said with a nod. "Download and destroy."

"Thank you. Do you have time for a little side project?"

Maeve reached into the bottom drawer of her desk and pulled out a cable, using it to connect the phone to the computer. "What kind of side project?"

"Tessa offered information on her father in exchange for trying to find her mother."

Maeve glanced up at him, brows raised in question. "And you said yes? Interesting."

"I didn't say anything. I doubt she knows much anyway."

"But you're considering it. Very interesting indeed," she murmured when he nodded, ignoring him when he glared at her. "Finding people who might not want to be found is probably something Sienna would be better at. Or faster, at least."

Shaking his head, Matteo stepped around her desk toward his office door. "I don't want the others to know about this yet. I don't need to give Luca more reasons to lecture me over this. So let's keep it between us for now."

"Will do."

"Has Antonetti reached out?"

"No, but the men we have sitting on his house and hotels say he appears to be scrambling to replace the men we killed. So he could be planning a strike."

"He'll find himself disappointed in his results."

"Of course he will. Davide sent over updated numbers for Q4. I put them on your desk along with Luca's reports for the casinos. No new movement on the sale of Gallo Industries," she added before he could ask. "It is only the first of the year, after all. Everyone is still sluggish from the holidays. But as soon as I know something, you'll know something."

"What am I going to do without you?"

She smiled, tapping a few keys to copy the information from one device to the other. "Flounder and drown. Oh, I almost forgot. Callum called last night. He had better luck in Frankfurt than he thought he would. There's an updated list of known Antonetti contacts on top of the stack on your desk."

"No one will ever match you, Maeve."

"I know. You'll be fucked without me."

Chuckling, Matteo let himself into his office and crossed to his desk. He picked up the list of names and quickly scanned it. Most of them he recognized, but a few were unknown. He didn't like not knowing things. He'd have to put calls in to his own contacts in Belgium and Greece and see if the Quinns knew anyone in Spain to get more information on these new additions.

He knew exactly where he wanted to start. Jurgen Braun. Matteo had run in overlapping circles with Braun during his time in Germany. He'd never had occasion to use Braun's services, but the guy was like a Swiss Army knife. Any tool, person, location, vehicle, or equipment you needed for a job, he could get it for you or tell you where to find it.

Braun was a neutral party, unaffiliated with any group or organization. All he cared about was getting paid. And he got paid well for his information and connections.

The guy was richer than anyone had a right to be. He could have retired ten times over by now, but when Matteo had run into him the previous Christmas at a party in Berlin, he'd been working. Bringing together a Russian arms dealer and a French trafficker.

Braun dealt in information and favors, and if he knew Antonetti well, he'd know who might be the best people on Antonetti's list to go after, and who they might not even know about yet.

Matteo wasn't interested in dragging this out. It had been a long eight months already, and he would not have a repeat of the near failure bringing down Gallo Industries had been. As grateful as he was for Sienna's inside knowledge that kept them from flailing around in the dark, her involvement had created a lot of complications too.

Least of which had been letting Drago poke too far into his business and then escape from the Gallo villa during their raid. If not for that mishap forcing him to go to Syracuse and take care of the boy himself, Matteo wouldn't be sleeping across the hall from a woman ten years his junior with a body he couldn't stop thinking about.

Shaking Tessa from his thoughts, he reached for the receiver of his office phone and dialed the number scribbled next to Braun's name. It rang three times and then went to voicemail. Matteo left his name and number and then asked about Braun's selection of wines. Code for a desire to solicit services.

Hanging up, Matteo turned his attention to the rest of his work while he waited. If he were Braun, he'd ask around before returning a call from an unknown entity. Matteo had plenty of friends across Europe who would vouch for him. That was the game. That was the part of all of this his father had never understood.

Power could no longer thrive in the vacuum of Sicily. If they wanted to outlast the zealous politicians hell-bent on eradicating the Mafia and their way of life, they needed to think bigger. They needed to go beyond Italy and establish alliances and understandings across Europe and even into Asia and the Americas.

Matteo had tried to explain this to his father many times before, but Lorenzo had never been interested. *This is the way it's always been done*, his father had said. *If you can't handle it, tell me, and I'll name Dom instead.*

Matteo yanked open the first folder in the stack, gritting his teeth against his father's words in his head. Being replaced by Dom had been his father's favorite threat. Things had really deteriorated between them when that particular threat no longer worked.

Not that it mattered much anymore. Lorenzo was dead, Matteo was in charge, and Dom was busy maintaining their hold on the Varda territory they'd acquired a few months ago. They were each playing to their strengths now, Luca and Carina included. It was nice.

And it was paying off. Profits were up at the casinos. Q4 always did well for them with the holidays, with people either celebrating or avoiding something. The renovations on the high-stakes poker lounges above two of the casinos were already paying for themselves, and Matteo made a note to revisit the discussion with Luca about hosting tournaments to garner more interest.

The strip clubs in the old Romano territory were likewise doing well. In fact, compared to the last two years of data they'd been able to find, money was better than ever, thanks to new girls, better menus, and the themed nights Davide had suggested.

Matteo spent the next hour signing paperwork where Maeve had indicated with little sticky notes, stacking them up for her to take care of on the corner of his desk. Lorenzo had hated this part, the tedium of paperwork and logistics, but Matteo thrived on it.

When everything was in order, it was easier to see where something was lagging. Something his father had been blind to. So much so he'd nearly run the casinos into the ground with his apathy. If Lorenzo hadn't killed himself when he did, there might not have been much of an estate to come back to.

His office door opened, and Matteo looked up, expecting to see Maeve, but it was Luca standing in the doorway instead. He'd only recently started working from the second corner office Matteo had set up for him, usually with Sienna. He had no idea how the two tolerated each other after being together from sunup to sundown seven days a week.

"Maeve said you gave the girl the new phone," Luca said by way of a greeting.

"I did. Maeve is running a full scan."

"She's finished." Luca closed the door behind him and crossed to one of the chairs across from Matteo's desk. "Nothing out of the ordinary. The girl doesn't appear to have many friends or people she communicates with regularly. Either she wiped it before we could get our hands on it, or her life in Syracuse was pretty bleak."

Matteo frowned. He couldn't say why, but he didn't like the idea that she might have been lonely before. "She fought pretty hard to keep it, so I don't think she wiped it."

"Unless she was faking it."

"Fuck's sake, Luca," Matteo said with a roll of his eyes. "You've got her pinned as some kind of criminal mastermind. I confiscated the phone. What else do you want?"

"She doesn't go anywhere without a driver until we know for sure she's not a plant."

"Fine." Matteo had no problem agreeing to that. He didn't like the idea of her going out on her own anyway. "And before you ask, no, I haven't heard from Antonetti about her."

"Don't you find that strange?"

Matteo shrugged. "Not particularly. We both know Antonetti doesn't exactly value women, and she said he wouldn't miss her."

"And you're satisfied with just taking her at her word, I guess."

"Give it a rest, Luca. You've been screaming in my ear about it since I woke up. If Antonetti tries to get to her, I'll handle it. But I would bet money he's more worried about the threat I pose to him to spend much time and effort reclaiming the daughter he loves with his fists."

"You don't know he—"

"A call on line one, *Il Signore*," Maeve's voice said over the intercom. "A Mr. Jurgen Braun about some wine."

Making eye contact with Luca, Matteo accepted the call and put it on speaker. "Mr. Braun, thanks for returning my call."

"I can't say it did not intrigue me. Then I spoke to Franz Schmidt in Frankfurt, and he further piqued my interest."

Matteo glanced at Luca, whose brows had shot up. He'd never mentioned Schmidt by name before. "We've known each other quite a long time. He vouched for me, I hope."

"He did." Static crackled over the line when Braun paused. "What can I help you with, Mr. Bianchi?"

Matteo smiled. "What can you tell me about Salvatore Antonetti?"

Chapter Eight

Pacing the short stretch of space beside the bed, Tessa kept glancing at the clock. Matteo had left his room nearly two hours ago. A week into her stay, she knew he should be coming back right about now. Then he'd spend close to an hour in his room again and emerge dressed in a beautiful suit that fit every inch of him perfectly.

She had no idea what he did in those two hours he was gone, but he hadn't deviated from this routine for seven days in a row. And if she didn't catch him now, he wouldn't be back until dinner. She couldn't wait that long.

A noise on the other side of the door stopped her, and she pressed her ear to the wood. Matteo or a maid? It was impossible to tell. It's not like the man made a lot of noise.

Heart beating wildly in her chest, she yanked the door open, instantly deflating when she saw one of the younger maids on the other side. Matteo's door was closed, but that didn't mean much. It was always closed. And locked.

"Good morning, signorina. Do you mind if I change your sheets and towels?"

Tessa glanced down at the laundry basket in the woman's

hands. Did that mean she'd already changed Matteo's sheets and towels and he was gone? Shit. He'd said she wasn't trapped here, but she still couldn't leave without his permission. Or assistance.

It was unlikely Luca would help her. He very obviously hated her. Despite the fact that they'd spent fewer than ten minutes alone together the entire time she'd known him.

It didn't matter. She didn't require Luca's approval. She had one goal here, and if Matteo wasn't going to take her up on her offer to help, she'd have to do whatever she could to find her mother on her own. Once she had her back, they'd get the fuck out of here. They'd leave Sicily. Hell, they could leave Italy altogether. Tessa wouldn't miss it. There hadn't been anything here for her since her mother disappeared.

Then Matteo and her father could battle it out until one of them killed the other for whatever shred of power helped them sleep at night. She wanted no part of that either. They could have the island. All she wanted was her mother and some fucking peace.

"Signorina?"

The maid's soft voice snapped Tessa out of her thoughts. "I'm sorry. Yes. I'll get out of your way..." She tried and failed to recall the woman's name. She was much better with faces.

"Cinzia, signorina," the woman replied with a polite smile.

"Cinzia," Tessa repeated. "Thank you."

Stepping back so the maid could enter, Tessa grabbed her phone off the nightstand and left the woman to her work. She was two paces down the hall when she heard Matteo's door open behind her. Forcing herself not to turn around but slowing her steps, she waited to see if Matteo would catch up with her.

He'd done his best to avoid her since the kissing incident.

Or maybe more accurately, he hadn't bothered to deviate from his normal routine that kept him out of the house more than in it.

Which was fine. There couldn't be a repeat of that damn kiss. Even if she couldn't stop thinking about it.

"Good morning," Matteo said, appearing at her elbow.

His voice was rich and deep, and it wrapped around her like a caress. She hated that about him. It made her think of the way his hands felt on her hips, of how he hadn't recoiled at the feel of her softness the way she expected him to.

"Morning. You're usually gone before I go in search of breakfast."

He checked the time on his watch, adjusting it before dropping his arm again. "You must be early then. I'm right on schedule."

He matched her pace down the hall instead of walking ahead of her, a courtesy she'd never experienced from a man before. She didn't know what to make of it. And it annoyed her that she wanted to make anything of it at all. She really needed to get a fucking grip.

Another maid met them at the bottom of the stairs with Matteo's travel mug and a *bombolone*—her favorite. Hopefully there were more where that came from. And filled with blueberry jam. When Matteo turned toward the front of the house instead of the direction of the dining room, the maid followed, and so did Tessa.

She watched him shrug into a beautiful navy cashmere coat, adjusting the collar and the cuffs of his suit. Once he was buttoned up, the woman handed both the mug and the *bombolone* to Matteo, dipped into a neat curtsy, and left.

Before he could stick the donut into his mouth to open the door, she reached around him and pulled it open. He nodded his thanks and stepped over the threshold.

"I was wondering if I could ask you for a favor," she said

in a rush.

He did a slow turn, head tilted. "A favor?"

"I've been here for a week."

"Yes."

"And you still haven't asked me for any information." That wasn't what she meant to say, but the words had already tumbled free, and she couldn't take them back.

His jaw tightened, but he nodded. "Correct."

"Why not?"

"I'm not sure you could give me anything I don't already know."

Tessa crossed her arms over her chest, forcing herself not to react to his snide tone. She needed his help today; playing nice was the best way to get it.

"Why don't you try me?"

He sighed, taking a sip of his coffee as he considered. "Fine, then. Tell me."

"My father has contacts in Spain. A drug supplier. I don't think their relationship is going so well."

"What makes you say that?"

"I heard him arguing with them over the phone right before Christmas. Something about my father not being pleased with the quality and wanting a discount."

Nodding slowly, Matteo took another sip of his coffee. "All right. I'll take that into consideration. Now what about your favor?"

She couldn't tell if he believed her, but that would have to be enough for now.

"Right. I need a ride or a car or something."

His eyes narrowed, and he tilted his head. "Why?"

"Because I've been here almost a week, and I'm running out of pretty much everything I found in the bathroom cabinets. Shampoo and conditioner and lotion. And call me vain, but I'd like to pick up some makeup too. Girl stuff."

"Sure."

"It won't take long."

He nodded again, holding out his coffee and donut to her until she took them. He reached into the inside pocket of his suit and pulled out a wallet. With barely a glance, he slipped out several bills and folded them. Taking the coffee back, he pressed the bills into her hand, then took the donut in the other.

"I'll call a driver for you. Is an hour good?"

"A driver?" Her eyes darted to the garage. "Isn't there an old car I can borrow or something?"

He met her gaze with a level stare, his face expressionless. "No. I'd feel better if you had a driver. Until we're certain your father isn't going to come after you."

"I told you he won't." She wrapped her arms around her waist and squeezed.

"I know. Go back inside. It's freezing," Matteo said. It was a command, but a gentle one. "I'll send someone over to drive you." He took two steps backward toward the garage. "One hour."

Once he'd gone, she counted out the bills. Three hundred euros. She couldn't remember if she'd ever been allowed to hold that much money before. Not because her father didn't have it to spare. But because he didn't trust her with it. He didn't trust her with much of anything.

True to Matteo's word, an SUV showed up an hour later. A short man with close-cropped blond hair swung down out of the driver's seat and opened the door for her. When she requested a specific store, he didn't bat an eye, expertly navigating through traffic and pulling into a parking spot within view of the front door of the shop.

He got out to open her door and tailed her inside. He didn't speak, which was fine if a little awkward. She didn't want to have a conversation about toiletries with a strange man anyway. But she didn't want him following her around all afternoon either.

Up ahead of her, a man with dark hair in a thick wool coat ducked into an aisle, and she had an idea. Hopefully this would work and buy her at least a few minutes. Adding body wash to her basket, she turned for the next aisle. Feminine products.

Once her guard realized where he was standing, his face went beet red, and he cleared his throat. She sent him an apologetic smile.

"This is the last thing I need."

He glanced around at the array of colorful boxes, and his cheeks darkened to an even deeper shade of crimson. "I'll just meet you at the front, then."

"Okay. I won't be long."

He nodded once and then raced up to the front of the shop like the tampons might actually chase him down if he wasn't fast enough. Tessa shook her head. Men were ridiculous.

"Fucking finally. You're thirty minutes late. And you didn't answer my text."

Tessa steeled herself before facing the voice at her back. "They took my phone and gave me a new one the other day. I didn't want to risk texting."

"Doesn't explain why you're late," her father grumbled. "You know how I hate it when you break the rules." He reached up and gripped her hair, but didn't tug. If anyone walked by and saw them, they might think he had his hand on the back of her neck. "What do you have for me?"

Tessa reached into her pocket and pulled out a crumpled-up slip of paper. Handing it to her father, she held her breath, hoping it was the kind of information he needed. By the way his fingers tightened in her hair, she assumed it wasn't.

"I already know about this shit, Tessa." He shoved the

paper roughly into his jeans and yanked her down to the end of the aisle and around the side, hiding them from view of the main aisle. "You're not there on vacation. If you want to see your mother again, you need to do better than that."

"It's not as if they trust me and tell me all their secrets. I had to dig that out of a trash can. Besides, they rarely talk business at the house. At least not when I'm around."

"Sounds like you need to get closer, then," her father said through gritted teeth. "I saw how Matteo looked at you that day in my office. He wants you."

"He doesn't. I can promise you that."

"Don't lie to me, girl. The Bianchi Don is not an indulgent man. He agreed to take you for a reason, and that reason is dangling between his legs."

"We haven't spent more than a handful of minutes at a time alone together in five days. What do you suggest I do?"

Tessa bit the inside of her cheek to keep from crying out when her father's grip tightened enough to have tears springing to her eyes.

"I suggest you get on your knees and give him a good suck," he whispered against her ear, voice low and dangerous. "I told you what happens if you disappoint or defy me, Tessa. Do you remember?"

She squeezed her eyes shut and tried to force the mental image from her mind. "You'll send me my mother in pieces."

"That's right." He released her hair so suddenly she swayed forward, catching herself on the edge of a display. "Give me your phone."

Tessa dug it out of her purse and laid it in his palm. He created a new contact—Luna, the name of her old dog—and typed in a number she didn't recognize.

"That's the number for a burner phone. I'll be in touch." He turned to go and then stopped, moving to stand in front of her again and crowding her against the shelves. "Don't do anything stupid, Tessa. The only way for you to see your mother again is if I give her back to you. If I find out you're lying to me—about anything—I'll kill you both."

Tessa stood there trembling long after he was gone. She didn't want to do this. She didn't want to spy on the Bianchis or be stuck in the middle of this war. A war that would never benefit someone like her. What did she have to gain if her father won? If Matteo did? Nothing.

What she wanted was her mother back in one piece and to get off this fucking island for good. She'd seduce Matteo to get the information her father was so desperate for. She'd do anything to free her mother from her father's clutches. Free them both.

But she didn't trust her father either, and it would be just as easy to feed Matteo what she knew about Antonetti business dealings too. She'd given him something this morning; now all she had to do was make sure he followed through on his end and actually searched for her mother.

Running a hand through her hair to smooth it, she headed up to the front of the store before her guard came looking for her and set her purchases down on the belt. He walked over and surveyed the items as they were rung up, brows drawing together when he noticed she hadn't grabbed any tampons.

"They didn't have the size I needed," she said casually, silencing his question and watching his face redden again.

He gave a curt nod and made no other moves to speak, following her out to the car and helping her and her bags into the backseat. Once they were in motion, Tessa slumped against the window with a sigh.

She needed to stomp out whatever shred of conscience she had left. This wasn't about right or wrong, good or bad, anymore. This was about survival. And she intended to make it out of this alive.

Chapter Nine

Drawing the blanket tighter around her shoulders, Tessa tucked her feet underneath her and scooted closer to the ring of warmth emanating from the outdoor heater. Enjoying the fresh air until the cold became too much and chased her back inside again was often the best part of her day. She didn't think anyone noticed she snuck onto the balcony off the second-story library overlooking the sea every afternoon.

But someone must have because today, the heater and a stack of thick blankets had been here waiting for her. If it was Matteo—and she suspected it was—it was the most he'd acknowledged her presence since she'd asked for a ride, save for the family's stilted and awkward conversation over dinner every night.

She'd tried everything she could think of to entice Matteo into kissing her again. A short list, given her limited experience with men. She didn't think he'd take well to her dropping to her knees and reaching for his zipper, so instead she'd acted shy and sweet and innocent. A regular damsel in distress. He seemed to like those. Why else would he agree to rescue her from her father's clutches?

Not that he'd done all that much rescuing. Her father still had her by the throat. He'd been texting multiple times a day, asking how she was. His code for updates. When she had news, she was supposed to ask if he wanted to grab coffee. But there was no news to share.

Matteo clearly thought his kiss in her bedroom had been a mistake. Or it really was just a ploy to get close enough to grab her phone. She hated how much that idea stung, but it wouldn't exactly surprise her. He struck her as the kind of man who did whatever needed doing to get what he wanted.

On that, at least, they were the same. She needed information, and since pawing through the trash in Matteo's office on the rare occasion she'd been able to manage it had yielded nothing, she had to up her game.

Maybe she needed to play up their age difference. He was at least ten years older than she was. Didn't men like being hit on by younger women? The ancient guys her father had always tried to marry her off to seemed to enjoy the idea of being with a woman young enough to be their daughter. Or granddaughter.

She grimaced at the memory of standing in front of men two and three times her age while they appraised her, talking about her as if she was a piece of property and not a person.

Truthfully, she'd be happy to avoid the company of men altogether until the end of time. They never seemed to add much to her life except fear, anxiety, and a sense of being trapped.

But that wasn't an option. At least not yet. Matteo had seemingly ignored her information about her father's business in Spain and refused to give her the slightest indication he was looking for her mother.

Which meant she needed to figure out a way to get Matteo

alone long enough to kiss him again. And hopefully more. Two things that were impossible to do when she only saw him at dinner, sitting around the dining room table with Luca and Sienna in silence.

He still watched her in that intense and searching way he had. In the nearly two weeks since her arrival, he'd never stopped watching her. But now she was beginning to wonder if she'd miscalculated the reason.

Maybe he watched her because he didn't trust her and not because he wanted her. Maybe she'd overplayed her hand by offering to help take her father down, and now he was determined to keep her at arm's length. If that was the case, she'd just have to do her best. No point wasting time being upset about it. She had too many other things to worry about.

The distant growl of an engine caught her attention, and from her spot, she had the perfect vantage point to see a flash of red through the trees lining the driveway. Matteo sometimes drove a bright red Alfa Romeo.

Checking the time on her phone, she ignored yet another request for an update from her father and let herself in from the balcony. She flexed her fingers and toes in the warmth of the house as she made her way down the winding stairs.

Usually when Matteo came home this early, he locked himself in his study until dinner. She wanted to catch him first. Finally get some forward momentum on this whole damn thing so she could be one step closer to washing her hands of it.

The front door was closing just as she hit the bottom stair. She couldn't have timed it better if she tried. When Matteo spotted her, he faltered, and she smiled.

"You're home early," she said, twirling a strand of hair around her finger, satisfied when his eyes tracked her movements.

He seemed to like her hair, and she couldn't deny she

wanted to feel his fingers sliding through it. She wouldn't mind letting him erase all the memories of the way her father liked to use it as a chain to...no. Dark thoughts like that wouldn't help her coax Matteo into kissing her again.

"Yes, I am."

She expected him to move past her down the hall, but when he remained rooted in place, she tried again. "Thank you. For the heater. It was very sweet."

He glanced up at the ceiling and then back at her face. "I'm glad you like it."

She stepped down from the last step and moved closer to him. When her lips parted, trying to think of what to say, his eyes dropped to them. Maybe he wanted her a little more than she gave him credit for.

He leaned in slightly, and she shifted her body closer still. She didn't want him to have any doubts about whether she wanted him to kiss her.

At the moment when he might have dipped his head to taste her lips, he suddenly straightened and moved quickly around her and down the hall. The man was going to drive her to fucking drink. His level of self-control might be impressive if it wasn't constantly in the way of getting what she needed from him.

Unwilling to give up so easily this time, Tessa spun on her heel and jogged to catch up with him. She followed him soundlessly into his office, pausing by the door and watching him cross to the desk.

The room was too big to be called cozy, but it still felt intimate. Floor-to-ceiling bookshelves lined the back wall, and a ladder hooked to a long metal bar gave access to the top shelves. She wondered how many of the books were useful and how many were just put there to look nice.

A small table sat in front of the shelves. A place to read or study if you were looking for something in particular and needed a spot to spread out. Between the table and the door was a large seating area with two couches in dark brown leather facing each other and chairs on either end. A perfect spot for meetings or stretching out to watch the TV mounted on the far wall.

The antique desk sat to the left between two windows and faced the room, with a large painting taking up most of the wall behind it. She wasn't one for art, really, but something about this one seemed familiar, homey even.

Trees with thin, twisted trunks speared up out of dense bushes, obstructing the view of a little village and the sea beyond. The colors were rich and vibrant, but the image itself was slightly distorted, like the artist had been peering through fogged glass when they painted the scene.

Matteo tracked her eyes to the painting and raised a brow. "Big fan of Monet?"

"I didn't know it was Monet. I thought he only painted pictures of fields and flowers."

Glancing over his shoulder, Matteo smiled. "That's what he's best known for. This is one from a collection he did while visiting Italy in the late 1800s."

She took a step into the room to examine it more closely. Maybe that's why it felt so familiar. Not because she'd seen the painting before, but because the tableau spoke to her. She'd happily go wherever she needed to go in order to survive after this, but she doubted anywhere else in the world would ever compare to Italy or its beaches.

"What's it called?"

"*Bordighera.*"

"Like the town?"

He smiled. "Like the town. He painted there for months after intending to stay for only a few weeks. Created something like forty works."

"You like art?"

Matteo shrugged. "A hobby. Did you need something?" He indicated the stack of folders he'd carried in with him from the car. "I have a lot of work to do."

Damn it. She'd meant to come in here and get him to kiss her, and instead they'd talked about art she didn't care about. She needed a change of venue. Something more romantic to set the mood.

"I wanted to ask if you'd like to sit out on the balcony with me tonight. Enjoy the new space heater together." She sent him what she hoped was a flirty smile.

Matteo stared at her for a long moment. "Do you have something in your eye?"

Thrown off guard, she blinked. "What?"

"You keep fluttering your eyelids. Do you have dirt in your eye or something?" He frowned, and she tried to figure out if he was actually concerned or making fun of her.

"My eye is fine," she said, her irritation warring with her desire to keep that sweet, innocent facade in place.

"I can ask Giulia to get you some drops."

"I don't need fucking eyedrops," she snapped. "Do you want to sit out on the balcony later or not?"

A smile tugged at the corner of his mouth, but he didn't give in to it. Instead he lifted his hand and crooked a finger at her, beckoning her closer. Her instinct was to disobey purely on principle, but she needed him to say yes, needed him to kiss her, needed him to do more. Need. Not want. That's what she kept reminding herself.

"Tessa, are you trying to get me alone with you?" he asked when she stopped in front of the desk.

"What?" Fuck's sake, she never knew what this man was going to say next. "Why would I need to get you alone? We're alone right now."

"Yes," he agreed, eyes darkening as he rounded the desk

to stand in front of her. "We are. Why do you want to sit on the balcony with me?"

"To say..." She wet her lips with the tip of her tongue, stomach tightening when his eyes fixated on her mouth. "To say thank you. For the heater. And for..." He took a step closer, and every thought drained from her head.

"For?" he prompted.

He was so close she could feel the heat radiating off his skin. He was so warm, so inviting. And he smelled good. Were men supposed to smell that good? Seemed like it might be a crime.

Jesus. Focus. She had to focus. This was what she needed him to do. To kiss her again so she could get him to take it to the next step and be closer to freedom.

"For everything you've done for me. I wanted to say thank you." She cleared her throat, drawing his attention back to her eyes.

He didn't speak, and the silence made her feel stupid. She was obviously reading these signs and signals of his all wrong. Maybe she should kiss him and be the one to make the first move. The rejection might sting in the moment, but at least she'd know exactly where they stood and how much work she had left to do.

"Fuck it," she muttered, pushing onto her tiptoes and tugging the lapels of his jacket to pull him closer.

Her mouth crashed into his, and she couldn't help the little sigh that escaped her. His hands immediately found her hips, kneading and squeezing while her tongue darted out to trace across his lower lip.

He groaned at the contact, and the sound reverberated into her bones. It was such a perfect sound, deep and gravelly. She wanted to hear it again, so she gently sucked his upper lip into her mouth and nibbled it with her teeth.

This time his groan was louder, and his hands tightened

on her hips, tugging her closer at the same time he rotated their bodies and pushed her back against the edge of the desk. She was trapped between his body and the solid wood, but she didn't care. This was exactly what she needed from him, and it felt damn good too.

Pulling her up onto her toes again, he shifted her back onto the edge of the desk and pressed her legs apart so he could step between her thighs. He trailed his hand up her back and fisted it in her hair, tugging her head back gently and exposing the skin of her neck.

Her bruises were mostly faded, but he pressed kisses against each one that remained, heating her skin and making her tremble. Jesus, the man was good with his mouth, and the rough feel of his beard on sensitive skin was its own kind of aphrodisiac.

Something toppled over behind her when she leaned back on her hands so his lips could roam further south, but she didn't care what it was as long as he kept doing that thing with his teeth. He tugged her shirt down enough to expose cleavage, pressing kisses to the tops of her breasts.

Halting his exploration, he brought his face level with hers, his breath warm on her lips when he spoke. "I've been thinking about kissing you again since I took your phone."

"Me too," she admitted. "And more."

He claimed her mouth again, rough and needy, and she gasped when his hand found her nipple through the fabric of her shirt and bra. He pinched the bud with two fingers, and she arched against the sensation.

She'd done that to herself many times, but nothing beat the feeling of someone else doing it to her. Of not controlling the pain and being at the mercy of his fingers, his desires, his will.

He skimmed his lips across her jaw to her earlobe, fingers

tightening on her nipple while he whispered in her ear. "What else have you thought about, *piccola*?"

This was it. This was her perfect moment. On her back, legs spread. She shook her father's voice from her mind. This might mean different things to Matteo than it did to her, but that didn't mean she had to ruin the experience for herself.

"I want—"

She was cut off by the sharp ring of his phone, the noise so loud and unexpected she jumped. Matteo released her nipple with a groan. But not the good kind.

"One second. Let me just…"

He wrestled the phone from his pocket, and for the first time, she realized how hard he was. For her. She wanted to touch him, feel how he'd reacted to her touch and her kiss and her body pressed against his. But he swore under his breath and stepped away.

"I'm sorry. I have to take this." He shot a look at the door and then back at her.

"Right. Of course."

She hopped off the desk and wobbled her way to the door, hoping he didn't notice how badly she was still shaking. The smile on his face told her he knew just what kind of effect he had on her. Let him stroke his ego with that for a while. It could only work in her favor.

"Close the door," he said when she reached it.

Once the latch clicked in the frame, she pressed her ear against it and listened for any sound. Nothing. The door was too thick, or Matteo was talking too quietly. She'd have to push on with her plan to seduce him. At least now she knew if she kissed him, he'd kiss her back.

She didn't like the idea of whoring herself out for her father's benefit. But she couldn't deny she wanted Matteo's lips and hands on her again. If this was the path she was forced to take, she could at least enjoy the ride.

Chapter Ten

It was dark by the time Matteo finished his calls. He'd been busy laying the groundwork for their first big strike against Antonetti's network. Well, technically, it was two strikes. One a distraction for a mid-level Russian mob boss and the other an effort to poach his Spanish drug supplier.

Tessa's information had proven useful, making it easy to identify one of the names he hadn't recognized on the list of contacts he'd gotten from Callum. The relationship was breaking down because Antonetti was attempting to go behind their backs and do business with the Columbians directly. Cut out the middleman. Bad for him, good for them.

Within a week, they'd hit Antonetti in two directions. Cutting off drug money he laundered through his hotels and distracting an ally with a lot of muscle so they couldn't be relied on for backup should Antonetti require it. Once they were dealt with, he'd drill down into the next layer of Antonetti's international circle.

The goal was to strip him of enough allies that Matteo could take the rest by force. Unlike Gallo, Antonetti didn't trust politicians. He preferred to align himself with other criminals. Matteo liked to do both.

But like politicians, some criminals were loyal to a fault. You couldn't always pay them to turn the other cheek or switch sides. The trick was weeding out the ones who were loyal only to what Antonetti could do for them and not to the man himself.

He'd already pegged a few, but it would be easier to go after them once he sidelined the Russians and made a deal with the Spaniards. The Spanish were rumored to be the only entry point for Colombian cocaine into Europe. If Matteo could out Antonetti as a snake and strike a deal with them, he'd line his pockets nicely.

More drug profits meant more money to build up the legitimate businesses he envisioned, including a complete overhaul of Gallo Industries under the Bianchi name. Sienna had come to him with some great ideas he wouldn't mind implementing.

But this first. He'd already started laying the foundation for pitting the Russians against their biggest enemy. Alexei had been translating messages from their contact for days. And in two days' time, Alexei would head to Russia himself to set the fire and fan the flames.

While Alexei was in Russia, Luca would be in Spain with Sienna, who spoke fluent Spanish. Matteo would prefer to go; his Spanish was good enough to negotiate a deal, and this wasn't normally something he would task someone else with. But there was too much to see to at home. Too many irons in the fire, too much to think about.

Not the least of which was the curvy, raven-haired siren sleeping across the hall. She'd been flirting with him all week. Or trying to. He had no interest in the demure act she was putting on. That wasn't what he liked about her. He liked her quick wit and razor-sharp tongue.

He liked the fire he'd seen in her eyes when she'd told him to wait and asked him to take her away from Syracuse. God help him, he liked the attitude when she'd refused to give up her phone.

Most of all, he liked that she'd given up on subtlety and taken what she wanted. He'd given it to her without hesitation. And he would have gone a lot farther than his lips and teeth on her skin if not for work intruding on their moment of sin.

But work was over now. And there was plenty of time between now and sunrise for sinning.

Pushing away from the desk, he crossed the room and turned off the light, locking the door behind him. A new habit. Another concession to get Luca to shut the fuck up about Tessa being in the house.

Matteo climbed the stairs, already loosening his tie and unbuttoning his vest. Her light was on, a thin gold line against the tile, and he stared at it while he undid his cufflinks and set them in the velvet-lined box on top of his dresser.

Making his way across the hall, he stopped outside her door and lifted his fist to knock, hesitating when he heard voices on the other side. Was she on the phone with someone? He strained to hear words, but all he could make out was raised voices.

He knocked quickly, and the voices immediately went silent. When she opened the door, she was still fully dressed, and his eyebrows shot up at the sight of her in jeans and a long-sleeved shirt at this hour.

"Is that what you wear to bed?"

Tessa looked down at herself and then crossed her arms over her chest. "You knocked on my door at almost two in the morning to check my sleeping attire?"

"No." There was that attitude he enjoyed so much. "I was just curious."

"I don't have any pajamas. I've had to…get creative."

A quick flash of her sleeping naked under the soft, pale pink sheets the maids always put on this bed seared through his mind, and he gripped the doorjamb with white knuckles and bit back a groan. As much as he enjoyed that mental image, the woman needed clothes.

He could take her shopping this weekend. Dom wouldn't be coming for their next check-in meeting until Sunday afternoon. If he shuffled some things around, he could… He stopped himself. What the hell was he doing?

He wanted to fuck the woman, maybe get some more intel out of her, not be her personal chauffeur and errand boy. He'd give her some cash and send her to the shops with Russo. He hadn't reported any oddities the last time he'd driven her to pick up some things she needed.

"Was there something else?" she asked, tugging him back to the moment.

"I heard voices," he said, a little gruffer than he meant to.

"I was watching a show." She grabbed her phone off the nightstand and turned it around to show him the American sitcom paused on the screen. "The one where Ross and Rachel break up. The first time."

He had no idea what she was talking about but nodded anyway.

"If that's it, I should—"

Backing her up against the frame before he could change his mind, he tilted her chin up with his finger and pressed a kiss to her lips, deepening it slowly until her body relaxed against him and her arms circled his neck. She was always so hesitant to touch him, but he liked the feel of her skin against his.

Dipping his head, he kissed the hollow of her throat,

smiling when she sighed and slid her fingers into his hair. Kissing across her collarbone, he tugged her shirt off her shoulder and nipped the exposed skin at the edge of her bra strap. It wasn't enough. He wanted more.

"Tessa."

"Hmm?" she murmured, using her fingers in his hair to guide his lips over her skin.

"If you don't want me to fuck you, you need to tell me right now."

Her breath was ragged in his ear, and she shivered when he dragged his teeth over her shoulder. "What if I do want you to fuck me?"

"Then we're both wearing entirely too many clothes."

He gripped the hem of her shirt and started to tug it up before pausing. No one was likely to happen on them at this hour. But he wanted to savor her lying down, not devour her standing up.

Grabbing her hand, he led her across the hall to his room, kicking the door closed and pressing her back against it. Her lips were swollen from his kiss, the skin around her mouth and across her chest was red from his beard. Her eyes were as big as saucers, and her breath raced in and out of her lungs.

When she reached for the buttons on his shirt, his gaze dropped to watch her fingers undo them slowly. He hadn't noticed the pink polish on her fingernails earlier, but it stood out sharply against the white of his button-down. As she neared his belt buckle, he helped her pull the tails out of his waistband, groaning when her fingers hovered dangerously close to his cock as she undid the last button.

She ran her hands up over his abs and chest, pushing the shirt off his shoulders and down his arms. He let her explore his body with her fingertips, but when she leaned in to touch her lips to his shoulder, it took everything he had not to spin her around, bend her over, and drive his cock inside her.

Her slow, methodical exploration was making him crazy, but he'd gladly let her drive him into madness if it was going to feel like this. Her teeth followed her lips and then her tongue, her hands skimming down to the buckle of his belt, undoing it and the button and dragging down the zipper.

She slid her hand inside, wrapping her fingers around his length, and he gritted his teeth as she gave him one long, lazy stroke. The woman was trying to fucking kill him.

Licking her lips as she watched her hand move up and down his shaft, she slowly lowered herself to her knees, looking up at him with those big brown eyes. Her tongue darted out to swirl around his tip, and he fisted his hands against the door to keep from surging his hips forward.

When she sucked him into her mouth, he let out a low groan, which only seemed to encourage her, and she slid more of his cock into her mouth, hollowing her cheeks around it. She pushed down until her eyes welled up with tears and she gagged, and he'd never heard a sweeter fucking sound in all his life.

What she seemingly lacked in experience, she made up for in enthusiasm, bobbing her mouth on his cock and working the rest of his length with her hand in quick strokes.

"Tessa," he gritted out in warning. "I'm going to fill your mouth if you don't stop."

She looked up at him again, sucking harder and pumping her fist faster. Fuck. She looked so fucking good on her knees, taking his cock like that.

"Is that what you want, *piccola*? My cum down your throat?"

Her hum of agreement sent vibrations down his cock, his hips jerking forward with short, rough thrusts until he lost all control and emptied his balls in her mouth.

Sitting back on her heels, she looked up at him, tongue darting out to lick her lips clean.

"Christ," he growled, reaching down and yanking her to her feet.

"That was different than I thought it would be."

He paused in his move to peel off her shirt and looked down at her. "Different how?"

Color rose to her cheeks, and he raised a brow, prompting her to answer. "I just...didn't expect to like it that much my first time."

Matteo jerked back, his hands falling from her waist. "That was your first time giving a blow job?"

"Yeah." Her cheeks and now her chest flushed an even deeper shade of red.

"The guys you've been with are idiots if they didn't take advantage of your mouth before now. And your hands." He reached for her hand, pulling her against him and pressing a kiss to each fingertip. "You have very skilled hands, *piccola*. But mine are better. Let me show you."

Guiding her back to the bed, he stepped out of his shoes and pants and lifted the hem of her shirt.

"Wait." Her hands flew to his, and he stilled. "We should turn off the light."

He looked over her head at the lamp on the nightstand and then back to her face. "Why?"

"Because." Tessa trained her gaze on his shoulder and refused to make eye contact. "You might not like what you see."

The words arrowed through him, and he took a step closer, gripping her chin and forcing her face to his. "I already like what I see, and I want to see more."

She tried to pull away, but he held her fast, using his free hand to inch her shirt up over her waist. She didn't move when he dropped her chin and pulled her shirt off.

Reaching around her back to free the clasp of her bra, he slid it down her shoulders and arms, skimming his fingertips over the underside of her breasts and circling her nipples until her breathing was ragged. He made quick work of her jeans, shoving them down her thick thighs and helping her step out of them.

Every fucking inch of her was perfect, all soft curves and dimpled skin. He brushed his lips over her thigh, using his hands on her hips to ease her back onto the edge of the bed. He pressed her legs apart and kissed his way up her inner thigh to her pussy, dragging his tongue up her already wet slit without hesitation.

Tessa sucked in a sharp breath, her hands gripping the duvet as her thighs trembled under his fingers. That's what he wanted. He wanted to make her come undone, to lose control.

Leaving one hand on her inner thigh to keep her spread, he used the other to part her pussy lips for his tongue, delighting in the way her hips bucked against his mouth when he swirled his tongue over her clit. Every time he touched her, she rewarded him with a new sound. A gasp, a sigh, a soft, needy moan.

When he slipped first one and then two fingers inside her, he groaned at how tight she was. He kept constant pressure on her clit with this tongue as he pumped his fingers in and out, curling them against her G-spot while she moaned and writhed.

"That's it, *piccola*," he crooned when she started to grind on his fingers, her breath coming in shallow pants. "Show me how you come for me."

"Matteo," she whimpered, her pussy clenching tight around his fingers as he worked them in and out faster, deeper, pushing her closer and closer to the edge.

She cried out with her orgasm, her back bowing beautifully before her arms gave out, and she collapsed back on the bed. Matteo pressed a lingering kiss to her pussy, making her twitch, and then kissed his way up to her breasts, swirling his tongue around her nipple and giving it a gentle bite.

"Your pussy tastes incredible." She smiled softly, murmuring her agreement, and he kissed across to her other breast, tonguing her nipple until her breath caught in the back of her throat. "You want more, *piccola*?"

"Yes," she sighed, wrapping one leg around his hip when he slid his cock against her. "More."

He sank into her slowly, relishing the feel of her pussy gripping his cock inch by inch until he was balls deep inside her.

"Look at me," he said, waiting until her eyes opened and focused on him before he pulled back and slammed inside her to the hilt. "You are perfect exactly as you are." He ran his hands over the swell of her stomach and cupped her heavy breast in his palm, squeezing it roughly. "Every fucking inch of you." He tweaked her nipple, making her back arch. "Understand?"

"Yes," she nodded, grinding into him and then groaning low in her throat when he pulled out and thrust deep inside her again. "Matteo. Please."

"Please, what?" he asked, fucking her at a slow and steady pace. He wanted to go harder, deeper, faster. But he wanted her to beg for it first.

"More," she said, squirming when he didn't change his pace. "Harder. Faster."

"You want me to fuck you hard and fast, *piccola*?"

She nodded, tightening her leg around his waist when he slammed into her. "Yes," she groaned. "Just like that."

He dropped his head to suck her nipple into his mouth, hips slapping against hers with each brutal thrust inside her. She was close. He could sense it in the way her muscles tightened and her hips moved erratically against his.

Biting down on her nipple, he smiled when she came

undone around him with a gasp, her pussy squeezing him like a vise until he had no choice but to follow her over the edge with his own release.

"Oh my God," she said, her voice muffled in his shoulder.

He chuckled as he rolled onto his back, reaching out to pull her against his side. She laid her head on his chest, and he indulged himself by running his fingers through her hair.

They lay there in silence for a few moments until she finally said in a small voice, "I should go back to my room. You probably don't want the maids to find me here in the morning."

Matteo didn't care what the maids saw. Or anyone else in the house, for that matter. But he wasn't going to chain her to his bed against her will just because he wanted to sleep curled around her luscious body.

He watched her retrieve her clothes from the floor, bundling them up against her body to shield herself as much as she could to dart across the hall.

"Tessa," he said, drawing her gaze with her hand on the knob. He couldn't resist getting one last look at her, lingering on the exquisite curve of her ass before moving back up to her face. "Don't forget."

"Forget what?" she asked, voice a little breathy.

"How perfect you are."

Her cheeks flushed and she ducked out, closing the door softly behind her. Matteo collapsed back against the bed with a groan. That woman was going to be his undoing.

Chapter Eleven

Tessa sat in one of the wingback chairs in front of the fireplace in her room, staring out the window at the rain pelting the grass and trees. Her usual spot on the library balcony was soaked through, thanks to the rain and the wind, which left her stuck inside, wishing for fresh air instead.

She'd woken up sore this morning. Sore and alone. And even though alone had been her choice, it still left a dull ache in her chest. The ache was a problem.

Spending the night in Matteo's bed would have been a terrible idea. He'd far exceeded any expectations she might have had as a lover. She wasn't entirely sure what she'd been expecting, but it hadn't been a man who was gruff and short with everyone else but made her feel seen and sexy and desired.

If this was a mind game, Matteo was winning, and she couldn't afford for that to happen. He could have his pick of any woman he wanted; the things he said to her the night before were his own means to an end. He wanted to have sex with her, so he did what he had to do to get what he wanted.

She was doing the same.

As long as she remembered that, she could keep the guilt at bay.

Her phone signaled on the arm of the chair, and she knew who it was without looking. She didn't have many friends in Syracuse, but none of them had this number. And she didn't know any of them well enough to have their numbers memorized.

How are you today?

Tessa stared at the message. She had nothing for him. Just like yesterday and the day before that and the day before that. Knowing who she was dealing with, there was a very distinct possibility that her father would eventually get bored with her lack of results and kill her and her mother anyway.

Even if it wasn't true, she had to give him enough to make him think she was making progress.

Better than yesterday. I think I'm finally getting closer to where I need to be.

Not a total lie, at least. She was closer than yesterday, but she could hardly promise her father she'd have anything for him anytime soon. If Matteo was just in this for the sex, there was no guarantee he'd ever let his guard down enough to share anything with her at all.

Good. That's good. I'll check in again tomorrow.

A knock on her bedroom door made her jump, and she quickly deleted the text messages and hid her phone between her leg and the chair.

"Come in."

"Sorry if I'm interrupting," Sienna said, tucking her brown hair behind her ear and offering a small smile.

Interrupting what? It wasn't as if Tessa had a wildly active social life to get back to. Watching things on her phone's small screen gave her a headache after a while, and there were only so many books a person could read. In truth, she was starting to get a little bored.

She might not have a lot of friends to miss, but she had enough that there was always someone to call when she needed to get out of the house for lunch or to go shopping or see a movie. And as long as she kept to a certain distance from the compound, her father permitted her to leave.

Here was an entirely different story. She didn't even know the name of the man who'd driven her around the other day, let alone how to contact him for a ride. It didn't matter. This wasn't a vacation, as her father had pointed out. Fun wasn't required.

"You're not interrupting," Tessa assured her.

"Mind if I come in?"

"Of course not."

Tessa shifted away from the window and toward the other chair when Sienna sank into it, rubbing her hands nervously on her thighs. Something dropped in the pit of her stomach. Had Matteo sent Sienna to deliver bad news?

"Is it about my mother?" she blurted, unable to handle the silence another second.

Sienna frowned. "Your mother?"

"Yeah. Did you find her?"

"I thought your mother went missing years ago."

"She did." Tessa sat forward, confused. Sienna was good with computers and searches. She'd heard them talking around it a few times. "I think she might be alive, and Matteo said he would help me look for her if I gave him information about my father."

"I'm sorry," Sienna said, giving her an apologetic look. "I don't know anything about that."

Tessa picked at a thread poking out from the cuff of her sweater. Like every other man she'd ever known, Matteo had lied to get his way.

"Just because I'm not looking doesn't mean someone else isn't."

"Who then?"

"Probably Maeve. Matteo's assistant. Her skill set is different from mine, but she's not bad with stuff like that. If anyone's looking, she is," Sienna added, as if reading Tessa's thoughts.

Tessa forced herself to smile. "I'm sure you're right. So what can I do for you?"

Scrubbing her hands on her thighs again, Sienna took a deep breath. "I actually wanted to apologize."

Tessa's brows shot up. An apology was the last thing she expected from any of them, but definitely not from Luca's woman. Luca loathed her. He'd made that opinion loud and clear. Tessa just assumed Sienna felt the same.

"Apologize for what?"

"For Luca. For myself." She smiled softly. "He could have handled your arrival with a lot more grace and respect, and I could have done more to encourage him to not be such an asshole about it."

"He hates me." Tessa waved a hand in the air. "It's fine. I'd probably hate me too if I were in his shoes."

"He doesn't hate you. He doesn't," Sienna insisted when Tessa raised a brow. "The relationship between the Bianchi siblings is...complicated. Matteo was gone for a long time, and now he's back and..."

"Conquering Sicily?" Tessa offered.

"Yes," Sienna replied with a soft chuckle. "I'm just saying there's a lot of unresolved shit between them. So it's not about you specifically. It wouldn't matter who you were or where you came from. Luca would still be upset about the situation."

"Because of the way Matteo treated you?"

"Luca is very protective of the people he loves. But so is

Matteo. And they both have very different ways of showing it. Which causes them to butt heads a lot."

Tessa snorted. "I noticed. They're either silent or shouting, and dinner is a graveyard when Matteo isn't trying to force conversation."

"The most awkward," Sienna agreed with a laugh. "We can change that. I'd like to change that. Get to know you better. Maybe we can grab lunch sometime."

The offer caught Tessa off guard. It seemed genuine enough, but even if it wasn't, she wasn't really in a position to be turning down opportunities to get out of this fucking house.

"Lunch sounds great."

"Good. There's this little place not far from here that has the best tiramisu. I was working the last time I was there, so I didn't get to enjoy myself. I've wanted to go back."

"Sounds good to me."

"Luca and I are leaving tomorrow to visit some friends in Spain," Sienna said, and Tessa's brows shot up.

So Matteo was using her intel, just not sticking to his side of the bargain. The asshole.

"We shouldn't be gone too long. I'll come find you when we're back."

"I'll be here," Tessa said, watching Sienna push to her feet and cross to the door.

Genuine or not, having lunch with Sienna was an opportunity to gather information. If Matteo wasn't going to keep up his end, then she needed something good for her father, and Matteo wasn't the only one in this house who knew things. His brothers knew what they had planned just the same, and Tessa would bet money Luca told Sienna everything.

Getting details out of Sienna would be a different beast entirely, but it probably wouldn't hurt to cultivate another source of information. Guilt surfaced in the pit of her stomach, and she immediately smothered it.

No doubt Sienna had her own motives for inviting Tessa out to lunch. Tessa refused to believe they were as altruistic as wanting to get to know each other. These people were not her friends. She couldn't forget that.

They were trying to destroy her father in the same way she was trying to destroy them. Although for entirely different reasons. None of them were innocent here.

So what if they were feeding her and housing her and not treating her like garbage? It didn't mean anything other than they were humane enemies. Much more humane than her father would be if he found himself in the same situation.

At the end of the day, she only cared about getting what she wanted. As long as she had her mother back at the end of all of this, she didn't care who got hurt along the way. She'd suffered enough these last eight years without her mother as a buffer between her and her father's wrath.

If this was what she had to do to have the freedom and peace she deserved, she'd do it a thousand times over and not feel bad about it for a second.

Chapter Twelve

"Alexei called when he landed in Moscow. He said everything's a go for him there."

"And Carina?"

"She's meeting him in Sochi once his work is finished. They're only planning on staying a few days."

Matteo frowned. He didn't like the idea of Carina in Russia right after Alexei did his part to stir up trouble. But she would have gone whether he approved or not. At least this way, he was able to get her on a private flight with people who would keep her safe until she met up with Alexei.

"And Spain?"

"We're on track there too."

"Our flight leaves early tomorrow, and I'm looking forward to practicing my Spanish," Sienna said, leaning into Luca when he squeezed her elbow.

"The meeting is set for tomorrow night over dinner," Luca added. "I'll update you after."

Matteo nodded. "Good."

"What?" Luca raised a brow. "No lecture about how we

need to be on our best behavior and not embarrass the family?"

Tossing his notepad and pen on the table in front of him, Matteo hung his head between his shoulders with a huff. "Why do you always expect the worst from me?"

"Because that's what I always get from you. Don't start," Luca snapped when Matteo opened his mouth to speak. "If you say you're doing what's best for the family one more time, I'm going to hurl."

"Maybe if I say it enough, you'll start to believe me," Matteo bit off. "How much longer are you going to make me pay for the past, little brother?"

"Get the fuck over yourself, Matteo."

"Can we not do this tonight, Luca?" Sienna asked.

"I'm just answering my brother's question," Luca informed her, turning back to Matteo. "This isn't about the years you were gone as much as it's about every decision you've made for the last eight months. On your own. Like you know best and none of us deserve a say in how this family runs."

"It's my responsibility."

"Maybe," Luca agreed. "But you can't keep saying we're in this together while continually shutting us out. If you—"

Luca cut himself off sharply, his eyes trained on a spot over Matteo's head. Sitting up, Matteo turned toward the door to see Tessa standing in the center of the soaring arch, a book in one hand and a glass of wine in the other.

"I'm sorry," she said, looking from Luca to Matteo and back, shifting on her feet. "There isn't usually anyone in here at this time of night. I'll go," she added when no one broke the heavy silence.

"Stop," Matteo said before she could sprint away. He hadn't seen her since she left his room the night before. Inviting her to stay would save him the extra step of seeking her out to see how she was doing since they had sex. That was all. "We were just finishing up."

Luca scoffed and shoved to his feet, extending a hand to Sienna. "I'll call you tomorrow when we land. Alexei should be checking in with you around eleven." He swept Tessa with a searing glare. "Try not to be too busy."

"Luca," Sienna scolded, elbowing him in the side.

"I'm only reminding my dear brother where his focus should be."

"Watch yourself," Matteo said, his voice a warning.

Giving a mocking bow, Luca's grin was razor-sharp. "I will if you will."

He gave Tessa a wide berth and a final disapproving look before stepping into the hall, and Sienna followed with an apologetic one. Tessa stared at Matteo, a deep crease between her brows.

"I didn't mean to start an argument."

"This one wasn't about you." He waved a hand in the air at the skeptical tilt of her head. "It wasn't only about you. There are plenty of reasons for Luca to be pissed at me. You just happen to make the list. Sit, Tessa. Please," he added, softening his tone.

"I didn't think you worked outside of your office," she said, crossing the room and sinking onto the far end of the couch he was sitting on.

She had her hair piled on top of her head in a messy bun, and her sweater hung off one shoulder, exposing the lace strap of her bra. All day she'd been running through his mind. The taste, the sound, the smell of her.

It was distracting enough to irritate Maeve, who suggested he go home after the fifth time he asked her to repeat something. Not that he'd gotten much more work done here. He'd abandoned his study to work in the family room partly because it had a fireplace when his study did not and partly because he hoped to catch a glimpse of her.

Pathetic yet effective.

"I needed a change of scenery. And a fire." He indicated the flames dancing behind the grate.

Smiling softly, she took a sip of wine. "The fire is why I like this room too. A cozy spot to read and have a glass of Cabernet before bed." She moved to set her glass on the table beside her and stopped, shooting him a worried frown. "I hope it's okay I borrowed this from the library."

He glanced at the book she held up, a historical romance by the look of it, and smiled. "You're welcome to whatever you find in the upstairs library. It was my mother's favorite room in the house. Most of the books were hers."

"She must have really liked to read. The shelves are stuffed full."

A pang hit him deep in the center of his chest. A memory of his mother sitting in the overstuffed wingback in the library, a blanket draped over her legs as she read. The cancer had taken all her hair by that point, and she opted to cover up her bald head with colorful scarves instead of wigs.

He would slip away from meetings his father never included him in to check on her. Watching her read with her head bent over the book, lips moving as her eyes tracked the page. Eventually she would call to him to stop staring and get back to work.

Before he headed back downstairs, he would always cross the room, press a kiss to her forehead, and tuck the blanket tighter around her legs.

Guarisci, Mama, he would whisper. But the cancer was too far gone by then. Her death had torn them all apart. And every time he thought he was finished collecting the pieces, he seemed to drop them again.

"You miss her," she breathed.

"About as much as you miss yours, I imagine. My assistant is working on locating her."

"Is she?"

"You sound surprised."

Tessa shrugged, fingering the edge of the pages. "When I asked Sienna about it earlier, she didn't know anything about it. I thought you'd gone back on our deal."

He stilled. Since when did she talk to Sienna? And why would she mention her mother? "I wasn't aware you two spoke."

His answer made her frown, and she tucked a loose tendril of hair behind her ear. "She came to talk to me. To apologize for Luca." Her eyes were defiant when they met his. "I didn't know I wasn't allowed to talk about my own mother."

"I never said you couldn't," he replied, shifting slightly to face her.

"If you're not actually going to help me find her, why are you keeping me here?"

"I'm not keeping you here, and I am going to help you find her."

"Well, I can't exactly leave on my own." She pursed her lips, staring into the fire. "It's been two weeks, and I'm no closer to finding her than I was when I left Syracuse. How do I even know you're actually looking?"

"Because I said I'm looking," Matteo snapped. "Why the hell would I lie to you about that?"

"I don't know. According to my father, you'll say whatever you have to say to get what you want."

On a growl, Matteo moved closer and reached for her wrist, tugging her into his lap and wrapping his arm tight around her waist when she struggled against him.

"Let's not put any stock in what your father says about anything," he said, voice low. He skimmed his hand up her arm and across her shoulder, tracing his fingertips gently down the column of her throat. "I told you I'm going to do something, and I will. My assistant is looking into your mother's disappearance. She has been since I corroborated your information about your father's dealings in Spain."

She swallowed, her throat bobbing under his fingers, and he shifted to trace the line of her jaw. "Turns out it's not that easy to find a woman who's been missing for nearly a decade."

"What if she's dead?"

Matteo's gaze slid up to meet hers, her eyes sparkling with unshed tears. He hooked his hand around the back of her neck and brought her closer, biting back a groan when she shifted in his lap and rubbed her ass against his cock.

"Then we'll find that out too, and you can decide what you want to do next."

"What if I want to leave?" Her gaze dropped to his lips and lingered there.

"Then I'll take you anywhere you want to go," he promised, but he wasn't so sure.

The idea of not having her here, of not being able to touch her or taste her or hear her voice again, felt wrong somehow. Before the thought could take root, he brushed it aside. It wouldn't do him any good to get weighed down by the impossible.

He was still fighting a war, and she was the daughter of his enemy. Despite what he wanted to believe about her, Luca was right. He didn't know if he could trust her. But he didn't have to trust her to take her to bed.

"Did you sleep well last night?" He pressed a kiss to her jaw. "After you came for me?"

She blushed a pretty shade of pink, and he kissed the apple of her cheek.

"I slept like a baby." She captured her bottom lip between

her teeth, then slowly released it. "I wouldn't mind a repeat performance."

He grinned, nipping her jaw and nibbling up to her earlobe. "Is that right?"

"Mmm," she murmured when he slid his tongue over the sensitive spot behind her ear. "We could just start from the top and work our way down."

"Sounds good to me," he replied, slipping his hand under the hem of her sweater and pushing up until he closed his fingers around her nipple. "But maybe we can add a few new things to the list. Because I want to see if I can make you come just from playing with your nipples."

She groaned in his ear, and he squeezed his fingers tighter, giving it a gentle twist. He wanted to make her vibrate with need and beg him to slide inside her. He wanted to watch her face as she came for him over and over, savor the way her body responded to him.

"I've never tried that," she said, breath catching. "But it would be a shame not to."

He chuckled. "A complete shame. We should—"

The shrill ring of his phone silenced his invitation, and he bit off a curse. He was forever being interrupted at the worst possible moments with her. She slid off his lap before he could ask, and he picked up his phone from the coffee table. Alexei.

He looked up at her, but she was already moving away, collecting her book where she'd discarded it on the couch cushions and her glass of wine from the table.

"*Piccola,*" he called to draw her attention. "Wait for me in my room. I won't be long." Her eyes darkened, and she smiled before rounding the corner into the hallway.

Matteo accepted the call and pressed the phone to his ear. He needed Alexei to make it quick. For the first time in a long time, he had something better to do than worry about work.

Chapter Thirteen

Matteo was already seated at the breakfast table when she came down the next morning, and she stopped short in the doorway to the family dining room. Usually he was gone at this hour. The man didn't really seem to take a day off.

She'd hoped to avoid him after falling asleep in his bed the night before and then sneaking out in the early hours of the morning. Getting up and going back to her own room had been the plan after he fucked her brainless, but his body had been so warm and his fingers combing through her hair so soothing, she'd fallen asleep before she even knew what was happening.

Sneaking out just before sunrise had taken more effort than she wanted to admit. And not just because she was trying not to wake him.

Nibbling her bottom lip, Tessa debated whether she should skip breakfast and this awkward conversation or push through and pretend it wasn't weird that she kept leaving his bed for her own. It shouldn't be weird, but it shouldn't be so difficult either.

Matteo spotted her as he reached for his cappuccino, smiling at her over the rim of his mug. He gestured to her usual spot on his right with a tilt of his head, and she crossed to the chair, sinking into it when the butler held it out.

A maid set a latte and a cornetto filled with what looked like raspberry jam in front of her and stepped back into the corner of the room. The silence felt heavy, oppressive. She twisted her fingers in her lap.

"Did you sleep well last night?"

"I…" She didn't know quite how to answer. After she'd left his room, she'd tossed and turned until the sun came up. But he didn't need to know that. "I did. Thanks. You?"

"Moderately well. A little cold."

His eyes swept over her outfit. The same one she'd been wearing when she asked him to take her from Syracuse. She was stuck rotating her clothes as best she could. It was becoming tiresome.

"Would you like to go shopping today?"

She paused in her reach for her coffee and blinked at him. "Shopping?"

"I noticed you didn't have many clothes."

Cheeks heating, she glanced down at the navy blue top and white pants. She could use more…everything in her wardrobe. But she only knew of one shop on the island that carried her size in clothes that were actually fashionable, and it was a little too close to home for comfort.

"I don't have enough left over from what you gave me the other day to get much. But I could use a few things."

He sipped slowly, his eyes again taking her in from head to toe. "I didn't ask if you had money. I asked if you needed clothes."

"Technically you asked if I wanted to go shopping."

Expecting him to be angry for pointing out his slip, she

was surprised when Matteo barked out a laugh, taking another sip of his cappuccino.

"Do you need clothes, Tessa? Pants, tops, underwear?" A smirk played at the corner of his mouth. "You don't wear any."

"One less thing for you to take off," she said before she could stop herself.

"Maybe I like to unwrap you. But if you need clothes, I can arrange a trip."

"With the guy from the other day?" He was nice enough, but she didn't know if he'd indulge a few hours of shopping in quite the same way.

"No, I'll take you." He almost seemed to regret his offer, but he recovered quickly and took a deep breath. "I have some work to do, but if you can wait an hour, I'll take you wherever you'd like to go."

"There's really only one place I can shop in Sicily. That carries...my size."

"Okay."

"It's forty minutes outside Syracuse."

Matteo twisted his watch around his wrist, something he seemed to do when he was thinking. "I'll make it work. One hour," he added, rising from the table and striding from the room.

Tessa sat staring after him. Her father wanted another meeting soon, and this was the perfect opportunity. But the idea of meeting with him with Matteo close by had knots twisting in her stomach. She didn't know if she could keep Matteo safe. More importantly, she didn't know why she wanted to.

True to his word, Matteo came to collect her within the hour. Leading her to his car with a hand on the small of her back, he held the door open and waited for her to position herself inside before closing it and rounding the hood.

They rode in silence, but he indulged her request to find something on the radio. And even though he gripped the steering wheel with tense fingers and gritted his teeth, he didn't demand she shut it off.

The boutique was busier than she expected, but Matteo nodded to the driver of an SUV she hadn't noticed had been following them as they crossed the parking lot. He'd arranged for backup, knowing they were close to her father's compound, and she wondered if it was for her safety or his.

The bell over the door greeted them with a cheerful ding when they pushed inside, and she sighed at the array of colorful clothes in every size. A friend had introduced her to this shop a few years ago, and it had been a lifesaver. Shopping only online was a pain in the ass.

She wandered over to the closest rack of sweaters in bright colors and flipped through them until she found one in a pretty golden yellow and another in deep purple.

Another display of tops caught her eye, and she grabbed a beautiful silk blouse with lace overlay from the hanger. Holding it up to her chest, she studied her reflection in the mirror across the room. It would either fit perfectly or pull too tightly across her breasts.

She didn't imagine Matteo's patience for this trip extended to trying things on, so she put it back. Best to stick with things she knew would fit so they could get in and get out. Her father hadn't responded to her text about being nearby, and the longer it took, the more she found herself wishing she could avoid him altogether.

Matteo followed behind her as she browsed, watching her carefully but saying nothing. He never looked away when she caught him staring, only grinned or raised a brow or nodded in approval. There was something intoxicating about having his undivided attention.

After amassing a stack of clothes that would last her at least a few months, she carried them to the counter and handed them to the clerk.

"This purple will look beautiful with your skin tone," the woman said as she rang it up and folded it. Tessa thought she heard Matteo murmur in agreement behind her. "We have a dress in this color I think would look stunning on you if you'd like to try it on."

"Oh, I don't think—"

"You should," Matteo insisted.

Tessa peeked at him over her shoulder. "I don't have much need for a dress."

Matteo lifted a brow. "Humor me."

Without waiting for Tessa to agree, the clerk scurried off in search of the dress. "Here we are," the woman said, holding the dress up like a prize. "Fitting rooms are back this way."

Before Tessa could follow, Matteo moved in closer, leaning down to whisper in her ear. "I have to check in with Alexei, but I want to see it on you before we leave."

"Is that an order?"

He grinned. "Yes. It is."

She shivered when he stepped away, her heart thumping in her chest. The way he could turn her insides to molten heat with a few words was unsettling. When she rounded the corner for the fitting rooms, the clerk was waiting with a smile.

"I set a few other items inside I think you might like in case you want to try those on too."

Tessa spotted the silk and lace blouse she'd seen earlier, as well as a few other tops and a skirt. When had the woman even had time to grab those things? Tessa stepped into the little room and closed the flimsy door before stripping out of her top and reaching for the silk and lace blouse.

It was nice but, as predicted, stretched too tightly across her breasts, creating hills and valleys in the fabric. An ever-present curse. Carefully peeling it off, she folded it and placed it in a separate pile before reaching for the next one. She was just pulling it on over her head when the door burst open and a man with a ball cap pulled low to hide his face pushed inside.

"What the fuck are you doing in here?" she demanded. "Get ou—"

A hand clamped down over her mouth, silencing the rest of her words, and she was shoved flat against the wall of the small cubicle.

"Shut up, it's only me," her father said, voice low. "Miss me?" He chuckled when she wrenched her face free from his grasp.

"You could have knocked. What if I was naked?"

He balled his hand into a fist by her head. "Two weeks away from my firm hand and you've already got a mouth on you. Do you need another lesson?" Swallowing hard, she shook her head. "I didn't think so. What do you have for me?"

"They're doing something in Russia," she said quickly, needing him gone before Matteo returned to see her in that dress.

"You'll have to be more specific than that," he said drily. "Russia is a big country."

Tessa tried to recall as many details as possible from Matteo's conversation with Alexei the night before. After he'd asked her to wait for him in his bedroom, she'd stood in the hall eavesdropping on their discussion for as long as she dared.

"Alexei's there. In Moscow. He's supposed to meet with someone named Ilyin today to discuss a..." What had Matteo called it? "A disruption."

Her father's eyes narrowed. "Dasha Ilyin?"

"I don't know. He only ever said Ilyin. That's everything I overheard."

He pushed away from her and stalked to the other corner. "That fucker. I know exactly what he's doing, but it won't work."

"Great. You need to go before he comes back."

He spun to face her, eyes bright with interest. "Who?"

"Matteo. He's taking a call, but then he's going to come looking for me. You should—"

"He's here?" Her father reached into his pocket and drew out a knife, flicking the blade open with his thumb and drawing it between his fingers. "I could kill him right now and be done with it all."

"No! No," she said again, fighting to keep the sudden panic from her voice. "You can't kill him."

"And why the fuck not? Don't tell me you're developing feelings for the bastard."

"Of course not," she replied with a shake of her head. "But if you kill him, the first thing the family will do is toss me out. And you'll lose your inside source."

"It will hardly matter then. It'll be done."

"It won't be," she insisted. "Dom will take over and keep pushing forward. They won't just stop because Matteo is dead."

She had no idea if what she was saying was true. She'd spent almost no time with Dom or Luca or Carina, had no idea if they would care about this crusade to rule Sicily if Matteo was gone. But that hardly mattered. All she cared about in this moment was keeping Matteo alive.

After what felt like an eternity, her father closed the knife in his hand and tucked it back into his pocket. "Fine. I'll let him live. For now. At least now I have a good idea of what his strategy is. I can head him off in a few different directions."

"You do that. But you need to get out of here," she said, gesturing toward the door.

"I don't take orders from you, little girl," her father snapped. "You might not be under my roof anymore, but you are mine until I say otherwise. Don't make the same mistakes your mother did."

A chill settled into her bones, but he disappeared before she could ask him what he meant by that.

Someone knocked on the door, and she jumped, clapping a hand over her mouth to muffle a yelp.

"Everything okay in there?" the clerk asked.

"Yes. It's fine. You just scared me."

"Sorry about that. Let me know if you need any help."

Ready to find Matteo and get the fuck out of this store and safely back to Palermo, she quickly changed back into her shirt and left the clothes discarded on the overstuffed ottoman. Whipping open the door, she stopped short when she saw Matteo standing in front of a pale pink settee. How long had he been standing there? Had he heard her talking with her father? Or seen him coming out of the dressing room?

He glanced up from his phone, his smile quickly replaced by a frown. "You didn't try on the dress."

"I told you, I don't need the dress."

Matteo tilted his head at her tone. "What's wrong?"

Crossing her arms over her chest, she took a deep breath. "Nothing's wrong. Just what I have at the counter is fine."

Matteo closed the distance between them in two quick strides, pushing her back into the room and closing the door behind them. "I want to see you in that dress, even if it means I have to strip you naked and do it myself."

"You wouldn't," she insisted, moving to push past him.

Gripping her wrist, Matteo shifted to press his body

against hers, pinning her to the wall. He dropped his head and traced the tip of his nose along her jaw to her ear.

"I absolutely would," he assured her. "So which is it going to be?"

Chapter Fourteen

If she knew how much the defiant fire snapping in her eyes made him want to push her to the brink until she was screaming his name, she'd do a better job of hiding her emotions from him. Or maybe she wouldn't. Maybe she liked this game they played as much as he did.

The nights he spent with her had been perfect, despite the way she kept disappearing from his bed. He loved to make her beg and scream. Now he wanted to see her squirm, hear her whimper.

Capturing the hem of her shirt, he lifted it over her stomach and chest, pulling it off and tossing it on the bench beside them. His eyes dipped down to her breasts, and he traced his fingertip over the lacy edges of her bra.

"This is ridiculous," she said when he moved to unbutton and unzip her pants.

He hooked his fingers in the waistband and slowly worked them down over her hips and ass. "Then tell me to stop."

"What?"

Her pussy slowly came into view as he tugged her pants

down her thighs to her knees, releasing them so the fabric pooled at her feet. He'd asked the clerk to select some matching bra and panty sets, but now he was considering leaving the panties behind.

He liked knowing she was bare under her clothes, ready and willing for him to touch her. Like she was right now.

"If it's so ridiculous, tell me to stop." When she said nothing, he smirked, lifting the dress from the hanger and working the zipper down. "Step out of those pants and put your arms up."

"I'm not a doll. I can dress myself."

"Up," he repeated, voice bordering on a growl.

She stared him down for a few moments—and Christ, if that didn't make his cock that much harder—before finally relenting and lifting her arms over her head. He helped her work the sleeves down her arms, adjusting the wide square neckline and the tight-fitting bodice.

The skirt flared out from her waist and swished around her knees. But it was the simple ruffles lining the collar down one shoulder, across her breasts, and up the other that he couldn't stop staring at. She looked delicate, decorated, and good enough to eat.

"Perfect," he murmured, leaning down to press a kiss to her exposed cleavage. "You should buy this in every color." Another kiss. "One for every day of the week."

"Maybe you should buy one for yourself if you like it that much."

Grinning, he reached for her wrist and moved both of her arms above her head, pinning them to the wall with his hand.

"You wear it better, *piccola*."

He skimmed his fingers over her breasts, circling her nipples with the pad of his thumb before sliding farther south, caressing her tummy and down her thighs. When he slipped his hand under the hem of the dress and dragged his fingernails up her inner thigh, she captured her lip between her teeth.

"You're going to get us in trouble."

"That depends on you." He circled her clit with his thumb, then pressed against it, making her knees wobble. "I know you like to scream, but let's see if you can come quietly like a good girl."

Sliding his middle finger against her clit and down the length of her pussy, he pushed it slowly inside her, her hips jerking against his hand as he filled her. She watched him, teeth digging into the flesh of her lip while he pumped his finger in and out.

He waited for her breathing to become needy and ragged before adding a second finger. She groaned low in her throat, and he captured the sound with his lips, fucking her with his fingers while he sucked and nipped at her tongue.

The harder and deeper he pumped inside her, the more erratically her hips moved, slapping into the wall as she thrust and rocked against him. Her hands balled into fists, nails digging into her palms as she whimpered and bucked.

"That's it, *piccola*," he whispered in her ear. "Don't let them hear what a good girl you are for me. Come nice and hard on my fingers." He pressed his thumb against her clit, working his fingers in and out at a dizzying pace. "I know you need it."

"Yes," she hissed, pushed onto her tiptoes for better leverage to fuck him back, her movements rough, desperate. "Matteo."

Her orgasm washed over her like a tidal wave, and he watched in awe as it rippled through her body, her neck straining with the effort not to cry out as her back arched and her hips jerked and her thighs trembled.

She collapsed against him, breaths coming in shallow pants,

and buried her face against his shoulder. Releasing her arms, he pulled her away from the wall and twisted them both until she was standing in front of the ottoman piled with clothes.

"Sit down."

Peeking over her shoulder, she shook her head. "I'm not wearing any underwear. I'm going to make a mess."

"I don't care. Sit down."

"Matteo," she said, getting her breath back and crossing her arms over her chest. "You're going to have to buy all these clothes. Definitely this dress, and I—"

It didn't take more than a gentle push to have her tumbling back onto the ottoman with a disgruntled squeak. Matteo sank to his knees and pried her legs open with his hands on her thighs.

"I don't care what I have to buy. I'm not leaving here without putting my mouth on this pretty pussy."

She dropped her head back against the wall with a soft thud when he shoved the dress up to her hips and brushed a soft kiss against her soaked pussy lips. Swiping his tongue up the length of her slit, he slid a finger back inside her.

"Jesus fuck," she gasped, and he grinned.

"Careful, *piccola*. You still have to be a good girl for me. And good girls are quiet when they're coming on my tongue and my fingers like this."

Wrapping his lips around her clit, he sucked hard, slowly moving his fingers in and out, matching the pace of the subtle rocking of her hips as he devoured her. She blew out a shuddering breath, throat bobbing when she swallowed as he nipped her clit gently with his teeth.

Watching her try to maintain control while he pushed her closer and closer to the edge of madness was intoxicating, all-consuming, an addiction he could get lost in. She writhed against him when he added a second finger, concentrating his lips and teeth and tongue on her clit as he pumped them in and out faster.

He loved to watch her come, the way her brows drew together and her eyes squeezed shut and her mouth dropped open in a gasp or a scream. She made such beautiful sounds for him, but he was having just as much fun forcing her to be quiet.

The way her body trembled with need and the effort of not screaming his name the way she did at home was fucking perfection. He would never get tired of giving her pleasure, of watching her take it.

He thrust his fingers deep inside her and then curled them up, dragging them against her G-spot as he pulled them out, making her entire body shudder.

"Matteo," she said, her voice a strained whisper.

"Yes, Tessa," he urged. "Come for me. Show me how much you need it."

She bit down on the heel of her hand to muffle the sob that escaped her when the orgasm overtook her. Bucking and squirming against his mouth and fingers, she clamped down on him deep inside her as she came.

Breathing hard, she slid her fingers into his hair and used it to pull him closer, planting a kiss on his lips that made them both groan. "We're definitely buying this dress," she said against his mouth.

He chuckled. "This dress and everything you just ruined."

"You insisted."

"Yes, I did. I—"

"How's it going in here?" the clerk said, making Tessa jump.

"Everything's good," Tessa squeaked. "We—I'll be right out." She shoved at Matteo's shoulder when he chuckled again. "That's not funny. She can't know you're in here with me. They'll never let me shop here again."

"I'm about to give that woman one of the best commissions of her life. She'd probably let us fuck anywhere we wanted."

Tessa snorted and reached for her pants, frowning when Matteo stopped her. "I have to get dressed so we can buy this."

He turned toward her, pressing his hard cock against the curve of her ass as he tugged the zipper up and readjusted the skirt. Ripping the tag off, he clenched it in his palm and scooped the rest of the discarded clothes off the ottoman.

"I want you to wear that out. So I can play with you on the drive home."

He left her standing in the dressing room with her mouth hanging open, carrying the rest of the clothes to the checkout and dropping them unceremoniously on the flat surface.

"I hope you found everything you need," the clerk said, a wry grin tugging at her lips.

"And then some," Matteo assured her.

Chapter Fifteen

Tessa studied the handwritten menu, careful to avoid the food stains, and tried to imagine Sienna eating at this restaurant willingly. She didn't know the woman that well, but this hole-in-the-wall place across the street from a seedy motel didn't exactly seem like Sienna's usual scene.

"I know it doesn't look like much, but if the rest of the food is as good as the tiramisu I had the last time I was here, we won't regret it," Sienna said from across the table.

The dingy blue tablecloths and chipping tile floors might leave a lot to be desired, but the view was beautiful. Beyond the abandoned patio, with its pergola strung with fairy lights, was a rocky beach leading down to the sea. Waves capped with white foam churned over the rocks and receded again and again.

With the right lighting and a couple glasses of wine, the whole place could be considered quaint, especially with the pulse of the waves just under the thrum of conversation. Besides, it was pretty busy during lunch on a weekday, and that seemed like a good sign that nothing she ate here would poison her.

Turning back to the menu, she was distracted by a flash of pale pink at the edge of her vision and glanced up to see Carina weaving through the tables. Tessa shifted in her seat, suddenly uncomfortable with the prospect of facing both of them down over a meal that had already been full of awkward silences.

Sienna followed Tessa's gaze and gave her a sheepish smile. "I told Carina we were having lunch today, and she asked if she could join us. I hope that's all right."

"Of course." As if she had any other option.

She plastered a smile on her face, but it felt too wide, fake, and she hoped neither of them noticed. She hadn't spent much time in either woman's company, but they made her nervous.

"This place is…interesting," Carina said, slipping out of her wool coat and draping it over the back of the chair. "Did you spend so much time hiding in Berlin you forgot what good Italian food was?"

Tessa's eyes widened at the jab, but Sienna threw her head back with a laugh. "I can only vouch for the tiramisu, but it made me curious enough to want to try the rest of their food."

Carina swept a glance over the worn edges of the menu and raised a brow. "I guess we'll see." She looked over at Tessa and offered a small smile, even though her gaze was sharp. "Are you settling in at the villa okay?"

"I am. Thank you," Tessa replied, taking a quick sip of wine to calm her nerves. "Everyone has been very…" She tried to find the right word.

Sienna snorted. "Don't lie. The only one who hasn't been an asshole is Matteo."

"Seems very out of character for my brother." Carina

studied Tessa closely, ignoring the waiter when he set a decanter of wine on the table and scurried away again. "Why are you really here?"

"Jesus, Carina," Sienna muttered. "Subtle much?"

"I wasn't subtle with you when we had a similar lunch last month." Her eyes never left Tessa's as she spoke. "Subtlety is not in my nature. So?"

"My mother might be alive. And the only way to find out for sure was to leave Syracuse."

The half-truth felt more and more like an outright lie each time she said it. This part was supposed to be easier. She wasn't supposed to feel guilty for lying to these people. Lying to her father to escape his wrath or get what she wanted was second nature to her now. Lying to the Bianchis shouldn't bother her nearly as much as it was beginning to.

For the last two nights, she'd allowed herself to fall asleep in Matteo's bed. And for the last two nights, she'd burrowed closer to him when she woke in the dark instead of slipping out quietly and back to her own room.

It was a dangerous game she was playing, letting herself get this comfortable with him, with his family. But it's the game she'd been forced to play. She had every right to make the most of it.

"Has Maeve had any luck?" Sienna wondered.

Tessa sighed. "If she has, I haven't heard anything from Matteo." Not that they spent much time talking. "I just..." She blinked back the sudden onslaught of tears, annoyed with herself for the display of emotion. "I feel so helpless."

"I absolutely know that feeling," Sienna assured her.

"I spent years wishing she'd come back, and after a while I just assumed she was dead. To find out she might not be but have no real way to look for her myself..." She blew out a deep breath. "It feels impossible."

Sienna reached across the table and gave Tessa's hand a

squeeze as the waiter stepped up to take their order. When he left with their menus, she spotted a familiar figure seated two tables away.

Her father's favorite hired man stared back at her, predatory gaze landing on hers with a grin. If her father was having her followed, that could mean only one thing. He was losing faith in her ability to help him get what he wanted. And if that happened, she was sure to be left collecting only bits of her mother.

"Are you okay?"

Carina's voice dragged her back to the conversation, and Tessa nodded, forcing a smile.

"Yeah. I think I'm just going to run to the bathroom and freshen up."

Grabbing her purse off the back of her chair, she wound through the tables, catching the eye of her father's man and indicating the narrow hallway to the bathrooms with a tilt of her chin.

She wasn't sure if he would take the hint or just ignore her, but her heartbeat quickened when she heard footsteps following her. A moment after she entered the bathroom, he did the same, locking the door behind him.

"What are you doing here?"

"I've been tasked with following the Gallo bitch."

Tessa let out a small sigh of relief. So her father hadn't lost faith in her. Yet. But the confession only led to more questions.

"Why?"

"I guess so she can't negotiate any more deals and steal business away from him." He took a step forward, reaching up to twirl a strand of her hair around his finger. "He's been pretty disappointed with your lack of progress. But maybe if you help me out today, I'll tell him how cooperative you were."

Shoving his hand away, Tessa moved as far away from him as the small space would allow and eyed the door.

"You need to leave. If the Bianchis find out my father is having one of their women tailed, they'll retaliate."

"Well, after today, she won't need to be tailed anymore. She'll be dead."

"What?" She jerked away from his sinister grin. "You can't kill her."

"Who's going to stop me? You?" He took a step closer, crowding her against the wall. "I take my orders from your father. And he wants to throw them off balance, halt the sale of Gallo Industries by taking out the only surviving heir."

"I thought the sale was already final."

"That's because you're stupid." He reached up to stroke a finger down the side of her face, his tone softening. "You don't need to worry about any of that. All you need to do is what you're told. There's a little covered market not far from here."

He backed away, reaching into his pocket and producing a knife. "After lunch, suggest that you stop in to check it out. I can attack in the crowd and then disappear without anyone seeing me."

She watched him flip the blade out and then balance it between his thumb and forefinger. The evil glint in his eye and the image of Sienna bleeding out on the ground from a fatal knife wound nauseated her.

"No."

He barked out a laugh, sobering when he saw she was serious. "What do you mean 'no'?"

"I mean, I'm not going to help you kill her."

He darted forward, gripping her hair and yanking her head back. "You know what your father gave me permission to do if you didn't cooperate?"

Sliding his hand down her stomach, he cupped her

between her legs, squeezing and grinding his dick into her ass. Tears sprang to her eyes, and she tried to wiggle free.

"I wouldn't exactly be able to take my time with you in this shitty bathroom, but I've wanted to give you a ride for years. So I could make do."

"Fuck you," she snapped, fingers inching slowly into her purse and closing around the only thing she had to protect herself with.

"No." He grinned, wrapping her hair in his fist. "That's what I'm going to be doing to you!"

"Over my dead goddamn body."

Before he could reply, she gripped the can of pepper spray she always kept in her bag and hit him right in his beady little eyes with it. He yelped, the knife in his hand clattering to the floor when he leapt away.

Stumbling backward, he rammed his hip into the edge of the sink, cursing under his breath while he struggled to rub the burning mist from his eyes. When he charged, she hit him with it again, causing him to thrash and snarl and grab for her.

He was thrown off, but he still blocked the door, and she needed to escape. Weaving on his feet, he tried to both switch on the faucet to splash water over his face and reclaim his weapon.

But he couldn't do one without losing focus on the other. And while he was distracted, she dove for the knife he'd discarded in his mad dash to relieve himself of the torturous burning.

When he finally looked at her with swollen, red-rimmed eyes, water dripping off his jaw and soaking the front of his shirt, the knife was clutched tight in her fist. His eyes trailed from the blade to her face, and he paused for a fraction of a moment before throwing his head back with a laugh.

"What are you going to do? Stab me? You don't have the balls."

He advanced on her then, reaching for the knife, but she twisted her body to the side, and when he got close enough, she rammed the blade between his ribs with a sickening squelch. Pulling it free when he staggered back, she lunged forward and stabbed him again, burying it to the hilt and twisting until his mouth distorted into a silent, anguished scream and blood trickled down his chin.

Breaths coming in sharp, terrified pants, she darted out of reach when he fell to his knees. His mouth moved, but no sound came out, and blood bubbled out of the wound in his chest like macabre soap suds, making her wonder if she'd pierced his lung.

He grabbed for her again, but she was too far, and the move threw him off balance until he teetered forward and collapsed face-first on the floor. He didn't move, his body still blocking the door, and she stared down at the bloody knife in her hand with disbelief. What the fuck was she supposed to do now?

A knock on the door made her yelp, spinning toward the sound.

"Tessa? What's wrong?"

Carina's worried voice only made her heart beat faster. How was she going to explain what happened? And what would her father do to her mother when he found out?

"Tessa. Open the door."

Stepping around the body as best she could, intent on not disturbing the growing pool of blood underneath him, Tessa opened the door enough to stick her head out. Carina's face, pinched with worry, nearly made her sob with relief. But she had to keep it together. She had no idea how much trouble she was about to be in.

"Something happened."

Scanning the hallway to make sure no one else was walking by, Tessa opened the door a little wider, revealing the dead man on the dirty yellow tile behind her.

To Carina's credit, she didn't react, her face remaining completely impassive when she pushed into the bathroom and closed the door, locking it behind her. Tessa watched as she dug her phone out of her pocket and dialed.

"Alexei. I need you to meet me at the address I'm about to send you. I need help cleaning up a body." She paused. "Bring them with you."

With no further explanation, she hung up and stuffed her phone back in her pocket, eyes scanning the scene.

"Didn't he want to know why you needed help cleaning up a body?"

"All Alexei ever needs to know is I need him."

"And he'll drop whatever he's doing to come help you?"

Carina looked at Tessa like the question was absurd. "Of course he will. Now, put that knife in the sink, wash your hands, and try to take deep breaths. He's about thirty minutes out, and there's nothing to do but wait."

Once Carina made sure Tessa could leave the bathroom without breaking down, she sent Tessa out to tell Sienna what happened and wait for Alexei. The man cut thirty minutes into twenty, breezing through the door of the restaurant and stalking toward them. He was tall and intimidating, with bright green eyes, dark blond hair, and a jagged scar running down the side of his face.

"Where is she?"

"In the bathroom," Sienna supplied, trailing a comforting hand up and down Tessa's arm when she could only point.

"Stay here. Luca and Matteo are right behind me."

Alexei gestured to another man standing by the door, and they made their way down the short hall toward the mess she'd made. Wrapping her arms tight around herself as an

SUV squealed into the parking lot and Matteo and Luca jumped out, Tessa braced herself for Matteo's temper.

What she didn't expect was the way he wrapped her up tight in his arms and kissed her forehead. His hands roamed from her shoulders to her wrists and up her back as if he was assuring himself she was safe and whole.

"People are starting to stare," Sienna said softly.

Matteo pivoted to stand next to her, dropping some bills on the table before wrapping his arm around her waist and leading her from the restaurant. Luca and Sienna were right behind them, and it didn't take long before a black SUV pulled around the side of the building and onto the road, Carina and Alexei joining them moments later.

"What the fuck happened?" Luca demanded, tugging Sienna in tight against his side.

Tessa's throat constricted even as Matteo ran a soothing hand up and down her back. She was too shaken up to tell them anything but the truth. Or some version of it, anyway.

"He works for my father. Worked," she added, squeezing her eyes shut.

"How did he know you were here?"

Luca's tone was accusatory, but Tessa laid a hand on Matteo's chest before he could snap at his brother.

"He said he's been following Sienna since you got back from Spain."

Sienna's eyes widened in shock. "Me? Why?"

"He said my father wanted you dead. To try and stop the sale of Gallo Industries."

"And you decided to kill him out of the kindness of your heart? To protect Sienna?"

"Christ's sake, Luca," Matteo snarled. "Would you rather she let him leave the bathroom alive?"

"He threatened to rape me before he killed Sienna," she whispered. "So it wasn't entirely selfless."

Matteo's hand slid up her back to her neck, and he squeezed, pressing his lips to her temple and lingering there for a moment.

"Not a single one of you goes anywhere without an armed escort, understand?" Matteo said.

"I won't be a prisoner on my own island," Carina replied, crossing her arms over her chest. "I can take care of myself."

"It's not up for debate," Alexei said, pinning Carina with a meaningful look until she relented with a sigh.

"Fine. But I hope you're planning on ending this soon, Matteo. I don't need an entourage while I plan the wedding."

"It'll be done soon enough," he assured her. "Though I don't know how Antonetti might respond to this little hiccup in his plans."

"I'm sorry," Tessa murmured.

"Don't be," Matteo replied, cupping her face in his hands and brushing his thumbs over her cheeks. "You did what you needed to do."

"And I'm grateful," Sienna said, reaching out to squeeze her shoulder.

"I want to move up our next meeting. If Antonetti wants to change the game, then let's fucking change it."

Matteo glanced at Luca, who nodded.

"I'll reach out to Dom. But first I'm going to take Sienna home."

"I'll meet you back at the casino," Alexei said to Luca, leading Carina toward a silver Aston Martin and leaning down to kiss her before helping her in.

No sooner had doors slammed and engines started than Matteo's lips were on hers, his hands gripping the curve of her hips to hold her tight against him. She clung to him the way he clung to her, soaking up every ounce of comfort he was willing to give and using it to banish the images of blood and death.

He pulled away sharply, leaving her feeling empty and wanting more of him. Without a word, he guided her around to the passenger side and gave her a hand up. They rode in silence back to Palermo, his hand reaching for hers over the center console, and she wondered if she could somehow salvage today's turn of events with her father or if he would take this as a declaration of loyalty to the Bianchis.

She wasn't sure if she'd be able to convince him otherwise. Moreover, she wasn't sure she wanted to.

Chapter Sixteen

The former Varda mansion rose from behind the low stone wall lining the sidewalk. Matteo hadn't relished the idea of driving from Palermo to Agrigento for today's meeting. Not after Tessa was attacked at the restaurant.

But Dom had two new shipments of weapons coming in today and was actively training a new cohort of soldiers. Coming to Agrigento just made sense. And he'd left plenty of men back at the villa to ensure no one got to Tessa while he was gone for a few hours.

Plus, now he could see firsthand all the renovations he'd paid for. They'd assumed control over the sprawling villa months ago when Dom killed Varda, or rather, when Emilia killed Varda to save Dom and her sister.

Before moving his ready-made family in, Dom had filled in the vulnerabilities and upgraded the security systems. Then once they were safely behind its walls, he'd given Emilia free rein to redecorate, claiming the property was in desperate need of some modern female touches. If the outside was any indication, Dom wasn't wrong.

The wrought iron gate guarding the driveway swung in at the touch of the security code Dom had given them, and Matteo pulled through and around to an inner courtyard. Tall trees shaded the brick, and a raised balcony ringed the first floor.

Emilia had taken what she initially described as a bare prison courtyard, where Varda's men would gather to smoke and drink while waiting for orders, and turned it into a pretty little oasis with flower beds and a bubbling fountain.

Dom stood in the break of the iron railing at the top of a short set of stairs, one hand in his pocket, the other resting protectively on Emilia's hip. His stance was challenging, the set of his jaw defiant.

Matteo bit back a sigh. Why did these interactions with his brothers never seem to get easier? Each one was more exhausting than the last.

He was the first one out of the car but the last one up the steps, giving Dom a small nod before following the others inside. It was simply and elegantly decorated in shades of blue and white, and Matteo had to admit, a huge improvement over the gaudy gold everything before they all but gutted the interior.

Dom led them down a short hallway and around a corner to a large family room. Matteo recognized some of the art on the walls from the family collection and had to stop himself from pausing to study each piece. Like their father, Dom preferred Italian painters. Or maybe it was Emilia's preference here.

Maids setting up coffee service on a side table quickly bobbed into curtsies when Dom entered, stumbling when they saw Matteo and doing another quick curtsy before disappearing through a seamless back door hidden by the wallpaper.

"You've outdone yourself, Emilia," Carina said, kissing Emilia on each cheek. "The house looks amazing."

Emilia smiled, pride evident on her face. "Thank you. And thanks for recommending that tile guy. He did such great work on the bathrooms upstairs."

"My pleasure. We have him redoing the whole house after the wedding."

"When is that officially?" Dom wondered, pressing a kiss to Emilia's temple and handing her a cup of coffee.

"Well, if you would all finally come out to Marsala for dinner, I would tell you."

"Christ," Luca muttered. "What is it with you and this dinner invitation? You've been on us for months."

"Yes. I have. Catch a clue that it's important to me, why don't you?"

"We'll put something on the calendar," Sienna insisted before Luca could snipe back. "Between the three of us, we'll make sure it happens."

Matteo tried to picture the seven of them seated around the dinner table at the Marsala house Carina had purchased from him a few months ago, making small talk and play-acting at being a real family. It's not like they had much to discuss beyond business and mundane small talk.

"How are the kids adjusting to their new school?" Carina asked of the expensive private school Emilia's younger brother and sister were now attending.

Matteo watched the women naturally gravitate toward one another. They hadn't known each other long—he'd only just found out Sienna was alive a month ago—but they already seemed easy with each other. He tried to imagine Tessa among them, and the fact he even let his mind wander to such a ridiculous notion was an annoyance.

It was enough that he'd been battling images of the worst happening to her in that bathroom. Of Carina finding a different body on the floor. It was an image he desperately wanted to scrub out of his mind forever.

He'd tried distracting himself with work, but the only thing that seemed to work was Tessa. And he didn't like that he was getting so close, so distracted. So attached.

"Good, I think," Emilia replied. "Antonio is—"

"Maybe we can save the family small talk for Carina's dinner party," Matteo said, voice clipped, earning him an eye roll from Carina and a glare from Dom. "We have business matters to discuss."

He waited for them to pair up on the couches and chairs before taking his own seat.

"It would appear Antonetti has finally figured out what we're up to," Matteo began.

"The little bird sleeping in your bed must be whispering in his ear."

Clenching his jaw, Matteo twisted his watch around his wrist. He supposed he deserved barbs like that. He'd said much the same about both Emilia and Sienna in the last several months.

Still, after Tessa had killed a man to save Sienna's life, he'd hoped his brother would soften toward her at least the tiniest degree. Those hopes had been quickly dashed.

But Tessa knew nothing about their plans for her father. They didn't spend their time alone together on conversation, and even if they did, it would hardly be about the next step in their strategy, as his brothers so often seemed to do with their women.

"Or Antonetti figured it out when his man didn't come back with Sienna's body. And we haven't exactly been quiet about any of this. He was bound to put it all together eventually," Matteo reminded them. "Besides, it doesn't matter if he knows or not, anyway. He's given us a gift."

"What gift is that?" Carina wondered.

"I've been monitoring his outbound calls," Sienna said, pulling a laptop out of the bag at her feet and opening the lid.

"So we know everyone he's contacted?" Alexei leaned forward, eyebrows raised.

Sienna grinned, fingers flying over the keys. "We do."

"And because we do," Matteo continued, "we can guess which alliances he values the most based on who he's tried to contact."

"And which are those?"

"Russia was a big blow," Sienna said to Dom. "If the number of times he's tried to contact them and failed is any indication."

"How do you know he's failed to contact them?" Emilia asked.

"Because all the calls are ten seconds or less."

Emilia nodded slowly. "So no one's answering, or he's being sent to voicemail."

"That's our guess," Luca agreed. "For too long, the Antonettis have relied on their own family for their numbers. And with the last two generations being much smaller, he needs the foreign muscle."

"And we've just cut him off from it."

"Yes," Matteo replied. "And a huge revenue source now that the Spaniards are supplying us instead. Thanks to Tessa," he added, pinning Luca with a look. "His hotels are doing well, but not well enough to pay the number of men he needs to stand against us. He had an arrangement with the Russians that is useless to him while they're busy fighting each other."

"So we've got him, then," Dom said. "We can take him down and be done with the whole thing."

"Not quite." Matteo glanced at Sienna. "There's one number he's called almost a dozen times within the last week."

Carina tilted her head. "Don't leave us in suspense, brother."

"An angel investor."

"All the money Antonetti makes from his hotels and his illegal dealings, and he needed an infusion of cash?" Carina asked. "When?"

"About eight years ago, when his wife went missing."

"Interesting timing," Luca murmured, and Matteo nodded. He'd had the same thought.

"They don't own a controlling stake in the company. Only about 35 percent."

"But he can and would fight us for it if given the chance," Dom guessed.

"She," Matteo corrected. "His angel investor is Nicolette Dumas."

Luca whistled. "Of Dumas-Theroux International?"

"That's right."

"That's one of the largest investment companies in Europe," Carina said.

"I can't imagine they'd stand idly by during a takeover when their investment can't be guaranteed."

Matteo nodded at Alexei. "They wouldn't. They like money too much not to fight for what's owed to them."

"And how would you know that?" Dom asked, ignoring Emilia's light elbow to his side. "Another one of your mysterious foreign trysts we know nothing about?"

"My foreign contacts have made all this possible," Matteo snapped. "Trying showing a little more gratitude."

Alexei snorted. "I don't see your precious foreign contacts here doing your dirty work."

"Maybe not. But without them, we wouldn't know half the things we know, and Antonetti would be all but untouchable. Now that we know his weakest spot, we can press it. Then we can make our move."

"Press it how?" Luca demanded.

"I've only met Nicolette once, but I know her partner. Or her father's partner before he died and Nicolette took his place. Laurent Theroux." Matteo shifted as everyone stared. "We've done business together once or twice. I can request a meeting."

"I don't speak French very well. I'm better at reading and writing it," Sienna said.

"He wouldn't meet with you anyway. Theroux doesn't do emissaries."

"Which means…" Carina began.

"I'd have to go to Paris for a few days."

Luca tapped his fingers on the arm of the sofa. "I could go with you if you can wait until next week."

"I'm going to take Tessa."

The mood in the room changed in a finger snap, and Matteo braced himself against the angry protests. They could say what they liked. He knew this business better than they did.

Theroux preferred to play at being a good host before talking business. The easiest way to get him to sit down and talk about anything beyond opera or wine or his newest thoroughbred stallion was to bring a beautiful woman to have dinner with him and his favorite mistress.

The last two times Matteo had met with him, he'd taken Maeve. She was sharp, and even though Theroux didn't allow women into the business discussion after dinner, she always had some interesting insight to share on the way back to the hotel.

He knew his brothers and sister would disapprove of his taking Tessa, but he didn't much care. He was not going to leave her alone for several days while he was out of the country. Not knowing her father had the means and the balls to follow her.

Who knew what Antonetti might do if he found out Matteo was out of the country on business. He would not leave her vulnerable, and he didn't trust Luca to protect Tessa the way he would. She was going, and they'd all just have to get over it.

They were in the home stretch of this. Working out a deal with Theroux to purchase the stake Dumas-Theroux International had in Antonetti's hotels or negotiating a peaceful transition of power when they assumed control was their biggest hurdle in taking the final step and eliminating Antonetti.

With this piece of the puzzle secured, taking out Antonetti would be easy. Then the Bianchis would sit on Sicily's throne at long last, and with her father dead, Tessa would have less of a reason to leave. He was starting to want that as much as he wanted the throne.

"It's not a discussion," Matteo barked over the buzz of squabbling voices. "I know what brings Theroux to the table. And if bringing Tessa means we get what we need, then that's what I'll do."

"You're suddenly keen to take entirely too many liberties with this family and its safety," Dom growled, shoving to his feet. "Hopefully you don't get us all killed while you're distracted by what's between Tessa's legs."

"Domenico!" Emilia scolded.

"Don't Domenico me," Dom replied, his tone harsh even while he wrapped an arm around Emilia's shoulders and pulled her close. "After the way he treated you and Sienna and even Carina, we're all supposed to pretend we're not seeing what's right in front of our faces?"

"I don't think that's entirely fair," Carina said. "I admit I have my reservations. But after what happened at the restaurant, I'm willing to give her a little grace and see if she surprises me."

"We still don't know much about her," Dom reminded them.

"I know enough to know she'll be fine if I take her to Paris for a few days in order to close the most important deal of the last eight months."

"I'd feel better if you took Maeve." Luca pinned him with a hard stare. "I think we all would."

"Lucky for me, this isn't a democracy," Matteo replied. "This is my judgment call, and I'll make it how I see fit. If you don't agree with my choices, if you don't think I'm doing the best job I can to get us all what we want…challenge me. If you best me, you can run this family and this island however you damn well please."

He stalked to the door, stopping short at the threshold. "Until that time, my word is law, and you'd all do well to remember that."

Chapter Seventeen

Tessa checked the time on the large antique clock hanging in the hall, twisting her phone in her fingers in case someone walked by and she needed to look busy. Matteo, Luca, and Sienna were all gone to Agrigento today. Another meeting to decide the best way to overthrow and take down her father.

Matteo hadn't wanted to leave her alone, staying curled around her in bed well past when he'd normally be up and going about his day. It warmed her in a way she knew it shouldn't, but every time Matteo touched her, a little piece of her slid back into place. His touch erased the memories of the man she'd killed.

She didn't feel bad about killing him, not knowing the fate she'd saved Sienna from, saved herself from. But she hadn't heard from her father since it happened, and she was beginning to worry that there'd be an unwelcome gift with his message the next time she did.

Which is why, as much as she hated it, she was going to force herself to use the empty house as an opportunity to send her father something she hoped he could use. If only to keep her mother breathing a little longer.

But the more time she spent with Matteo, the more she hoped Maeve would find her mother so Tessa could do everything in her power to help the Bianchis bring her father down. She wanted his end, just not more than she wanted her mother back.

A noise at the top of the stairs drew her attention, and she melted into the shadows of a potted palm. Whether because of Matteo's orders or sloppiness, the maids had begun leaving Matteo's bedroom door unlocked after cleaning it.

The study remained a vault she couldn't get into, but Matteo sometimes brought work to bed. She'd seen a stack of file folders on his nightstand last night before he took her across the hall to her room and they made use of the giant claw foot tub in her bathroom. Matteo had taught her a new love of bubble baths.

The way he touched her, as if he'd never get enough of her, was addicting. She was constantly reminding herself it meant nothing, that he wouldn't want to have anything to do with her if he knew the truth about why she was here.

Her head would be on the chopping block right next to her father's if Matteo or any of them found out she was passing information to him. Even if that information never seemed to be as helpful as Salvatore wanted it to be. He was growing increasingly agitated that everything she'd sent him so far still left him a few steps behind.

The maids descended the stairs, talking animatedly while they lugged their buckets and vacuums from one room to the next. They always cleaned Matteo's room last, so she knew she'd have the whole upstairs to herself for a while. Matteo said he wasn't due back until midafternoon.

Waiting until their voices faded, she darted quickly up the steps, jogging down the hallway and around the corner. Her heart pounded and her palms grew damp when she noticed the sliver of light peeking out from the crack in Matteo's bedroom door. Open.

Checking that the coast was clear, she pushed in, leaving the door the way she'd found it. She slept in here often enough now that if someone happened in and found her here, she could say she was looking for a piece of clothing or an earring easily enough.

She rounded the bed and stared at the haphazard stack of manila folders where Matteo had left them on the nightstand. Bringing work to bed must be more of a habit than an intention for him these days. Since he rarely did more than worship her body until they both passed out once he came upstairs.

Reaching for the top file, she hesitated, bringing her hand back against her chest and curling it into a fist. Nothing about this felt right. Not helping her father, not betraying Matteo, none of it. But she wasn't doing this for herself. She was doing it for her mother. And getting her mother back alive was worth the guilt constantly eating away at her insides.

The first folder felt heavy in her hands when she lifted it up and dropped it on the bed, but she wasn't sure if that was reality or her conscience. Sinking to her knees, she flipped the folder open and leafed through the first few pages. Casino business. Probably not what her father was looking for.

The next folder was nothing but information about the strip clubs Matteo had absorbed from the Romano territory. The third was a bunch of paperwork with notes in the margins about Gallo Industries, the deal her father had tried to sabotage with Sienna's death. A plan she'd most definitely foiled by killing the man tailing her.

The last folder was stuffed with miscellaneous papers, and it surprised her. Matteo was so ruthlessly organized she couldn't imagine him lumping everything together into one folder. But the handwriting on this one was different, a loopier script than Matteo's usual all-caps text. Something his assistant had put together, maybe. The illustrious Maeve everyone seemed to love so much.

This one had sample drink menus for the clubs and a page of text detailing some ideas for siphoning business away from her father's hotel casinos. None of it looked very useful until she saw the page at the very bottom of the stack.

This one was a list of names, some of whom she recognized. Men her father had invited to the house for dinner or mentioned over drinks with Tomaso. Some of the names were starred, others were highlighted, and still more had notes scribbled next to them.

Ilyin was crossed out. The Russians she'd already warned him about. Another name was crossed out too, Salgado, with a string of numbers that looked like dates or maybe times behind it. Probably the Spanish contact she'd given Matteo. She didn't know what all the shorthand was, but it was the only paper in the stack that struck any sort of chord for her.

Using her phone, she took a quick photo of it and sent it to her father. Carefully tucking things back into the folder, she stacked them on the nightstand as best she could so they didn't look disturbed. Hopefully if Matteo noticed they'd been moved, he'd assume the maids did it while dusting.

Crossing to the door, she held her ear up to the crack and listened for any noise. Hearing none, she slipped out, pulling it to and darting across the hall to her own room. Slumping against her door with a sigh, she dropped her head back against it with a dull thud. How much fucking longer until this nightmare was over?

Her phone rang a moment later, making her jump. Luna flashed across the screen. Mouth suddenly dry, she moved further into the room and accepted the call.

"Hello?"

"Is that it?" her father demanded.

"What do you mean?"

"What I mean, Tessa," he snapped, "is what the fuck am I supposed to do with a bunch of names and scribbled notes? I already know Matteo is going after my contacts, and I've shored myself up in that department. I need more. I need to know where he's going to try to undermine me next."

"What I sent you is what I have access to."

She jumped at the sound of a door slamming across the line. "And I'm telling you it's not fucking good enough! I'm tired of playing catch-up. I didn't know about the Russian thing in enough time to head it off, and he used it as a distraction to steal a Spanish supplier right out from under me. And since the Gallo bitch is still breathing, I'm fucked there too."

Tessa squeezed her eyes shut and dropped onto the edge of the bed. Her father must have assumed the Bianchis took him out directly. For now, at least, her cover was intact.

"I'm sorry. I—"

"Did I ask you to speak?"

Tessa drew the inside of her cheek between her teeth and bit down on it hard. What the fuck else did he expect her to do? She was tired of playing this dangerous game, of balancing on the razor's edge and it still not being enough.

"We're going to change tactics."

"Change them how?"

Something in his tone set her teeth on edge. Whatever he was about to suggest, she wasn't going to like it.

"I'm tired of reacting to all his plans. Apparently he doesn't like your cunt enough to keep you closer in his confidence." A chair creaked in her ear, and she gritted her teeth. "I want to play offense for once."

"Okay."

"I want information I can use against him."

Tessa gripped her phone so tight her fingers ached. "What kind of information would that be?"

"What are his weaknesses? Where can I strike against him and do the most damage? What is he most afraid of losing? You've been there almost a month. You might not be very intelligent, but you're observant. I know you've seen something that could help me."

Matteo's Achilles' heel was his family. They might fight constantly, but he would do absolutely anything for them. And the idea of giving her father that information, of putting any of the Bianchis directly in danger in an effort to bring Matteo to his knees, turned her stomach. Human sacrifice was not what she signed up for.

"No."

"Excuse me?"

Her father's voice was clipped and full of rage, and she was infinitely grateful he was on the other side of the island. No doubt if they were in the same room, he'd have his hands around her throat.

"I said no. I'm not offering him up to you on a silver platter. That wasn't the deal."

"The deal," her father bit off, "was you pass me information that helps me win this war in exchange for seeing your mother again. What did you think was going to happen when you gave me that information? You thought I was going to send him running with his tail between his legs?"

She'd always tried not to think about it. Better yet, she'd hoped to be long gone from this island before she ever knew the outcome of her treachery.

"If that is no longer proper motivation for you, then I suppose I'll have to send you a bit of your mother to get your head back in the game. What do you think, Tessa? A finger? An ear? What would be most instructive for you? Maybe her tongue. So you can never hear her voice aga—"

"Stop it," Tessa demanded, forcing a shaky breath out between pursed lips. "How do I know she's even alive? How do I know you aren't fucking with me?"

"I told you, you'll have to trust me."

"No." She shook her head even though he couldn't see her. "That's not good enough anymore. If you want me to do this, then I want proof of life."

Shoving off the bed and pacing in the silence her father held, she chewed the pad of her thumb. If he rejected her demand, she didn't want to think what piece of her mother might show up first.

"Fine. I'll send you another picture."

"No." The distance and her own determination had made her bold. "I want to hear her voice."

"Tessa. I don't have time for these games."

"I'm not playing games anymore, Father. If that's the kind of information you want, I've just named my price."

"You're hardly in a position to be negotiating," he spat.

"Apparently I am."

More silence engulfed her until her father finally said. "It'll take me some time. A few days. Maybe more."

"A few days, then."

"Tessa," her father snarled. "If you don't have something good for me when I call again, I'll kill your mother before I hang up the phone."

"Let me talk to my mother, and I'll have something good for you."

She disconnected the call before he could speak again, clearing the call and text history and deleting the photo out of habit before throwing it into the center of her bed. Shoving her hands through her hair, she stalked to the balcony doors and wrenched them open.

The air was cold, but the sun was warm, and they both

played over her skin in a war of the senses. She let the wind dry the tears gathering at the corner of her eyes.

The more her father pushed and hedged, the less she believed her mother might still be alive. But if she wasn't, Tessa had been doing all of this for nothing. And she wasn't ready to believe it was for nothing yet. She wouldn't let herself go there until she heard her mother's voice. Or she didn't.

Bending at the waist, she pressed her forehead to the cool railing and let the chill wash through her body. Her mother had to be alive. Why else would her father agree to let Tessa speak to her? He had to know she wouldn't give him a goddamn thing if she spoke to a stranger.

But the alternative wasn't better. If he was telling the truth, and this time next week her mother's voice played in her ear, Tessa would have to betray the only person who had been kind to her in such a long time. A person she was starting to miss when they weren't together. A person who made her feel wanted and beautiful and cherished.

The end goal had been so clear when this all began, when she agreed to do this thing for her father. Now she couldn't see a way out of this without someone she cared about getting hurt.

Chapter Eighteen

Tessa stared out the window as the SUV rolled to a stop in front of a towering office building. Palermo's business district was not where she expected to end up when Matteo texted and said he was sending a car for her.

The driver climbed out of the front seat, rounding the trunk and opening the door. Hopping down to the pavement, she craned her neck to look up at the gleaming steel and glass.

So this was where Matteo went every day. It certainly fit the image he insisted on projecting, businessman instead of Mafioso. Still, the idea that he would rent office space in a high-rise building just to maintain that image seemed a little silly. And why would he summon her here instead of just waiting to talk to her at home?

Only one way to find out.

Crossing to the revolving glass door, she pushed into a lobby with a soaring atrium that was at least three stories high. The floors were black marble polished to a mirrored shine, and potted plants in elegant black and chrome planters somehow managed to give the vast space a cozy, inviting feel.

A man with broad shoulders and tree trunk arms wearing a black suit and tie with a white button-down sat behind a desk topped with the same shiny black marble as the floor. He caught her eye as she approached but didn't smile.

"I'm here to see Matteo Bianchi. Do you know what floor—"

"Tessa?"

She turned at the sound of her name to see a willowy redhead walking toward her, tablet balanced in one hand, a bright smile on her face.

"I'm Maeve," the woman said, extending her free hand for Tessa to shake. "I'll take her up, Gio," she said to the guard, who nodded. "This way."

Tessa trailed away from the guard desk and followed Maeve around the corner to a bank of elevators. Maeve pressed a button to call the elevator, and the doors opened immediately. Once inside, she swiped a black card over a pad, waited for the light to go green, and pressed the button for the top floor.

As the car climbed, Tessa tried to study Maeve without staring. This thin, beautiful redhead was not at all who Tessa pictured as Matteo's assistant. She didn't know how she felt about the uncomfortable pinch of jealousy between her ribs at knowing this was who Matteo spent most of his time with.

"I was wondering if I could ask you some questions," Maeve said, breaking the silence.

"Questions?"

"About your mother." Maeve smiled. "I've tried all the usual avenues to find someone, but she must be living pretty far under the radar. Or under an assumed name, maybe."

Maeve tapped a perfectly manicured nail across the screen of her tablet, brows drawn together. "I found her maiden name in a records search and tried that, but didn't have any luck. Can you think of any other names she might be using that would have allowed her to stay hidden for so long?"

Tessa shifted on her feet. It was impossible to know what lengths her father might go to in order to hide the wife who had so thoroughly disappointed him. Would he give her enough freedom to need an assumed name?

"My mother was really close with her maternal grand-mother until she moved to Geneva when my mother was fifteen. Anna Maria De Luca was her married name."

The door opened with a ding, and Maeve stepped off, fingers darting over the screen of the tablet. "That's very helpful. Thank you."

"Maeve," Tessa said, trailing behind her through the empty cubicles. "Do you think my mother is still alive?"

Maeve hesitated, and Tessa couldn't tell if she was preparing to lie or tell the truth.

"Honestly, I don't know. If she wanted to be found, I probably would have by now. But that doesn't mean she's dead. I'm going to officially rope Sienna in on this as long as Matteo has no objections."

"Objections to what?"

Tessa looked up to see Matteo framed in the doorway to a large office. He'd removed his suit jacket and vest and rolled his sleeves up to his elbows, exposing muscled forearms and the tattoo she liked to trace her fingertips over while he was sleeping.

"Tessa gave me an international thread to tug for her mother. If I can bring Sienna in to help with the search, it'll go a lot faster."

"Let's do that then. Do you have the files—"

"For the Spanish deal, yes. And Callum called about the—"

"Belgian sale. I know. He texted me. I also want to follow up with Schmidt about—"

"Braun," Maeve finished. "Already on it."

"And you have the documents I asked for?"

Maeve set her tablet on the desk outside Matteo's office and leaned over it to open the top drawer. Pulling out a thick sealed packet, she handed it to him.

"Perfect, thank you. Tessa?"

He motioned toward his office, and Tessa looked between them one more time before stepping into it.

"You and Maeve must be very close," she said when the door closed behind her. "Finishing each other's sentences."

Expecting Matteo to round the desk, she jumped when he moved behind her and spoke low in her ear, his breath tickling her cheek.

"You're not jealous, are you, *piccola*?"

"Of course not," she lied, ignoring that pinching sensation in her chest as it galloped back to life. "Everyone mentions Maeve all the time. It's nice to finally put a face with a name. But I don't understand why I'm here."

"I would have come home to collect you, but this was more efficient."

She swallowed hard as he moved in front of her and unsealed the packet in his hands, sliding things out. Maybe he knew she'd been communicating with her father all this time. She shuddered to think how he might be planning to punish her if that was true. Though she couldn't imagine Maeve would have been so friendly if Tessa were truly in trouble.

"We're going to Paris."

She stomped out the white-hot flare of jealousy and disappointment. "I'm pretty sure you could have just texted me that you and Maeve were going to Paris."

The next few days would be an exercise in not torturing

herself with images of what the hell Maeve and Matteo would be doing together in Paris. Hell, what they probably did every spare moment at the office. Maeve was very pretty. And they were so in tune…

"Not me and Maeve. Me and you."

"What?" Tessa blinked up at him. "Why are you taking me to Paris?"

He shuffled through a stack of what looked like passports until finding the one he wanted and handing it to her. "Because I have business to attend to there, and I want to take you with me."

"Why?" She took the passport from him and flipped it open to a picture of her face and an unfamiliar name. Tessa Santoro.

"I need a woman on my arm, and I don't want to leave you here alone after what happened."

Her head snapped up, something softening inside her at the look on his face. This was the danger of getting too close.

"I'm not very good at business stuff. You should take Maeve."

Grinning, Matteo slipped on his vest and then his jacket, buttoning both. "You are jealous."

"I'm not!" She squirmed under his direct, teasing gaze. "Besides, I don't have anything to wear."

"I had our favorite clerk from that boutique you like send a dress over for you. It's all arranged."

Her cheeks heated at the memory of the looks they'd gotten from the clerk ringing them up when she emerged from the dressing room.

"When are we leaving?"

She didn't want to potentially miss a call from her father, but she didn't want to let him know she was leaving the country with Matteo either.

"Right now. My meeting is tomorrow, and we'll come back the day after."

She blinked. "But I'm not packed."

"I had the maids pack a bag for you."

Tessa's eyes dropped to his hand when he held it out to her. "Why didn't you tell me about this last night?"

"My mouth was busy doing other things to you last night." He pulled the door open and nodded to Maeve before leading Tessa to the elevators. "And I wanted to make sure I'd be able to get you a passport in time."

She looked down at the document in her hands. "Santoro?"

"In case your father is tracking your movements."

"Can he do that?"

Matteo pressed a kiss to her knuckles. "If he wanted to. Hence the fake passport. Don't worry, *piccola*. You're safe with me."

The drive to the airport was quick, and the SUV pulled alongside a small jet idling in the private aircraft section. A woman dressed in a navy blue and white skirt suit stood at the bottom of the stairs directing two men carrying bags back and forth from a second SUV.

Matteo climbed out first and then helped her from the car, nodding at the flight attendant, who greeted them both by name. Shaking her head when he gestured for her to go first, Tessa gripped the railing on both sides and followed Matteo up. He ducked to enter the plane ahead of her, and she paused before taking a deep breath and doing the same.

Tessa stumbled to a stop, and her breath caught in the back of her throat. She couldn't help but stare. The short, wood-paneled hallway opened into a wide seating area with plush leather chairs lining either side of the aisle. She counted four chairs clustered around a small table and two more beyond opposite a sofa with a closed door directly ahead of her and a small kitchen area behind.

Matteo claimed one of the chairs facing her, watching her with a bemused expression. "Never been on a private jet before?"

"I've never been on any kind of plane before," she breathed, taking the seat across from him and marveling at the china coffee service and tiered tray of finger sandwiches on the table between them.

Pulling his phone out of his pocket when it rang, Matteo checked the readout and set it on the table without answering. "Did you take the train on all your family holidays?"

Tessa leaned back in the chair, caressing the soft leather and refusing to meet his gaze. "I've never left Sicily. My father wasn't one for family trips. At least not with me. He and my mother went to New York once, though."

When she glanced up, Matteo was watching her intently, eyes never leaving hers even as the flight attendant boarded, closing and locking the door behind her.

"Your bags are all loaded, *Il Signore*," the woman said. "We should be ready for takeoff in about twenty minutes. Can I get you anything in the meantime?"

"You can take this." Matteo gestured at the coffee service and sandwiches. "And bring us two glasses of Prosecco."

"It's a little early for alcohol, isn't it?" Tessa wondered.

"Never too early to celebrate."

Tessa raised a brow. "Celebrate what?"

"One of many firsts for you on this trip." His phone rang, and he ignored it again. "The plane ride, leaving the country, seeing Paris."

"You've already given me several firsts."

Matteo gave her a questioning look, but she waited until the flight attendant set their glasses on the table and left before continuing.

"Blow jobs, sex, sex in public, sex in a...well, all the different places we've had sex, really."

He paused in his reach for his glass, eyes darkening. "Tessa," he said, his voice so low and gravelly it raised goosebumps over her skin. "Are you telling me you were a virgin the first time I fucked you?"

She bit her lip, unsure if the truth would be in her best interest. It was hard to tell whether the offhanded confession had upset him.

"Well, I...um...technically. Yes. You're the first man I've ever slept with."

He was up in a flash, yanking her out of her seat and tugging her hard into his lap. Hands sliding into her hair, he brought her mouth a hair's breadth from his.

"Say that again."

"You're the only man I've ever had sex with," she whispered.

He crushed his mouth to hers, tongue sliding past her lips to take, hands fisting in her hair to hold her in place. She groaned against his roughness, but that only seemed to spur him on, shifting her on his lap and angling her jaw to take the kiss deeper.

"I would have gone slower if I knew," he said, tilting his head to trail a line of kisses down the column of her throat.

"I didn't want you to go slower. I wanted exactly what you gave me, what I asked for."

He nibbled her shoulder, hands sliding up under her shirt to graze his thumb over her nipple through her sheer lace bra. "I could have hurt you," he said, sounding outraged at the thought.

"You didn't."

"You were innocent."

She laughed, and he pulled away sharply. "I said I was a virgin, Matteo, not a saint. You have heard of dildos before, right? Vibrators." He growled low in his chest, his fingers tightening on her nipple. "Toys," she said, gasping softly.

"Toys," he murmured, scraping his teeth against her jaw. "Now I know exactly what to buy you next."

She groaned, squirming on his lap, then jolting when the flight attendant cleared her throat.

"We're ready for takeoff, *Il Signore.*"

Matteo made a grunt of acknowledgment, but didn't stop his exploration of Tessa's skin with his lips.

"I think that means we need to put our seatbelts on," Tessa said, giving his shoulder a light shove even as she leaned into his kisses.

Sighing, Matteo shifted her into the chair next to his and reached for her belt, buckling it over her lap.

"We are absolutely not finished with the direction of this conversation," he assured her, securing his own seatbelt and gesturing to the flight attendant that they were ready.

"That can be another first," she said with a grin. "Joining the mile-high club."

Chapter Nineteen

They had barely reached cruising altitude before Matteo was fumbling for her seatbelt, popping the catch and yanking her back onto his lap. Tessa's heart was pounding furiously; from the way his hands urgently roamed her body or the speed of takeoff, she wasn't sure.

His lips found hers again, demanding and possessive, as he pushed the hem of her sweater over her hips and stomach. He'd exposed the lacy underside of her bra before she came to her senses and pushed his hands back down.

"Wait."

"I did wait." He pressed his hand against her lower back to grind his cock against her ass. "We're in the air, and I want to see how many times I can make you come in two hours." He started to peel her shirt off again.

"Matteo. The dressing room was one thing, but I'm not having sex with you in full view of three other people."

"The cockpit door is closed," he assured her, sighing when she crossed her arms over her chest. "Fine," he grumbled, motioning for her to stand and taking her hand.

He moved to the back of the plane, taking a seat on the sofa and pulling her down to straddle his thighs before reaching around her to a control pad. After quickly tapping a series of buttons, a partition behind them slid closed, hiding the rest of the plane and staff from view.

She looked at him with wide eyes, and he chuckled.

"This couch folds out into a small bed, so there's a door for privacy." He gripped the hem of her shirt. "Feel better?"

"Yes. Thank you."

"Good."

Tugging the sweater over her head in one swift motion, Matteo leaned in and scored her breast with his teeth, smiling when she gasped. His hands skimmed up her thighs to the button of her jeans, undoing them and tugging the denim down just enough for him to get his hand inside.

"Fuck," he groaned. "You're wearing the panties that match the bra."

"You bought them. I figured you wanted me to wear them."

"I want to see you in them," he corrected. "Stand up and take your jeans off."

She stilled. "What?"

"This is my favorite set." He traced a finger over the teal bow between the black lace cups. "And I want to see what you look like wearing it."

"Matteo." She moved to stand when he planted his hands on her waist and eased her off his lap. "I've never…"

He grinned when her words trailed off. "Another first for me. Excellent. Come on, *piccola*. Let me see."

Biting her bottom lip, she hooked her thumbs in the waistband of her pants and shimmied them down over her hips. She'd been naked in front of the man plenty of times, but somehow stripping down to her underwear and putting herself on display for him made her more self-conscious than anything else.

His eyes were hungry as they roamed her from head to toe, his hand moving to rub his cock through his suit pants. When they were pleasuring each other, she knew what to expect. She could make up for where her body felt lacking with her hands or her mouth, but there was nothing to be done standing in front of him like this—vulnerable, exposed.

"Cold?" he murmured, reaching out to trace a fingertip over the goosebumps gathered on her stomach.

She flinched, but he didn't seem to notice, slipping his fingers into her panties and easing them slowly down her thighs—torturously slowly—until they pooled at her feet. Curling his fingers into her skin, the drag of his nails up her calves and over the back of her thighs made her shiver.

He traced the round globes of her ass, squeezing roughly while he leaned in and pressed a kiss to her belly button. His beard both tickled and set her on fire at the same time. Heat raced along her skin as her awkwardness slowly subsided the more he touched her.

This she knew what to do with. The giving and receiving. She could actually feel sexy as long as he wasn't studying her, as long as she could escape from her own head instead of incessantly listing all her flaws.

He brought his fingers up to trace over her slit, slipping one easily inside her and instantly curling it up to tap against her G-spot. Her legs wobbled, and he took her hands and placed them on his shoulders before adding a second finger.

Not a single fucking toy in the world could replace how Matteo touched her. Like she was everything. Like he never wanted to stop. She knew enough about her own pleasure before sleeping with him to ask for what she wanted, but Matteo showed her things she'd never even dreamed about.

Or maybe it was just nice to be touched by someone else

after convincing herself for so long she would never be with a man who actually wanted her. Not with the matches her father had been trying to set up her entire life. Men who saw the alliance or the money or the proximity to her father and not her, not Tessa, the woman.

His lips trailed across her stomach, the scratch of his beard adding a new layer of sensation as he pumped his fingers in and out, using one hand on her ass to guide the rocking of her hips. She dug her nails into his shoulders, capturing her lip between her teeth as he urged her closer and closer to the peak.

It wouldn't satisfy him, her release. The man was never satisfied until she was a heap of limbs, unable to move or think or speak. He enjoyed leaving her boneless in the middle of his bed so he could collect her in his arms and run his fingers through her hair until she fell asleep. Then he'd wake her up a few hours later by sliding his cock inside her, and they'd do it all over again.

He nipped her hip, pressing his thumb against her clit until she gasped before rubbing quick circles over it, need sparking over her skin like electricity as his fingers thrust deep.

"Matteo," she whispered, afraid her legs would give out the second she let go.

"Good girl," he crooned, eyes locked on hers. "I've got you. Come for me."

The second those words left his lips, she followed his command, pussy clenching around his fingers as she let go, the orgasm washing over her in waves.

He drew her into his lap, claiming her mouth as his hands fumbled with his belt buckle. When feeling rushed back into her body to replace the numbing euphoria, she reached between them and pushed his hands away. Fighting to pull down his zipper, she finally freed his cock, wrapping her hand around it and making him groan.

Shifting beneath her, Matteo pulled her higher up on his lap, flexing his hips to slide the head against her slit.

"Tessa," he ground out when she squeezed the base of his cock. "I need to be inside you."

"Okay."

She gauged the width of the couch. Not big enough. The carpet didn't look all that soft, but she was too desperate to feel him thrusting into her to care about how much her knees would protest later. When she started to slide off his lap, he stopped her.

"I want to watch you ride me, *piccola*."

"But I—"

He growled, shoving her hand away and slamming his cock inside her in one swift movement, holding her hips in a punishing grip and rocking her back and forth.

"Every time you say you've never done something before, it only makes me want to claim it more. To do every first with you."

He slid his hands around to the backs of her thighs, lifting her up and lowering her again until she was controlling the movements herself.

Her breath hitched each time she sank down on him, letting him fill her completely. And when he moved his hand up to press against her shoulder and tilt her body forward, she groaned as he seated deeper, the angle changing and making her shudder.

"Good girl," he panted in her ear. "Just like that until I come inside you."

Gripping the back of his neck for leverage, she fucked him. Slow at first and then faster, satisfied that she was driving him crazy each time she ground against him and made his cock twitch inside her. She loved to drive him wild, to push him to the edge until he lost all control, loved knowing she had the power to do that to a man. The power to do that to him.

"Tessa," he growled against her neck, his breath heating her skin. "Are you going to come for me again?"

"Yes," she whimpered, shuddering when his hand inched up her thigh and between her legs. "Matteo."

"Be a good girl, *piccola*," he said, swiping his fingers roughly over her clit. "And come all over me."

"Fuck," Tessa gasped, fingernails digging into the back of his neck, body shaking as he shoved her over the cliff and followed her into the abyss.

"Jesus fucking Christ," he breathed, groaning when she laughed and her pussy clenched around him. "You're so fucking perfect."

"Two times."

"What?" He picked his head up off her shoulder to look at her.

"That's how many times you can make me come in a two-hour plane ride."

Matteo lifted a challenging brow, his softening cock instantly going hard again inside her.

"You think that's it? We still have plenty of time left." He pinched her clit, rolling it between his fingers. "And I haven't even made you scream my name yet."

Chapter Twenty

Matteo scanned the email update from Maeve, ignoring her postscript about scheduling interviews for her replacement, and sent back a quick reply. The email from Luca was comforting, if curt. So far, Antonetti didn't seem to know they were in France. He'd made no moves to contact anyone since they'd left, and Nicolette hadn't contacted him either.

Closing the lid on his laptop, Matteo crossed to the bedroom to check on Tessa. They needed to leave in ten minutes if they didn't want to be late, and Laurent hated to be kept waiting.

The bedroom was empty, but the light was on in the bathroom, and he made his way around the settee at the foot of the bed and across the plush antique carpet. He caught her reflection in the mirror, stopping short at the sight of her.

She'd swept her thick mane of hair to one side and pulled it over her shoulder, pinning it up with a pretty clip she'd purchased when they went shopping earlier. Whatever she'd done to her eyes made them pop against the dress the boutique had delivered.

He hadn't picked it out as much as he'd asked the clerk for something in red that showed off the curves he loved to look at so much. It far exceeded his expectations.

Sheer red sleeves from shoulder to wrist wouldn't keep her warm, but they added a fairytale feel to a dress that left nothing else to the imagination. It hugged her curves from the swell of her breasts under the sweetheart neckline to her knees. She kept adjusting the ruching over her stomach and staring at herself with a frown.

When he walked in behind her, she glanced up at his reflection over her shoulder and then back at herself in the mirror, tilting her head and studying the dress with shrewd eyes.

"Are you sure this is what you want me to wear? It's so…"

"So?" He lifted a brow when she didn't continue.

"Tight. You don't think it's too tight?"

Wrapping his arm around her, he pressed his hand against the curve of her stomach and pulled her back against him. "I think it's perfect," he whispered in her ear. "I'm really going to enjoy taking it off you later."

She drew her lip between her teeth and leaned her head back against his shoulder. "I think I might enjoy that too."

He gave her a squeeze and pressed a quick kiss to the side of her neck. "Ready?"

"Ready." Her hand went to her bare throat. "Normally I'd wear a simple necklace with something like this. But I didn't see anything in my bag that would go."

"I have just the thing," he said, snapping his fingers and disappearing from the room.

Digging around in the side pocket of his suitcase, he produced a velvet box he'd pulled from the safe in his study after buying the dress for her. Lifting the necklace out, he carried it back into the bathroom and laid it over her neck, smiling when she gasped.

"Matteo. I can't wear this," she breathed, running her fingers over the pear-shaped ruby pendant hanging from the diamond-studded chain.

"Of course you can. This necklace is why I wanted the dress to be red. Besides, Laurent appreciates a nice display of wealth."

He slipped it under her hair and fastened it, watching as she adjusted it to lie flat. The large ruby did exactly what he wanted it to, sitting just above the cleft of her cleavage.

Tonight's casual dinner was as much a part of the dance as the actual negotiations would be once they left the women to their coffee and retired to discuss business. Matteo wanted Tessa on full display and for everyone to know exactly who she was going home with.

The restaurant wasn't far from the hotel. Laurent was a creature of habit and usually chose only one of two places. Tonight he'd chosen Paris's most exclusive and expensive restaurant. This place had a ten-month waiting list. A subtle reminder of who had the power.

The driver pulled up in front of the valet stand, and the uniformed valet opened their door, giving them both a quick bow of the head when Matteo slid from his seat and reached in to help Tessa out.

Tucking her hand into his elbow, he led them up a wide burgundy carpet and through a set of ornate gold doors. The maître d' smiled indulgently when Matteo gave him the name for the reservation and motioned them to follow.

"I can't eat here," Tessa whispered as they snaked through the tables toward the rear of the restaurant. "I have no idea what fork I'm supposed to use."

Matteo chuckled. "They'll bring you a new fork with each course."

"I have a very serious confession, then."

He wrapped his arm around her waist, squeezing her hip as they turned down a short hallway toward private dining rooms. "What confession is that?"

"I hate French wine."

Laughing, he pressed a kiss to her temple. "That's because it's disgusting. A few sips with each course and you'll be fine. Just do what I do and wash it down with water."

They finally turned into a room beautifully decorated in gold and teal with a table set for four in the center. A couple was seated in front of an unlit fireplace, heads bent together, backs to the door. The maître d' took both their coats and cleared his throat to announce their presence before leaving the room and closing the door behind him.

Laurent stood from his chair and turned, a dashing smile spread across his face. He reached a hand down to help the woman up, pulling her close and kissing her cheek.

"Matteo, it's so good to see you again," Laurent said in French, sweeping an appraising gaze over Tessa and nodding politely. "I'm glad you could join us for dinner. I hope you don't mind, I've ordered the chef's menu for the table."

"He'll switch to Italian eventually," Matteo whispered in her ear as they followed Laurent to the table and took their seats.

She raised a brow before turning to Laurent with a soft smile. "*Le menu du chef a l'air délicieux. Merci.*"

Laurent laughed, clapping his hands. "*Très bien! Vous avez trouvé un trésor,* Matteo."

"*Bien sûr,*" Matteo agreed, reaching for Tessa's hand and bringing her knuckles to his lips. "I appreciate you meeting with me on such short notice."

"Margot and I love a reason to socialize," Laurent said. "And you and I have worked well together in the past. But we'll save that for later," he said, leaning back in his chair as the first course arrived.

"Margot is Laurent's favorite mistress," Matteo explained to Tessa under his breath. "Don't confuse her for Mrs. Theroux. Laurent hates that, despite almost never being seen in public with his actual wife."

Tessa glanced across the table. "She looks so familiar."

"She's a film actress."

Her eyes widened slightly in recognition. "American."

"French American," Matteo amended. "Don't mention that either."

The waiter set a small plate down in front of her, and she looked at it and then back up at him. "How many courses did you say this was again?"

His lips twitched. "Thirteen."

"Dear God," she muttered as another waiter poured them each a small glass of wine.

"For tonight's amuse-bouche, you have a caramelized fig wrapped in thinly sliced prosciutto and topped with a nugget of Roquefort cheese and a toasted walnut. Enjoy."

"So, Matteo," Laurent said, drawing his attention away from Tessa, who was waiting to see how everyone else ate this tiny bite of food before digging in. "Maeve is well, I take it?"

"She is. She sends her regrets."

"She's a smart girl, that one. Even if her French leaves a little something to be desired. This one, however."

"Tessa," Tessa supplied with a smile.

"Your French is perfect."

"Thank you." She cut the fig in half the way Margot did. "I had a lot of time to teach myself and a very patient housekeeper who would let me practice."

"You're Italian too, I take it?"

"Guilty," Tessa replied, making Laurent smile. "But your city is beautiful. I'm enjoying my stay very much."

"You'll have to come back in the spring. Nothing beats Paris in the spring."

"It's true," Margot agreed. "The blooms in the city's gardens and parks are unmatched."

"I've also read the cherry orchard at Parc de Sceaux is a must see," Tessa replied.

"Oh, yes. Perfect for a day trip outside of the city."

Tessa was a natural, as if she'd been born schmoozing self-absorbed billionaires. Laurent was enchanted, continually challenging and being impressed by Tessa's command of French and her knowledge of French history. Matteo almost wished his brothers were here to see how right a decision he'd made in bringing her.

By the time dessert was served, Tessa was deep in conversation with Margot about the merits and drawbacks of method acting. When Laurent suggested they step into another room, Matteo almost didn't want to leave her.

Rising from his chair, he leaned over and captured her chin in his hand, brushing a lingering kiss across her lips. She smiled when he released her, and if he could, he'd snap his fingers and deposit them both right into bed.

Grabbing his cognac, he followed Laurent into a smaller adjoining room that looked more like a parlor than a private dining room, despite the intimate table for two in the center.

"I don't know where you found her, Matteo, but she's absolutely exquisite," Laurent said as soon as the doors were closed.

"Yes," Matteo agreed. "She is."

"You'll have to bring her again. Now, let's get down to business so we can get back to our women."

Matteo crossed to the window and watched the lights from the boats gliding down the Seine through the trees.

Normally he'd have spent dinner rehearsing this part, but he was too enthralled with Tessa to have bothered.

"There's a company I want to acquire in Sicily."

"I would have thought you were well beyond needing my capital for buying companies."

Matteo swirled the dark amber liquid in his glass and took a sip. "I don't need your capital to buy it. I'm here because you're already invested in the company I want."

"A fascinating turn of events," Laurent said after a beat. "Which company would that be?"

"The Antonetti Hotel Group."

"Fascinating indeed," Laurent murmured. "You're talking about a takeover, then. I know Salvatore Antonetti isn't in the market to sell. Nicolette would have told me."

"Something like that. He's cutting into my casino profits, and aside from that, he's a pain in my ass I'd like to get rid of."

"So you want to buy out our stake."

Matteo lifted a shoulder and took another drink. "If that's your preference, we can discuss that."

"And if it's not?

"A continued stake and an additional investment for renovations. Of the seven hotels, at least three of them need modern upgrades. Milan, Venice, and Naples. With those upgrades in place, we could increase rates, attract more international business, conferences, things like that. Grow profits year over year."

"I told Nicolette not to invest eight years ago. We certainly haven't seen the return we were promised. But she has a soft spot for Salvatore. I suspect they were having an affair, as he spent quite a bit of time in Paris that year."

"Is that going to be a problem?"

Laurent studied Matteo with a tilt of his head. "You've got a good head for business. The deals we made last year netted me more profit in six months than Antonetti has in eight years. No, it won't be a problem."

Matteo grinned, reaching out to give Laurent's hand a firm shake. He loved it when closing a deal was this easy.

"You do whatever it is you need to do to gain legal control of Antonetti Hotel Group, and I will make sure the board votes in favor of your proposal."

"And Nicolette?"

Waving a dismissive hand, Laurent downed the rest of his wine in one swallow. "She makes business decisions with her heart instead of her head. I've been looking for a good reason to get rid of her, and this might be it."

"So what you're saying is, don't fuck it up."

"Precisely," Laurent said with a chuckle, turning for the door.

"I hope it goes without saying I don't want any of this getting back to Nicolette or Salvatore before I've had a chance to make my move."

"Believe me when I say I want Nicolette out too badly to ruin this opportunity. Your secret is safe with me. Now"—he clapped Matteo's shoulder—"let's get back to our women. Another drink?"

"I think I'm going to take Tessa back to the hotel." Matteo drained the last of the cognac in his glass. "And get her out of that dress."

"Good man."

Laurent pulled open the door between the two rooms, and Matteo followed him through. Tessa and Margot sat in front of the dark fireplace, chatting in low voices, coffee forgotten on the table between them.

They looked up at the same time, and Tessa's eyes immediately found him, her whole body relaxing and her eyes going soft. He closed the distance between them and leaned down to kiss her because he could.

"Mind if I steal her away?" he asked Margot.

Margot gave him a knowing smile. "Not at all. Enjoy each other."

"Oh," Matteo said, reaching down to help Tessa to her feet, "I intend to."

Tessa blushed a pretty shade of pink as he led her to the door with his hand on the small of her back. Their coats were waiting for them at the front, and he helped Tessa into hers before shrugging into his own.

"Did you get what you needed?" Tessa said once they were in the car on the way back to the hotel.

"I did. And then some. You were fucking brilliant."

She grinned. "I was, wasn't I?"

He reached for her hand and pulled her up against his side, cupping her face in his palm and brushing his thumb over her cheek. "Absolutely fucking phenomenal. If I'd had you with me the last time I met with him, he might have given me a better deal on the loan I needed for the airport I wanted to buy."

"You own an airport?"

He pressed a quick kiss to her lips. "A small private one in Belgium."

The car slid to a stop in front of the hotel, and Matteo climbed out, reaching in to give her a hand. He nodded at the attendant who held the door for them and let his hand wander down to the curve of her ass as they crossed the lobby.

"I'm surprised you waited this long to grope me," she teased, pressing the button for the elevator.

"I won't be waiting much longer." The doors slid open and he tugged her inside, pushing her back against the wall and punching the button for the top floor. "I have been thinking about doing this all goddamn night."

Chapter Twenty-One

Tessa didn't get much time to prepare before Matteo's lips were on hers, his hands gripping her hips possessively while his tongue explored her mouth. She registered the faint beep as the elevator climbed, but she was too lost in him to notice the doors opening on their floor until someone cleared their throat.

Matteo took her hand, pulling her off the elevator and through the group of people with amused expressions waiting to get on. He fumbled the old-fashioned key, cursing under his breath before giving up and pushing her back against the door and taking her mouth again.

Fuck. If they didn't get inside this suite, he was going to end up fucking her in the hallway. And she would let him. Breaking the kiss, she turned in his arms and shoved the key against the lock until it finally slid home. Matteo painted kisses across her shoulders as she unlocked the door and it swung in.

He followed her inside, slamming the door shut and wrapping his arm around her waist to draw her back against his chest. Sliding his hands up to her breasts, he cupped one in each hand and gave them a rough squeeze.

"It's a miracle I was able to concentrate tonight with you in this fucking dress."

She smiled as he traced the underside of her breasts with his fingers and then slid them around to the zipper at her back, pulling it down with the click of metal teeth.

"You're the one who picked it out."

"I asked for red, and I asked for sexy." He pushed the sleeves off her shoulders and down her arms. "I didn't know they'd do such an expert job. And this goddamn bra and panty set."

The dress fell to the floor in a whisper of fabric, leaving her in only the black pumps, black lace bra, and matching thong. She wasn't usually one for thongs, but with the way Matteo was looking at her, she might have to wear them more often.

He twirled his finger in the air, indicating she should turn for him, and she obliged, catching sight of herself in the window across the room. She squeezed her eyes shut and moved quickly to face him. She would not ruin this moment or that look in his eyes with her insecurities.

Matteo shed his suit jacket, tossing it over a nearby chair and undoing his cuff links as his eyes raked her from head to toe. The desire in his gaze heated her from the inside out. That's what she wanted to see when he touched her, when he made her come alive.

"He was right," Matteo said, undoing the button of his suit pants but not moving to take them off.

"Who was?"

"Laurent. Tonight he said you were exquisite. He was right. You don't agree?" he asked when she snorted.

"I don't think me half naked is what he meant."

"Impossible." Matteo undid the buttons on his shirt as he moved closer. "I think about you naked all the time."

She chuckled, watching him reveal the tanned, toned muscles of his abs and biting her bottom lip. "You're biased."

He drew her up against his chest, smiling when she ran her hands up his torso to his shoulders and pushed his shirt onto the floor.

"I think about you naked all the time too."

"Do you?" he murmured, carefully removing the clip from her hair and setting it down with his cuff links.

"I do." She sighed when he fanned her hair over her shoulders, twirling the strands around his fingers. "Let's go into the bedroom, and I'll show you what I was thinking about at dinner."

"Why the bedroom?" He leaned down and nipped her bottom lip. "Plenty of surfaces out here for me to fuck you on."

"Because the curtains are closed in there, and I can't see my— People can't see us," she amended quickly.

He eased back slowly, studying her face for a long moment. When she tried to squirm away, he tightened his arm on her waist, holding her in place against his chest.

"You can't see your what?"

"Nothing. Just all the lights are on. People can see in here and watch us."

Matteo was silent for a long time, his fingers drawing lazy circles across her hip while he stared over her shoulder. Capturing her hand, he pulled her across the room to stand in front of the window. This close, she could see both of their reflections as if she was looking into a mirror.

"No one can see in." He skimmed his hands up her back, undoing her bra and easing it down her arms. "The balcony is lined with plants."

"Matteo." She sighed, peering over her shoulder at him.

"Turn around," he said, voice rough. "And put your hands on the glass." When she didn't move, he gripped both her wrists and placed them on the cold window on either side of her reflection. "I want you to watch me touch you."

"But, I—"

"Don't move," he commanded, reaching up to circle her nipples with his fingertips. "Keep your hands there until I give you permission to remove them. Don't close your eyes, don't look away, just watch my hands on your body. Your beautiful, soft, perfect fucking body."

His voice was low and gravelly, his breath hot on her shoulder. He held her gaze through their reflections for a beat before his eyes dropped to his hands on her breasts, and she did the same.

Unease settled in her stomach at the sight of her figure on full display like this, but he made quick work of that, brushing the pad of his thumb over her nipple as he leaned in to kiss her shoulder. His other hand wandered down to her stomach, caressing the soft curves before slipping into the waistband of her panties.

His fingertips grazed over her clit, and she gasped, hips twitching. Watching him touch her like this seemed to heighten every sensation. The slow, teasing glide of his fingers against her clit, the sweep of his thumb across her nipple, the warm, wet kisses from her shoulder to her neck.

All of it sent heat racing through her, electricity snapping across every nerve ending. Especially as he picked up the pace, gripping her nipple between two fingers and pinching it roughly, pulling it slowly away from her body until she whimpered from the pressure and the pain of it.

He let it fall from his fingers, watching her breast bounce before cupping it in his palm and squeezing. His breaths grew faster, harsher in time with her own, and he ground the hard length of his cock against the swell of her ass.

Sinking to his knees behind her, he trailed a line of kisses down her spine, watching his movements in the window as he pulled her thong down over her thighs to her feet. She groaned when his finger immediately traced along her slit before slipping inside her.

"I wanted you from the first moment I saw you. That day you interrupted our meeting."

"Why?" she gasped, rocking her hips forward when he added a second finger, pumping them deep.

"You're stunning." She snorted softly, and he gave her ass a hard smack in response. "I wanted to run my hands over every inch of you. Every curve, every dip. Everywhere. I wanted to make you mine."

Tessa dropped her head between her shoulders with a groan when he used his other hand to rub her clit as he fucked her with his fingers, picking up the pace until her legs wobbled.

"Eyes up," he commanded. "Watch yourself come."

Sucking in a sharp breath, she lifted her head and found his hand moving between her thighs at a frenzied pace. In, out, deeper, harder, faster, the pressure on her clit relentless. Her breath fogged the glass in front of her, and her body trembled, but he didn't slow or falter.

"That's my good girl," he said, voice hoarse, lips grazing her ass as she began to clench around him, and with one last painful squeeze of her clit, she tumbled over the edge.

She felt him stand behind her, heard the rustle of his clothes as he shoved his pants to the floor and stepped out of them. Then he was pressed against her, using his foot to position her legs further apart and pressing his palm to the small of her back to bend her forward.

Leaning over her, he brought his lips to her shoulder, then her jaw. "You're mine," he whispered as he slid deep inside her.

"Matteo," she groaned.

"Tell me I'm wrong." He pulled back and surged forward again with a brutal thrust.

He wasn't. That was the problem. But she couldn't be his, no matter how much she might want it. And once he found out she'd been passing information to her father, he'd want nothing to do with her ever again.

This moment with him, of watching herself become an object of desire, of feeling as sexy as he always told her she was, it was priceless. And it would have to last her a lifetime.

"Mine," he growled, punctuating the word with the slap of his hips. "Forever."

"Yes," she whimpered, fingers curling into the glass as he ravaged her.

Another lie. There would be no forever for them. Only this perfect encapsulation of how much he wanted her, frozen in time. She couldn't keep him, but she could keep this memory.

He reached up to grip her breasts as he slammed into her over and over, rocking her onto her toes and forcing low, needy moans from her throat. This was what she wanted to remember. The feel of him inside her, the feel of his hands on her skin, his fingers on her nipples, the ragged sound of his breath in her ear.

She wanted to remember the way her body felt like liquid fire whenever he touched her, whispered to her, coaxed orgasm after orgasm from her body until she was limp with exhaustion. Those were things that would last well after he hated her. That was her forever.

"Be a good girl," he breathed against the back of her neck, "and come hard for me."

He held her nipple tight in his fingers, increasing the pressure until she could barely breathe. When he wrenched it with a sharp twist of his fingers, she sobbed his name, her orgasm swamping her as his cock surged in and out of her pussy.

"Tessa," he said through gritted teeth, shoving deep and emptying himself inside her. "Do you believe me now?" he asked after a beat, flicking his tongue against her earlobe.

"About what?" she panted.

"About how perfect you are and how much I want you."

She chuckled in spite of herself. "I think I'm starting to."

He stepped away, and she groaned at the loss of him, leaning her forehead against the glass as she caught her breath. His fingers circled her wrist, pulling her body upright and spinning her slowly to face him. Pressing her back against the window, he kissed her, warming her to the core even as the cool glass sent a chill over her skin.

"I'm going to keep touching you, keep reminding you until you believe me," he promised her.

She bit her lip and glanced around the room over his shoulder. "On all these surfaces?"

He laughed, twisting his body and dropping onto the chaise. Pulling her into his lap, he pressed a kiss to the hollow of her throat. "There are so many surfaces in this place to try. But I want to watch you ride me again, *piccola*. You looked so pretty riding me on the plane."

Straddling his thighs, she looped her arms around his neck and brought his lips to hers. Her kiss was slow and deep, and he returned it without demanding more.

In that moment, she wanted nothing more than to tell him. To confess every single thing that had happened between when she saw him in her father's office and now and know that the two of them could find a solution together, find her mother, kill her father, and live happily ever after.

But that was a fairytale. And fairytales weren't real.

This was how it had to be. It would all come crashing down around her eventually. Hopefully she could escape

Sicily before he found out. She didn't think she could stand to see the look in his eyes when he learned of all the ways she had betrayed him.

"I'm never going to get enough of you, Tessa. I hope you know I'm going to keep you." He nipped her chin, groaning as she slid down his length. "Forever."

"Forever," she agreed.

For a little while longer, she would let them both have the fantasy that a future together was possible. She'd have plenty of time to think about all the ways this could go horribly wrong another day.

Chapter Twenty-Two

"Aren't you going to buy something for yourself?"

Matteo slid his sunglasses down his nose and looked at Tessa over the top. "And what do you call that?"

She glanced at the black and white bag he gestured to. "More lingerie than I will ever be able to wear in a single lifetime."

Wrapping an arm around her waist, he hauled her up against his chest, leaning down to kiss her. "Nonsense. I intend to make you model every single piece once we get home."

She tried to look stern, but it was broken by a grin when he dropped his hand and squeezed her ass.

"Matteo," she replied, a pleading note in her voice.

"Tessa."

"What about that watch you saw? We could go back and get that."

He darted a look back the way they'd come and checked the watch he was already wearing. "Maybe. Are you hungry?"

She lifted a shoulder in a casual shrug, pressing closer when a group of teenagers brushed past them. "I could eat. What time is our flight again?"

"Not for another couple of hours." Though he could spend weeks with her in Paris and still want more time.

Watching her experience the city for the first time was almost like experiencing it for the first time all over again himself. The sights, the shopping, the little cafés every ten paces. Everything enthralled her. And her French was better than his, something that never ceased to delight him.

Margot and Laurent were right; Paris was better in the spring. They could sit outside the cafés enjoying fresh croissants and café au lait or a nice lazy lunch or take a boat ride down the Seine for dinner. But she was a light against the dull days of winter bundled up in her bright blue coat, her thick black hair coming loose from the bun she'd swept it into and blowing across her face.

He reached up to hook a piece behind her ear, dropping a quick kiss to the tip of her nose. If not for everything waiting for him back home, he'd extend their stay by at least a day or two. But now that he had Laurent's promise not to stand in the way of the takeover, he had work to do.

"Let's get something to eat. Then maybe we'll see about the watch."

"If I had money, I'd buy it for you," she said, looping her arm through his and huddling into his side against the breeze.

"I gave you money."

"That doesn't count." She gave him a teasing bump with her hip. "That's your money. I don't have any of my own. I never have."

Her voice was sad, and he gave her waist a squeeze. "What would you do to earn your own money?"

They stopped outside a café to read a chalkboard sign

with the daily lunch specials, and Tessa was silent for a long moment.

"I don't know. No one's ever asked me that before."

They kept walking, bags rustling between them in the silence. The specials at the next restaurant looked better than the first, and they ducked in out of the cold, claiming a table by the front window.

"It should feel weird, shouldn't it?"

"What's that?" he wondered.

"Ultimately this whole trip is just another piece in a puzzle that ends with my father dead." She toyed with the edge of the menu, bending it back and forth with her fingernail. "What does it say about me that I don't feel bad about that?"

"Nothing."

She gave him a dubious look as the waiter approached the table and took their order.

"Do you want it to mean something?" he asked once they were alone again.

"No." She sighed. "I guess it doesn't have to. My father has never treated me as anything other than a nuisance to be dealt with. And my mother was a better buffer for his distaste of me than I realized. Once she was gone, there was no barrier there to save me anymore."

Matteo reached for her hand across the table, squeezing her fingers when she laid them in his. "I haven't had any updates from Maeve about it."

Her smile was sad, and it arrowed straight to his heart. "I haven't heard any from Sienna either." Tears gathered in her eyes, and she blinked them away rapidly. "She's probably dead," Tessa whispered.

"You don't know that," Matteo replied.

Though the longer it took Maeve to find someone, the greater the chance they weren't alive to be found. He had even less hope with Sienna digging into it too. Still, he didn't want to take that hope away from her if it was what she needed right now.

"We won't know until we know. Simple as that. And we'll keep looking until we find out. One way or another."

There was that sad smile again, the tears. "Thank you. You are better than I deserve."

Taken aback, Matteo blinked in surprise. But he didn't have an opportunity to ask her what she meant, interrupted by the sharp ring of his cell phone. Pulling it out of his pocket, he saw Luca's name flash across the screen. He almost silenced it and slid it back into his pocket, but Tessa waved a hand for him to answer it, so he accepted and pressed the phone to his ear.

"What can I do for you, brother?"

"There's a file I need in your office," Luca said. "What's the code for the door?"

Matteo frowned, leaning back in his seat as their waiter deposited their drinks and left again. "What file?"

"Numbers I crunched for the remodel on clubs three and four. Sienna's uncle on her mother's side is a contractor and thinks we're being gouged. Just let me in the damn office."

"Maeve can get you the file."

"Fuck's sake, Matteo," Luca snarled, a noise that sounded like something being thrown punctuating his words. "Maeve went home sick. Why do you trust some woman you met in Ireland three years ago and not your own fucking brother?"

"It's not that I don't trust you," Matteo said, trying to temper the irritation in his tone. "But I have a lot of sensitive paperwork in there."

"I have better things to do than rifle through your shit. It's one file. I can see it on the corner of your desk. Or I would be able to see it if you didn't seal your office up like some priceless tomb every time you left. A tomb only Maeve has the code to."

"I'll be home tonight. I'll get it for you tomorrow."

"Unbelievable," Luca said, ending the call.

Matteo dropped his phone on the table with a scowl. It wasn't that he didn't trust his brother. That wasn't it at all. It was that he was allowed a modicum of privacy. Privacy he couldn't maintain if everyone who wanted it had the keys and codes to his personal spaces.

"Everything okay?"

He glanced at Tessa's raised brows, shaking his head. "Just Luca throwing a hissy fit because I won't give him the code for my office."

"Why not?"

"Because." He found he didn't have a better answer when faced with her direct gaze, and he was grateful for the interruption of the waiter bringing their food.

"Because?" she prompted, dipping her spoon into her bowl of soup.

"Because I'll be back tomorrow, and I'll get it then."

He was aware of the defensiveness in his tone, and he hated it. He did not need to explain his choices. Not to his family, and not to Tessa.

"I thought all the locked doors were for me," she said softly. "Not them. Why are you so intent on shutting them out?"

Matteo dropped his spoon to the table with a clatter. "Jesus Christ. Now you sound just like them. I'm not shutting anyone out. Seven years of being on my own. No, scratch that. A lifetime of it. As if my father cared about my reasoning for anything. He taught me the Don's word was law. If only my brothers and sister respected that."

Tessa studied him, popping a piece of bread in her mouth

and chewing slowly. "And your father was a good man? A well-respected leader?"

Surprised by her questions, Matteo jerked. "No. I definitely wouldn't say that."

"Then why do you want to be just like him?"

Matteo opened his mouth, then closed it again. *Rule with an iron fist, or they'll walk all over your back, son.* Lorenzo had drilled that lesson into him for as long as he could remember. His father kept everyone at arm's length, including his children.

He refused to justify himself to anyone. He saw it as a weakness. And Lorenzo Bianchi could not tolerate even the perception of weakness.

"What's the point of winning the war if you all hate each other?" Tessa asked. "Believe me when I say it's a miserable existence. Being hated by people who are supposed to love you. Especially when you care."

"Who says I care?"

"Please." Tessa waved a dismissive hand in the air and spooned up another bite of soup. "If you didn't care what they thought about you, it wouldn't bother you so much."

He pursed his lips, staring down at his own soup before leaning back in his chair with a huff. Of course he cared about his family. Everything he was doing was for them. To make sure they avoided the cliff their father had been careening them toward. To preserve the family legacy for future generations.

The power and money and status and connections he was amassing weren't for himself. It was for every generation of Bianchis that would come after him. He wanted people to whisper Bianchi in international circles with the same reverence they whispered Callahan or Quinn or Verdugo. He wanted permanence for the Bianchi name long after he was gone.

"I don't know how to undo it all," he confessed quietly. "They're so angry at me for leaving all those years ago."

"Maybe you don't have to undo it. Maybe you can just move forward. They want what you want."

He raised a brow. "And how would you know that?"

"It seems pretty obvious to me. Your goals are the same. Maybe the reason your father's methods aren't working for you is because they didn't work for him either."

"How the fuck did you get so wise?"

Tessa chuckled. "A lifetime of wishing for my father to love me instead of hate me."

Lacing their fingers together, Matteo drew her into his lap, tucking her hair behind her ears and cupping her chin in his hand. He pressed a lingering kiss to her lips, wrapping an arm around her waist when she let out a satisfied little sigh.

"You deserve to be loved, *piccola*."

She smiled, leaning her forehead against his. "That's what my mother used to say." Her fingers stroked down the side of his face. "Be your own man, Matteo. You'll get better results that way."

Brushing a kiss against her cheek, he released her to return to her seat. Be his own man. That's what he thought he'd been doing. But maybe he hadn't run as far outside his father's shadow as he thought.

Chapter Twenty-Three

Tessa stood in her closet staring at the rows upon rows of new clothes Matteo had insisted on buying her. She'd sworn up and down she didn't need anything else, that what she had at home was fine, but the man wouldn't take no for an answer.

In fact, as soon as she'd agreed to go shopping on their final morning, he'd had them driven directly to a shop already waiting for them with champagne and items for her to try on. As if he knew he'd talk her into it eventually. Probably because he never failed to get his way.

It was nice to be dressed up by him. He knew what he wanted. And he wanted her. That might have been the best part. Being wanted after so many years of being discarded, forgotten, ignored.

She blew out a breath and stripped a pretty pink cable-knit sweater from the hanger, pulling it on and adjusting the sleeves. That was dangerous thinking.

They'd been back on the island for three days, and she still hadn't heard from her father. Not even a text message hounding her for information. It was starting to make her twitchy.

She wanted to believe that no news was good news, but all it did was settle a sickly feeling of dread in her stomach. If he knew exactly where her mother was, what was taking him so long to connect them by phone?

Smoothing the shirt down over her hips, Tessa slipped her feet into a pair of simple black flats and crossed into the bathroom. A second towel hung on the rack next to the tub, and it welled a deep ache inside her.

She shouldn't have let herself get this close to him. Aloof, detached, cold, unfeeling. That had been the goal, and it hadn't even taken her all that long to fuck it up. A handful of nice words from him, a few good orgasms, and suddenly she was putty in his hands.

Brushing her teeth quickly, she rinsed and turned off the light, stalking across the room to where she'd left her phone on the nightstand. Scooping it up, she brought up her contacts, her finger hovering over the call button for one of only a handful of people.

Luna. Her father's burner phone.

The name stared up at her, a taunt. One phone call. She'd demand a deadline to hear her mother's voice. She had a big juicy carrot to dangle in front of her father's face. Something better than how much Matteo loved his family, how vulnerable they made him. The airport in Belgium.

You didn't borrow money from a guy like Laurent Theroux to buy a private airport somewhere so far away unless you were planning on using it for something important. She didn't know what that important thing was, but her father would hardly care.

It was the perfect piece of information. The kind that would release her from this agreement with Salvatore Antonetti forever. Then she could pack her bags, get her mother, and never look back. That's the only thing she'd ever wanted.

It used to be the only thing she ever wanted. She tossed the phone on the bed and flopped down beside it, dropping her head into her hands. Now she wasn't so sure. Her desire to see her mother again warred with her want for Matteo until it was all a confusing jumble in her mind, and it was impossible to untangle the pieces for the truth.

Had she started to wonder if her mother was dead because of her feelings for Matteo or because it was the most likely outcome? If she let herself think about it too long, it became easier and easier to conjure up anger at her mother for not trying harder to find a way back to her instead of the intense relief she felt when her father first told Tessa her mother was alive.

That palpable relief had been a beacon of hope in a sea of darkness. Was that hopeful light fading because she was finally seeing the truth of her father's manipulation? Or because it made her feel less guilty about her warring desires?

It was impossible to know. Not really. At least, that's what she kept telling herself. She couldn't know for sure one way or another until she spoke to her mother. She wouldn't make any decisions until then.

Tucking her phone into her pocket, she headed downstairs for breakfast. Matteo had been up with the sunrise, raining kisses over her face and neck before leaving her to sleep. He likely wouldn't be back until late. They didn't ever talk about it, but she knew they were in the final planning stages of taking down her father.

It was an easy guess made even easier by the searching looks Luca would give her whenever he ran into her in the hallway, as if he was trying to see inside her soul and figure out if she was a traitor. She tried to avoid Luca as much as possible. Just in case she was becoming a little too transparent.

She heard a noise in the family dining room before she rounded the corner. If it was anyone at this time of day, it was Carina, who often stopped by the house if Alexei had club business close by she wasn't interested in.

From what Tessa could gather, Carina only cared about club business if she got to participate with a blade in her hand. There was something Tessa rather admired about that.

But the smile on her face died when she saw Luca seated at the table. Alone. He glanced up with his own smile, expecting to see Sienna, no doubt, and it quickly faded into a scowl when he caught sight of her.

Tessa contemplated retreating and asking Giulia to bring something up to her room or skipping breakfast entirely, but the butler was already setting out a place for her. Luca's eyes dropped to the extra place setting and then swiveled back to her face. He raised a brow, as if challenging her to be rude and leave now.

Dragging her feet across the floor, she sank into the chair the butler held out.

"Your usual latte and *bombolone*, signorina?" the butler asked.

"Yes, thank you, Taglia."

Luca's eyebrows shot up when she used the butler's name, but he wasn't looking at her; he was engrossed in the papers on the table in front of him. Or pretending to be, anyway. She wondered if it was the numbers he'd called and asked Matteo about on their last day in Paris. She also wondered if he knew she was the reason Matteo had picked up the phone again, called Luca back, and given him the passcode to his office.

Probably not. And even if he did know, she doubted it would make much of a difference anyway. Luca's suspicions had not ebbed since the incident at the restaurant, and even though Matteo didn't know it, Luca had every right to be. And Matteo would probably hate her soon enough too.

"Did you enjoy your holiday?"

There was a bite to Luca's question, a clear challenge, but she chose not to rise to it. Better to play dumb instead.

"More of a work trip, but Paris is very beautiful."

He snorted softly. "You call shopping work?"

Tessa bristled at that, but took a deep breath in through her nose and out through her mouth. If he was trying to goad her into an argument, it wouldn't work.

"Matteo insisted."

"Yes," he murmured, still pretending to study the pages in front of him. "He insists on a lot of things with you. It's certainly a departure from the norm where my brother is concerned."

The butler returned with her latte and donut, setting both on the table in front of her before retreating to the far corner of the room.

"I'm not sure I understand," she said.

Taking a sip of her latte, she watched Luca over the rim of the mug. He slowly organized the papers into a stack, tapping them on the table until they were perfectly straight and then slipping them into a pocket folder.

Pressing the flap closed, he sealed it with the metal pin and laid it on the table next to his plate, adjusting it with his fingertip until it was perfectly perpendicular to the table's edge. Only then did he look up at her.

The anger and disgust on his face were palpable, and she shrank as far away from him as the chair would allow.

"There isn't an impulsive bone in Matteo's body. For as long as I've known him, he's been steady, cold, calculating. Then you came along."

"Me?"

His scowl deepened. "Yes. You. I don't know what the fuck you said to him back in Syracuse, what sob story you're feeding him now, but he's the only one who believes it."

"I'm not feeding anyone any sob story."

"Please," Luca said with a derisive laugh. "Sienna told me about looking for your mother. You don't really think she's alive, do you? After all this time?"

She opened her mouth to speak, and he waved her words away.

"No, don't. It'll only piss me off when you lie." He shoved away from the table, leaning his knuckles against the edge to get as close to her as he dared. "I don't care how mesmerized my brother is with you. I don't trust you. And I'm going to figure out what your end game here is if it's the last fucking thing I do."

Snatching the folder off the table, Luca stormed out of the dining room and slammed out of the house. The mug rattled as Tessa set it slowly back in the saucer.

Luca shook her, and for good reason. If anyone was going to put together the pieces of what she was really doing here, it would be him. She desperately needed her father to call.

Because if her mother really was alive, the choice was simple. Or at least it used to be.

Chapter Twenty-Four

Scanning through the red pen edits from the lawyers for the Gallo contract, Matteo made notes of his own in the margins. Far enough out from the holidays, there was finally forward momentum.

Despite Antonetti's botched assassination attempt, the sale of Gallo Industries would go through in the next week or so. And hopefully not long after that, he'd slide Antonetti Hotel Group in right beside it. Then his empire would be booming.

Luca had been meticulous about the details of the deal for Gallo's foundering company, constantly offering notes and suggestions. He was adamant that it was fair and Sienna didn't get screwed somehow. He was half the reason the process had taken so damn long.

Matteo didn't see how he could screw her. The girl had a sizable inheritance after claiming what was owed to her from her father's estate, and she'd continue to benefit from its profits once Luca proposed and she became a Bianchi. Matteo had noticed the ring Luca thought he was concealing well.

Plus, it's not like he was stealing the damn company. He

was paying fair market value for a failing enterprise. It hardly mattered that he was the reason it was failing in the first place.

Setting the contract aside, he glanced through the glass walls of his office. He was eager to absorb both companies, eager to get on with the next phase of his plan. To fill up the sea of empty cubicles with employees to support the legitimate side of the empire.

The more money they made above ground, the more they could make below without drawing the ever-increasing suspicion of ambitious politicians wanting to take down the Mafia.

That was something the other Dons on the island couldn't seem to grasp. Not even his father. If they excelled at one, they inevitably failed at the other.

Varda had been so stuck in the old ways his men had started to splinter away, looking for better-paying work, making his takeover effortless. Romano had been so concentrated on his petty drug trade he'd ignored the failing health of his strip clubs. Gallo's weapons trade had been more of an afterthought than a business model in favor of Gallo Industries.

All of this made them easy targets. And if not for the hard work of Dom and Luca in his absence, Bianchi casinos would have gone under or been ripe for a takeover themselves. All of that was changing now. He was going to make damn sure they were never that vulnerable again.

Maeve poked her head in, drawing his attention. "Hey," she said, wiping her nose on a tissue. "Your brothers and Alexei are on their way up."

Matteo grabbed the legal pad he'd been making notes on and pushed away from his desk. "I thought I told you to go home an hour ago."

"I'm not going home. I'm fine," Maeve said, her voice thin and tinny from congestion.

"You're not fine. You're still sick." He stepped away from her when she started coughing into the tissue in her hand. "And you're getting your germs everywhere."

"I'm Irish," she replied. "We don't get sick."

"I hate to break it to you, but you—"

"Maeve." Luca weaved toward them with Dom and Alexei close behind. "What the hell are you doing here? You should be at home. Resting." Luca glared at Matteo as if he was keeping Maeve chained to her desk.

"I'm fine. I just need some tea and a—" She dissolved into another coughing fit, and all four men took a step back. "Men are such babies," she muttered.

"Get out," Matteo said, voice stern.

The firmness wouldn't work as much as the men standing around staring at them would. Maeve was a little sister to him, and she listened about as well as one when they were alone. But she understood and respected the chain of command when she needed to.

With an irritated huff, she yanked open the bottom drawer of her desk and pulled her purse out before slamming it shut. Grumbling to herself, she shuffled papers into a stack and stuffed them in her bag.

She glared daggers at Matteo, slinging her bag over her shoulder and stomping toward the elevators. Maeve hated to be sick, and he bit back a grin as he watched her sag against the wall while she waited for the elevator.

"It must be true what they say about the Irish and their tempers," Alexei said, scratching his fingertips over his jaw as Maeve shoved away from the wall and stepped into the elevator, angrily mashing the button to close the doors.

"You have no idea. No Carina today?" Matteo wondered.

He'd long since stopped trying to keep Carina from these

meetings. As much as he'd wanted to protect her from the harsh realities of this life like their father had their mother, she'd demanded a seat at the table. And he'd wasted far too much time and energy trying to keep her away from it.

"Something about table settings," Alexei said, following them into the conference room. "I'll brief her tonight."

Once they were all seated, Matteo claimed his spot at the head of the table and flipped his pad to the right page.

"As you know, Paris went off without a hitch. I talked with Theroux this morning. Not only is he eager for this transfer of power after seeing preliminary numbers from Antonetti's Q4 earnings, but he's also offered a sizable investment for renovations on the mainland properties."

"How's that change the deal already in place with Antonetti?"

"I'm still negotiating that piece."

"What's their current stake?" Luca asked, tapping his fingers on the edge of the table.

"Thirty-five."

Luca stared out the window, calculating in his head. "And how much were they promised as a return?"

"Four million in the first five years. They've seen less than half that in eight."

"Not surprising," Dom said. "According to some of my mainland contacts, Antonetti has been spreading himself too thin. It got worse after his brother died."

"He's been hiding his mismanagement well," Luca added.

"Very well," Matteo agreed.

"We could easily double profits in the next year."

Matteo smiled at the note of excitement in Luca's tone. Luca had a good head for business. One of many reasons the Bianchi name had survived while he was off island.

"At least. But this takeover has to be flawless. Just like Gallo, I cannot have a botched hit."

"Suicide then," Alexei said, voice just as eager as Luca's had been at the prospect. His father's old enforcer had always been a ruthless son of a bitch, a remorseless killer with a blade in his hand.

"I was thinking more like an accident," Matteo replied, chuckling when Alexei frowned. "Not as bloody as you'd prefer, I know. But again, this needs to look clean on paper."

Dom swiveled back and forth in his chair. "What did you have in mind?"

Matteo didn't need his notes for this. He'd been building this part of the plan for weeks. This was always going to end with Antonetti dead, but the closer he got to Tessa, the more Matteo wanted the man to suffer.

Salvatore Antonetti deserved to pay for every time he'd ever laid a finger on his daughter, ever bruised her skin, ever told her she wasn't good enough. He would give Alexei free rein to inflict as much pain as possible as long as the death ultimately looked like an accident.

"As far as anyone will ever know, this will be a legal sale from Antonetti to us. One that's been in the works for a while. Sienna can draft up the paperwork, fake correspondence between us, whatever needs to be done. Once Antonetti and his son are dead from a tragic accident, Theroux will help push the sale through to us based on Antonetti's final wishes."

"He's in on it?"

"No, but he knows enough about who I associate with to know the game we're playing isn't always an honest one. And Dumas-Theroux might not have a controlling stake in the company, but they have enough sway to push it right into our hands."

"It'll still look suspicious," Alexei pointed out. "To have him die so close on the heels of Gallo and suddenly you own both companies."

"It'll raise fewer alarm bells if we leak it to the press first."

"It'll raise Antonetti's alarm bells," Luca said. "He'll come after us when he gets wind of that."

"Not if I leak it to the right source," Matteo replied.

"And what source is that?"

Matteo swiveled to look at Dom, a skeptical brow raised. This was the usual point he'd offer some vague reference to his source or brush it off as none of their business. With Tessa's words ringing in his ear about being his own man to get better results, he decided to try something different.

"When I first left Sicily, I stayed in Rome for a few weeks, thinking I would just come home after I cooled off. Or after Father did." Ignoring the stunned expressions at his candor, Matteo pushed on. "I met a woman there. Regina. She was a beat reporter then, but she's a well-respected, award-winning journalist now. And she owes me a favor."

Luca shared a look with Dom and Alexei before asking, "Why would an award-winning journalist write a story about a business deal?"

"She wouldn't. But she'll hold the story until I give her the green light and pass it on to someone else at her paper."

"And we're sure we can trust her?" Alexei asked.

"I'm sure the favor she owes me is big enough she'll do exactly as I say."

Luca nodded, drumming his fingers on the table. "It would take a few days for a Roman news story to filter down to Antonetti, longer if he's not paying attention."

"We have enough people in our pocket to control the story after the fact. Give the accident enough time to die down, leave Theroux to handle Nicolette and make sure she doesn't do or say anything stupid to the press, and quietly close the deal behind the scenes. Maybe hold a press conference once we're ready."

"Do you care how he dies?" Alexei wondered.

"Not as long as it's painful."

Excitement lit Alexei's eyes. "How painful are we talking?"

Matteo set his pen on top of his legal pad and folded his hands in his lap. "As painful as possible while still making it look like an accident."

"A little retribution for your plaything?"

"Watch yourself, Luca."

"She's not wor—"

"We're finished here," Matteo snapped, pushing back from the table. "Dom, I'd like you to go with me to Rome. Can you take the time in two days?"

"Why me and not Luca?"

Matteo swept both his brothers with a look. "Because you're the second." Luca scoffed; Matteo ignored him. "So? Free?"

"Yeah, I can be free in two days."

"Great. I'll see you then."

Matteo swept out of the conference room and back into his office, slamming the door behind him and twisting the blinds closed to shut everyone out.

He was not going to spend the rest of his life justifying every single choice he made. This family was not a democracy. If Luca didn't like the way Matteo was running things, he was welcome to leave Sicily and make his own way in the world. Or Matteo might very well make the decision for him.

Because his patience with Luca was hanging on by a well-worn thread in danger of snapping.

Chapter Twenty-Five

Tessa squinted at the page she was reading and tried to focus. If her mind would stop racing, she might actually be able to read more than a single page. After re-reading the same paragraph for the fifth time, she gave up, tossing the book next to her on the loveseat with a frustrated sigh.

"Bad ending?"

Tessa squeaked, slapping a hand over her heart. "Jesus, Matteo. You scared me. How long have you been standing there?"

He smiled, pushing away from the doorframe where he'd been leaning and crossed to her, bending to brush a kiss over her lips, then her nose, then her forehead.

"Long enough. What's the matter, *piccola*?"

"Nothing," she lied. It's not like she could tell him she was anxious because she still hadn't heard from her father. "I just didn't sleep well last night, and now I can't concentrate on anything."

Matteo shifted the book to the coffee table and claimed the seat next to her. She instantly pivoted to lean back against his side, feeling better as soon as he wrapped his arm around her shoulders and pressed his cheek against the top of her head. This was the fucking problem.

She should get up, move away from him, put distance between them to remind her she wasn't here for Matteo. She wasn't even here for herself. She was here for her mother.

But he was so warm and comforting at her back, his presence grounding. So she stayed and let him drag her a little further into the darkness he didn't even know was looming beneath them.

"I didn't expect you home so early."

"Maeve is still sick, and I…"

She tensed, wondering if he was going to say he'd missed her and that's why he'd come home from the office early.

"I can work from home just as well as the office when she's out," he finished.

Of course. That made so much more sense. And it was better that way. She was already far too attached, far too invested. If she was smarter, she'd push him away, pick fights, make him hate her long before he found out what she'd done.

She wanted to be that cruel. But she couldn't bring herself to do it.

"I have to go to Rome tomorrow. I'll be gone most of the day."

"Is Luca going with you?"

"No." There was a hardness to Matteo's voice. "Do me a favor and stay away from my brother for a while."

"Don't have to tell me twice."

Matteo's arm tightened on her shoulders. "Did he say something to you?"

"Not since we ran into each other at breakfast."

"And?" Matteo's tone was rough and dark.

"More of the same. He doesn't like me, doesn't trust me."

His fingers flexed on her arm. "And that's it?"

"Of course."

The one thing she would not do was intentionally drive wedges between Matteo and his brothers. He had enough of an uphill battle trying to earn their trust. Her presence was bad enough. No need to make it worse.

"He'll get over it eventually," he promised her. "Once your father is gone and he realizes his accusations were wrong."

Guilt twisted painfully in her stomach, and she squeezed her eyes shut. She should tell him. Right now. It was the perfect moment to bare her soul, to beg for his forgiveness, to try and make things right.

"Matteo, I—"

His phone rang, and he shifted to dig it out of his pocket. "Sorry, *piccola*," he said, kissing the top of her head. "I've got to take this."

She sat up when he released her shoulders, and he spared her a single smile on his way to the door. Tessa collapsed onto the love seat, draping her legs over the arm and covering her eyes with her forearm. Stupid. She was stupid.

Another five seconds, and she'd have given away the whole fucking thing. And then what would she do about her mother? She snorted and shook her head, swallowing back tears.

Maybe that was what really made her stupid. Believing her mother was still alive. Luca was probably right. It was a sob story. One she wanted so badly to believe.

A tear slipped free from the corner of her eye, painting a trail to her temple and disappearing into her hair. She couldn't stop the rest. As much as she willed herself to stop crying, it was impossible, and that was as annoying as all the rest of it.

Sitting up, she picked up the pillow that had fallen from

the couch and launched it across the room with an angry shriek. So fucking satisfying. She picked up a second pillow and did it again. And again and again until all the pillows in the room were in a heap in the far corner.

"Everything okay in here?"

Tessa whirled to face the door, swiping at the tears on her face as Sienna stepped in, brow furrowed. She looked past Tessa to the pile of pillows and tilted her head.

"What did those pillows ever do to you?"

Tessa laughed, but it got stuck in the back of her throat and sounded as much like a sob as anything else. "I figured it was better pillows than vases," she said, eyeing the pretty hand-painted vases on either side table.

"Probably for the best. Luca says these were his mother's favorite. That this was her favorite room." Sienna indicated the books lining the floor-to-ceiling shelves.

At the mention of Luca and his dead mother, Tessa dissolved into tears again.

"Shit. Sorry," Sienna said. "I'm sorry. Here." She moved to the long couch opposite the balcony doors and patted the seat cushion next to her. "Come sit."

"I just want to know. I want to know one way or another if she's alive or dead." Tessa blew out a shuddering breath. "I thought I'd given up on this deep, aching hope a long time ago."

"If I had even the faintest inkling my mother might still be alive, there's no power on this earth that could convince me she was dead until I had proof."

"She smelled like roses." Tessa's gaze was fixed on the beams of light crisscrossing the floor, but she felt Sienna watching her. "I had forgotten that at some point, that she always smelled like roses. But we walked past a flower shop in Paris, and the smell and the memory of my mother's perfume hit me so strong."

"My mother smelled like apples. She didn't even like to eat apples," Sienna said with a wistful smile. "But she always smelled like them."

"Forgetting was better," Tessa whispered. "Forgetting didn't hurt this much."

"It comes in waves for me still. Some days it's at the very forefront of my mind because I think I hear her voice in a crowd or I see someone who looks like her. Other days I don't think about her at all. On those days, I feel incredibly guilty. I never want to forget her, but sometimes the pain of remembering is unbearable."

Tessa nodded slowly. She'd put this pain, these memories, in a box so long ago. Her father had forced her to dig them all out. He'd dangled this hope in front of her and turned her into someone she hated. Someone like him, willing to lie to and hurt and betray someone she loved to get what she wanted.

"I don't want to be like him," she murmured.

Sienna frowned. "Like who?"

"Like my father." Tessa blinked, realizing what she'd confessed, and quickly tried to cover her slip. "He felt nothing when my mother disappeared. He barely looked for her, didn't miss her, didn't mourn her. Eventually I gave up hope and started feeling nothing too. Now we're the same."

They sat staring quietly out the window for a long moment, Tessa's hands clenched tightly in her lap.

"We can choose."

Tessa looked up to find Sienna staring at her, some emotion Tessa couldn't name swirling in her eyes. Sienna cocked her head, studying Tessa as much as Tessa was studying her.

"We can choose which parts of our parents live on through us and which parts we stamp out. You don't have to be the same. Not if you don't want to be."

Tessa gave Sienna a small smile. "Thank you. I'm sorry for crying all over you." Pushing to her feet, she turned for the door then stopped herself. "Did you need something?"

"What?"

"You came to find me. I thought you needed me for something specific."

"Oh." Sienna seemed to hesitate, but ultimately smiled. "No. I just heard the great pillow toss and wanted to see if you were okay."

"I appreciate it."

Tessa slipped out, padding down the long hallway to the other wing. She could not afford to lose her composure around these people. She had to keep it together until her father called.

But she was tired of waiting. A week was plenty of time for him to find her mother and get in touch. And if he had nothing, then he needed to say that so she could play her next hand.

Closing her bedroom door behind her, she pulled her phone out of her pocket and brought up a new text message to her father.

I want to talk to Mama. Now.

Three dots appeared and disappeared on the screen. Then his message popped up.

I'm working on it. I've been a little busy, and it's been difficult convincing her to talk to you.

He could not have said a more hurtful thing if he tried. Swallowing a fresh wave of tears, Tessa quickly typed out a new message.

If she doesn't call me tomorrow, our deal's off, and I'll tell Matteo everything.

It was a risk, this particular brand of blackmail, but her father's response came through faster than she expected.

Fine. Noon.

Tessa tossed her phone on the bed. Shoving her hands through her hair, she stared down at it. By this time tomorrow, she'd be listening to the sound of her mother's voice for the first time in eight years.

And if it wasn't her mother on the other end of the line... She shook her head. It had to be. She needed it to be. She'd clung to hope for this long. She could hold on a little longer.

Chapter Twenty-Six

Tessa paced back and forth in front of the doors to her balcony. Rain lashed at the windows and ran down the panes in thick rivers. The trees whipped in the wind coming off the sea, swaying until they looked like they might snap in half before righting themselves again.

It was a wild, living, breathing thing beating against the glass. The fact that it matched her mood perfectly wrung a wry chuckle from her lips. She thought that kind of thing only happened in movies.

Her gaze swung to the clock on the nightstand, and her chest constricted as the neon numbers ticked over. Eleven fifty-seven. Just three more minutes before her phone would ring. The anticipation was eating her alive.

She'd realized sometime in the early hours of the morning there was really no good outcome here. She could no longer pretend she'd be able to walk away from Matteo as if nothing happened. Whether she betrayed him and had her mother back or she didn't, today was a linchpin moment that ended with someone suffering at her hands.

The distant hum of a vacuum caught her attention, and

she moved to the door to press her ear against it. It didn't sound like anyone was right outside the door. Most likely they were vacuuming the main hallway that led to the stairs. They'd been down here to clean her room and Matteo's hours ago.

Still, to ease her fluttering mind, she checked to make sure the lock was securely in place. In all the time she'd been here, she didn't remember ever once locking the bedroom door. No one had ever barged into her room here, not like her father did back home, but would they find it odd if they asked to come in and she had to cross the room to open the lock?

Taking three big steps back from the door, she checked the clock again. Eleven fifty-nine. One more minute. Sixty seconds. A lifetime of hope and longing boiled down into a single phone call.

The shrill ring of her phone made her jump, drawing a surprised shriek from her throat before she dove for it, snatching it off the edge of the bed and holding it up to her face.

Not her father's burner phone under the fake contact. A number she didn't recognize. Her heart leapt into her throat, and blood pounded through her ears. This was it.

Swallowing hard, she accepted the call.

"Hello?"

"That was fast."

She deflated a little at the sound of her father's voice. "Where's Mama?"

"Watch your tone, Tessa. I can take this gift away as easily as I can give it."

"You said I could talk to her. She's the only reason I'm doing any of this."

"Yes, yes. I know. It took some convincing, but she finally agreed. Here."

There was rustling over the line, maybe the scrape of a chair, the soft warble of voices. A crack and a pop.

"Hello?" a woman's voice said softly.

Tessa held her breath until she was dizzy from it, letting it out in a slow hiss. "Mama?"

"Tessa, baby. How are you?"

"I'm good." She squeezed her eyes shut to keep the tears at bay. "How are you?"

"Oh, fine. Enjoying this weather we're having."

Her eyes popped open, gaze landing on the window and the rain sliding down the glass. "I miss you, Mama," she whispered.

There was silence, more rustling. "I miss you too, baby. But I had to stay away. You were better off without me."

"I wasn't." She shook her head, fingernails digging into her palm. "I needed you. I was just a girl."

"You were practically a woman. And your father was able to give you everything I wasn't."

Tessa laughed, but it was an empty sound. "Are you safe? Are you happy?"

"Of course I'm happy, sweetheart. I'm happier than I've been in a long time."

Dropping onto the edge of the bed before her legs gave out, Tessa rubbed at the impossibly deep ache in her chest. This was not the reunion she'd been expecting.

"Are you satisfied now, Tessa? Your father went to a lot of trouble to arrange this conversation."

"Yes. I'm satisfied." She chewed the inside of her cheek, trying to decide if she should ask her next question. "Can I come see you?"

A pause and a scratching sound, like someone placed their hand over the receiver. "I don't think that's a good idea, Tessa. Just let the past be and move on with your life. Be a good daughter to your father and do as he says."

A tear slipped down Tessa's cheek, and she flicked it away with the tip of her finger. "Okay. I have one more question."

"What is it?" she asked, irritation edging her tone.

"Do you know where your emerald and diamond necklace is? The one that's always been passed down from mother to daughter. I looked for it after you left, but I couldn't find it."

Tessa gripped the edge of the bed until her knuckles went white and her fingers ached.

"The, uh, emerald and diamond choker, you mean?"

"Yeah. The one grandma gave you on your wedding day."

"I took that one with me. Sorry, baby. I couldn't bear to part with it."

"I understand," Tessa said softly. "Thank you."

"Happy now?" her father's gruff voice said.

Pinching the bridge of her nose, Tessa sat up straight and tightened her grip on the phone until her fingers stopped shaking. "Yes. That was all the proof I needed."

"Good." She heard the sound of a door slamming. "Now we can stop playing these fucking games. What information do you have for me?"

She cleared her throat, the plan slowly forming in her brain. "We need to meet in person."

"In person?" her father snapped. "Why?"

"Because it's too much information to send via text. If I could scan everything in using a computer and send it, that would be easier, but that's too risky. And taking photos of every single document would be a waste of time. It's better to meet."

"You have documents?" His tone dripped with greedy interest. She'd hooked him. "Of what?"

"Assets," she said simply. "Lots of assets."

An engine growled to life in the background, but her

father was silent for a beat. Calculating his next move. "I can send Tomaso to—"

"I'm not giving anything to your bastard." Tessa tried to lash her temper when her father snarled. She needed to keep a cool head to get her way.

"You do not call the shots here, girl. I do."

Her anger sparked, but she tamped it down and said evenly, "Since I'm the one who has the information you want and you can't get it anywhere else, then I'll call the shots just this once. You and me. In person."

He swore under his breath. "I have urgent business to take care of. I can't meet until Friday."

Three days. She could work with three days. "Friday is fine. Afternoon is better."

He gritted his teeth so loud she could hear it across the line. He really hated taking orders from her. But he wouldn't get to see her any other way. She was done letting him be in control.

"Two?"

"Yeah. Friday at two."

"Great," he replied, though the word was drenched in sarcasm. "We'll meet at the same store as the first time. And Tessa?" he added before she could hang up. "Don't forget who's really in charge here. I can kill your mother at a moment's notice if you do anything stupid."

"I'm not going to do anything stupid."

She disconnected the call and carefully set her phone on the edge of the nightstand. She was going to do what she should have done a long fucking time ago. Tell Matteo the truth. Because the woman on the other end of the phone today was not her mother.

Tessa had known it from the first word. Eliana Antonetti's voice had an almost musical quality to it. Lyrical and sweet.

The woman she talked to today sounded nothing like her mother. No matter how soft she tried to make her voice.

And her mother never would have said her father could do a better job as a parent. She was constantly apologizing for Salvatore's shortcomings and promising Tessa she would do everything in her power to make sure she had a good match with a good man who would love and cherish her in the way her father wasn't capable of.

The question about the emerald and diamond choker that didn't exist was just a final confirmation of what Tessa already knew. Her father never had any idea where her mother was, and he counted on Tessa being too stupid to realize it.

Running her fingers through her hair, she twisted it over her shoulder and pushed away from the bed, crossing to the closet and opening the top drawer. Unearthing the velvet bag with her mother's pearls, she dumped them into her palm.

Tessa had rescued them from her mother's jewelry box a few weeks after she disappeared. Once it was clear her mother wasn't coming back.

And she'd gone through her mother's things in the nick of time too. Two days later, without explanation, her father had ordered everything cleared out of her mother's bedroom, including all of her clothes and jewelry. Tessa had managed to save the pearls, her grandmother's engagement ring, and her mother's favorite scarf.

All she'd brought with her from the compound was the pearls. She regretted not grabbing the rest. Especially since she would probably never see it again.

Slipping the pearls back into the bag, she shoved them beneath her underwear again and slammed the drawer closed. She was an idiot for ever believing for a second her mother was alive. As with everything else, it had been a lie her father told her to get what he wanted. It was her fault for mistaking it for truth.

Matteo wouldn't be back from Rome until late, but she would wait up for him. She had to, had to do everything in her power to make this right. Her father deserved to pay. Not only for what he most likely did to her mother, but for every transgression against her. Every hit, every slap, every bruise, every broken bone, every ugly word.

She wanted him to experience at least a fraction of the pain she'd endured. It was no less than what he deserved. Payment for what he'd taken from her. It wouldn't be enough. It would never be enough. But she'd have to make do.

Before she slept, she would tell Matteo everything. He might hate her, and she'd have to use every hour between now and then to prepare herself for that, but only he could help her end this.

Her father would get nothing, but Matteo would get Salvatore Antonetti handed to him on a silver fucking platter. Because in three days, Tessa knew exactly where he was going to be and when. And her father would never see it coming.

Chapter Twenty-Seven

Climbing the stairs at a jog, Matteo rolled his neck to crack it and nodded at the maids who stepped out of his way before resuming their duties. His wing was empty and quiet, as instructed. He'd left Tessa sleeping in his bed this morning and didn't want her jolted awake by a vacuum cleaner or eager maid.

Turning the knob, he eased the door in and stepped inside, closing it behind him. She was still asleep, the sun slanting across the foot of the bed, and he smiled. Normally she wore her long black hair twisted in a bun on top of her head when she slept, but this morning it was down around her shoulders and shielding her face from his view.

He'd gotten in well past midnight and found her curled up in the middle of his bed with all the lights and her clothes still on. It was sweet that she'd waited up for him. Or tried to. He'd done his best to peel her out of her clothes without waking her up and slipped into bed behind her.

With the feel of her warm body against his and the way she snuggled into him and sighed, he'd been out in seconds, woken only by the demanding ring of his cell phone. Too much shit to deal with and too little time to deal with it. Maeve was still sick, which left him fielding all the usual phone calls. Sending her back to Ireland when her year was up was going to be hell.

Tessa stirred but didn't wake, and he crossed the room to set the bakery box next to her on the nightstand. He wanted nothing more than to crawl into bed and wake her up with his cock, but he only had time for a bite of breakfast. And he'd brought her back donuts from his favorite bakery in Rome.

Brushing her hair off her face, he leaned down and peppered kisses from her forehead to the tip of her nose, and finally, her lips. He felt her come awake by degrees, easing into the kiss until she was kissing him back, her hand sliding lazily up his arm to loop around his neck.

"Morning, sleepyhead." He pulled back to look down at her lips, rosy from his beard. "I brought you a present from Rome."

"You didn't have to do that."

She stretched, arching off the bed with her arms above her head. When the sheet slipped down to reveal her breasts, he ducked his head for a taste of her nipple, swirling his tongue around it and then grazing it gently with his teeth. She hummed low in her throat, and he sucked harder before pulling back and letting it fall out of his mouth with a pop.

"Was that my present?" she asked with a grin. "Is there more?"

He chuckled, kissing the side of her breast. "There will be later. Hungry?"

"For food or something else?" Her eyes dropped to his cock, already semi-hard, and he laughed again.

"For food, *piccola*. Later I'll feed you my cock all night long." She smiled, but then it faltered and fell, and he frowned. "You okay?"

"Yeah. I, ah, I tried to wait up for you last night."

"I know. It was sweet. I didn't have the heart to wake you, so I just undressed you and got into bed."

"I gathered that." She tugged the sheet up to cover her breasts and tucked her hair behind her ears. "But I need to talk to you about something. Do you have a minute this morning?"

He checked his watch. He had a delivery flying into Belgium any minute and two more flying out. Then there was the meeting down at the casinos and another with the contractors for the strip clubs to see if Sienna's uncle was right and they really were trying to gouge them. And he was still waiting to hear back from Alexei about his plan for taking out Antonetti.

"It's important," she said softly.

He leaned in to kiss her lips, cupping her face in his hand and tilting her head back to take it deeper. "Okay, *piccola*. For you, I have a few minutes. What is it?"

She clutched the sheet tight between her breasts. "Can I get dressed first?"

"Of course." He pointed to the bakery box. "And eat. Meet me downstairs in the study when you're ready."

Tessa nodded, but something in her expression seemed off, even if he couldn't quite put his finger on it. Kissing her forehead, he left her to dress and made his way back downstairs.

Luca was at the office with Sienna going over all the documents and correspondence they needed to create to make this fake sale of Antonetti Hotel Group look not just real, but like it had been months in the making. Once that was in place, he'd tap Regina to leak the story to her contact at the paper and let Alexei off the leash.

God willing, Antonetti and his son would be dead by this time next week. Then Tessa would be free, and they could talk about what came next. He'd been doing a lot of thinking about what came next lately. He had a few ideas, but he wanted to get her take on it. Especially while they continued searching for her mother.

He didn't have much hope her mother was still alive. They'd exhausted every avenue they could think of and come up empty. The hardest part was going to be breaking that to her. He didn't relish it, but he didn't want to leave it for too long either. Once this thing with Antonetti was done, they'd talk about all of it.

A knock on the door drew his attention. Dressed in a sweater he'd bought her in Paris and a pair of jeans, Tessa had her arms crossed over her middle and was hugging herself tightly. She looked uncomfortable, nervous, like she might change her mind and bolt at any minute.

"Are you sure everything's okay?" he asked, meeting her in the middle of the room and rubbing his hands up and down her arms.

She swallowed hard and gave him a thin smile. "It's just important, and I don't want to fuck it up."

"Tell me, *piccola.*"

She opened her mouth and took a deep breath but was cut off by his ringing phone. Fuck's sake. They were forever being interrupted by work. He glanced over his shoulder at the phone on his desk, willing it to be quiet so she could get whatever it was off her chest.

When it went silent, he turned to her, giving her shoulders a squeeze and urging her to continue. But she jumped when it went off again. He sighed and sent her an apologetic look.

"Hang on. Let me just…"

She nodded, and he jogged back to his desk, scooping it off the top and frowning at the readout. Why the hell was Peeters calling him when he should be handling the incoming and outgoing shipments?

"What do you need, Peeters?" he said by way of a greeting.

"We have a situation here," Peeters said, sounding more than a little out of breath.

Matteo snapped to attention. "What kind of situation?"

"Someone attacked the incoming and outgoing shipments. All three of them."

He flicked a glance at Tessa, who stood watching him in the center of the room. "Attacked them how?"

"They fucking blew them out of the sky. Fire brigade is on their way, and probably the cops. If you have favors you can call in, I'd do it and do it now."

Matteo hung up and immediately dialed Callum. "Someone attacked me in Belgium," he said as soon as his friend answered.

Callum bit off a curse. "Who?"

"I don't know yet. But I can't do much cover-up from here. Can you—"

"I'll send Roarke. He's finishing up business in Brussels and can be there inside of an hour. I'll call you with updates."

"Thank you."

Matteo ended the call, tapping his phone on his palm. He wondered if his guy in Frankfurt had any pull with the Belgian government. Couldn't hurt to at least ask. He had to take care of damage control and cover-up before he could focus on figuring out just who the fuck had taken such a big swipe at him.

None of these shipments would ruin him financially, but that didn't mean he would let something like this go unanswered. As soon as he found out who it was, the punishment would be swift and severe.

"What happened?"

Matteo's gaze traveled to Tessa again, and he sighed. "Someone blew up a couple flights at the airport." She sucked in a sharp breath. "Can whatever you have to say wait until tonight? I really need to get ahead of this as much as possible."

She hesitated a fraction of a second, but ultimately nodded and offered him a tentative smile. He really didn't like that look on her face. "Sure. We can talk about it later."

"I really am so—"

"Matteo!"

Luca's voice echoed down the hall seconds before he burst through the door with Sienna on his heels. He sent Tessa a look so scathing she stumbled back from him, and Matteo took a menacing step forward.

He really didn't have time to deal with Luca's temper and vitriol today. He had enough on his plate without piling on more.

"What do you want, Luca? I have a bit of a situation I need to handle."

Tessa turned for the door. "I'll go, and we'll—"

"No," Luca snarled, shooting out his arm to stop her. "You should stay. You'll definitely want to hear this." Luca nodded at Sienna.

"We've been monitoring Antonetti's call activity to make sure he hasn't been tipped off by anyone," Sienna said, tapping a series of keys and then looking at Matteo over the lid of the laptop.

"Right. And?"

"And yesterday"—she flicked a glance at Tessa—"we noticed a new contact pop up in his call history." She turned the screen to face him and hit the return key to make the number she'd highlighted bigger. "Recognize that phone number?"

Matteo squinted at it, trying to place it in his memory. When the realization hit him, his head snapped up, eyes narrowing on Tessa's face. She looked stricken, eyes wide, face pale, arms still tightly wrapped around her body.

"Your father called you?"

Her mouth opened and closed again, and her eyes flitted to each one of them before settling on Matteo's and filling up with tears.

He took a step forward, and she took one back. It had to be a mistake. He couldn't be this blind, this naive, this fucking stupid. But yesterday was the first time her number had shown up in his contacts. They'd been monitoring him for weeks, and her number had never shown up before.

"How long did the call last?"

"What?" Luca said. "Why does that matter? She—"

"How long," Matteo said through gritted teeth, "did the fucking call last?"

"Almost ten minutes."

His phone announced an incoming text message. Numb, unable to make all the details make sense in his brain, he glanced down at the screen. Roarke.

On my way to Bruges. Will send updates when I know more.

He read the text message twice more, and everything snapped sharply into focus.

"You told him about Belgium."

"No...I...Matteo," Tessa stammered. "I can explain."

"What's in Belgium?"

Ignoring Luca's question, Matteo stalked across the room and gripped her arm so hard she winced. "This isn't the first time, is it?"

She slowly shook her head, and he felt like all the air had been sucked out of the room.

"How? How were you contacting him?"

"A burner phone. Matteo, please."

"No," he barked, hauling her toward the door and into the

hallway. "How long have you been in communication with him?"

"Since the beginning."

She was crying now, tears streaming down her face and dripping off her jaw onto the collar of her sweater. He hated that there was still a part of him that wanted to comfort her, to wrap his arms around her and tell her everything would be okay. But everything wasn't okay.

All this time he thought he was protecting her, and Luca had been right. He'd been fucking the enemy. Pulling her in too close when he should have been pushing her away.

She stumbled going up the stairs, but he righted her, tightening his grip on her arm until she squeaked in protest. The maids hurried out of his way as he dragged her down the hall and around the corner.

Shoving her into her room, he quickly scanned it for her phone.

"Give me your phone."

She flinched at his unforgiving tone but turned to face him anyway. "Matteo. I can explain. Please. You have to let me explain."

Her voice hitched, and it cut a place deep inside him. The place that wanted her, that trusted her, that loved her. He buried it under the betrayal so he could focus on what needed to be done.

"You think I'm going to give you a chance to lie to me again?" He took a step forward, and she stumbled back against the post at the foot of her bed. "Give me your fucking phone."

It struck him that this was exactly the same position they'd found themselves in when she first arrived. Only this time, it wouldn't end with his lips on hers.

She pulled the phone out of her back pocket with trembling fingers and held it out to him. He unlocked it with his fingerprint. His own safety mechanism so he could go through her phone if the situation ever presented itself. He never had. He hadn't seen the need. Another mistake.

The only number on the phone he didn't recognize was someone named Luna. But there was no call history, no text history. She was erasing everything after every interaction. Not even the call they'd spotted on her father's phone was in her history here. She'd been carefully covering her tracks for almost two months.

"Luna was my—"

"Shut up," he growled, and she flinched again.

He couldn't bear to look at her. If he did, it might break him. Instead he turned on his heel for the door. Wrenching the key from the inside lock, he held it up and saw her eyes widen.

"You will not leave this room until I clean up this mess and figure out what the fuck to do with you. Lucky for you, you reminded me I'm not like my father. If I was, you'd be dead already."

Chapter Twenty-Eight

Matteo stood in the hallway for a few minutes listening to Tessa pound on the door, begging and pleading for him to come back, to just listen. But he didn't think he could stomach more of her lies. He had enough to deal with.

Unable to take any more, he stalked away from the door and moved back down the hallway to the stairs. Rather than turning toward his office, he headed for the kitchen. Activity ground to a halt when he pushed in, and Taglia quickly came over to stand in front of him.

"How can I help, *Il Signore*?"

Matteo held up the key. "Tessa is in her room. Tessa will stay in her room until I say otherwise. Three meals a day. Just leave a tray on the desk. Do not speak to her, do not give her anything, do not take anything from her. Clear?"

"Of course, *Il Signore*."

Accepting the key Matteo pressed into his palm, Taglia nodded his agreement. Satisfied, Matteo squared his shoulders, preparing to face down his brother, and backtracked to the study. Luca and Sienna were seated on one of the couches, and Luca sprang to his feet when he noticed Matteo.

"So you believe me now, then?"

"Not now, Luca. You can tell me I told you so later. Right now I have to figure out this bullshit in Belgium on top of all the other bullshit I have to deal with."

"What's in Belgium?"

Matteo rolled down the sleeves of his dress shirt and secured the cuffs. "I own a private airport there. It's how I met Laurent Theroux."

"A private airport for what?"

Slipping his arms into his jacket, Matteo adjusted the collar. "To more easily transport illegal goods across the continent."

Luca's eyebrows shot up, and he followed Matteo back into the hallway. "No wonder you wanted Gallo Industries so bad. It wasn't an acquisition as much as an expansion for you."

"I told you I haven't exactly been sitting on my ass these last seven years."

"Not that I would know." Luca sent Sienna a sheepish glance when she elbowed him in the side. "How did Tessa find out about it?"

Matteo faltered in his reach for the front door before gripping the knob and yanking it open. "I mentioned it in passing. In Paris."

He heard Luca suck his teeth as he dogged him across the driveway to the garage. To his brother's credit, Luca chose not to point out what a mistake that had been. Matteo had been making nothing but mistakes where Tessa was concerned since he agreed to take her from Syracuse.

Climbing behind the wheel of his SUV, he looked over at Luca when he got into the passenger seat and then in the rearview at Sienna when she slid into the back.

"What are you doing?"

"We're coming with you. Obviously. What?" Luca asked at Matteo's raised brow. "You thought you'd handle a direct attack against the family on your own?"

Matteo started the car and sped out of the driveway. "I assumed you'd be too busy gloating over being right to want to help. This is my mess, after all."

Snorting, Luca waved a hand in the air. "What you've always failed to understand, brother, is it doesn't have to be lonely at the top. Besides, I can gloat about Tessa later. Once we know Antonetti isn't going to take any more swipes at us."

Sienna leaned forward over the center console and smacked Luca on the arm. "What do you need?"

Glancing over at the two of them, Matteo's hands tightened on the steering wheel. "I want to know who the fuck blew up my shipments. Anything in Antonetti's call history to point to who he might have contacted for something like this?"

"None that I saw," Sienna said, sitting back in her seat and repositioning the laptop on her thighs. "Every call has been a local number. But he could have had someone else place the call to his contact in Europe. If someone told him we were monitoring him."

"Sh—" He started to say Tessa didn't know they were monitoring her father's phone. He'd never told her about it. But that didn't mean she hadn't found out by eavesdropping or snooping. Or maybe he talked in his goddamn sleep.

"And now we know he's using burner phones," Luca added. "He could have a lot of shit in play we don't know about."

Matteo tapped his fingers on the steering wheel. "We have the list of his allies. How hard would it be to find out their movements from the last forty-eight hours?"

"Time-consuming, maybe, but not hard as long as they're not running any additional security on their comms."

"Let's start with the contacts he has closest to Belgium and circle out from there until we find what we're looking for."

Punching the button for the parking garage, Matteo pulled into his assigned spot and buzzed them all into the elevator. Once on the top floor, Luca and Sienna split off for Luca's office, and Matteo crossed the empty expanse to his own.

"What are you doing here?" he demanded of Maeve sitting behind her desk with a scarf wrapped around her neck and a mug of still steaming tea at her elbow.

"Callum called me looking for something and told me what happened. I can't believe you didn't tell me yourself."

"I didn't tell you because you're sick. You need to go home and rest." He stepped around her and into his office, crossing to the desk and dropping into the chair.

"Like hell. Someone attacked us. I'm medicated. I'm fine. My organs are practically swimming in the tea my ma sent me."

Matteo gave her an appraising glance. She looked better than she did the other day. Her eyes weren't glassy with fever anymore, and her cheeks had more color. As much color as she got with her pale Irish complexion, anyway.

She crossed her arms over her chest and cocked her hip. "If you want me to leave, you'll have to toss me over your shoulder and carry me to the car."

"Like I did that time you almost brawled with the waitress at the pub and got us all arrested?"

Maeve dismissed his words with a wave of her hand, biting back a smile. "Bitch deserved it. I should have broken her ugly nose. I'm not leaving, Matteo. Tell me what you need."

Matteo sighed. Some battles weren't worth fighting. "Luca and Sienna are digging into who Antonetti might have called to get this done."

"Antonetti? How the hell would he know about Belgium? Oh shit," Maeve said at Matteo's raised brows. "I never would've thought… Never mind. Callum said Roarke was on his way to deal with the cops. Have you contacted Schmidt yet?"

"Not yet," Matteo confirmed. "But I seem to recall he had contacts in the Belgian government. Someone who might make sure everyone looks the other way on anything that doesn't add up."

"I think you're right. I'll call him and Grandda's people in Brussels. Between the Bianchis and the Quinns, we'll find someone who can lean on the right people."

"Thanks, Maeve."

"Don't think of it." Maeve stepped into the hall and paused in her reach to shut the door. "Matteo? I'm sorry."

He didn't have to ask what about. Maeve knew him too well for that. He nodded once, and she closed the door without another word, leaving him alone with his thoughts.

He'd been stupid. There was no other way around it. He saw what he wanted to see where Tessa was concerned, and he got burned because of it. He couldn't lay the blame anywhere but his own feet. And now he might be exposed in Belgium, vulnerable who knew where else, all because he'd been distracted by a great pair of tits and a willing mouth.

But as painful and expensive as this might be to come back from, he would come back from it. He would grease the right palms, put better security measures in place, and make sure he never found himself vulnerable to anything or anyone ever again.

That was really the problem here. He'd let himself get too

close to someone in a way he'd never allowed himself before. He'd gotten comfortable, and because he had, he'd seen what he wanted to see in Tessa. That was his mistake. One he wouldn't be repeating.

Pushing Tessa and her tears and her pleas from his mind, he got to work. There were plenty of threads he could pull and paths he could follow to figure out who fucked him over and who needed to be punished as a result.

Tessa might have known the airport existed, but someone else had to have given Antonetti the location for an attack and the time of incoming and outgoing shipments. And they were going to be dead as soon as Matteo learned their fucking name.

He was scanning through his contact list when the screen lit up with Roarke's name. Accepting the call, he put it on speaker.

"Talk to me."

"Somebody sure hates you," Roarke said.

Matteo's stomach clenched, and he got up to pace in front of the windows. "That bad?"

"They fired on your shipments with RPGs."

"Fucking hell." Where would Antonetti even get that kind of firepower on such short notice? "And the cops?"

"So far, they're calling it an act of terrorism. There wasn't much left of the flights in terms of wreckage, so I doubt they'll be able to pull out anything they can pin on you as illegal. And your paperwork did a damn good job covering you when it came to the manifests."

"I should give Peeters a raise."

Roarke snorted. "He could use it to put more food on the table. Man looks like a twig. I could snap him in half with one hand."

Matteo chuckled and then sobered. "Do I need to be worried about the authorities?"

"They'll probably pay you a visit to have a chat with you on the record, but I wouldn't say you have anything to worry about."

Leaning his forehead against the window, Matteo blew out a relieved breath. That was one thing he could check off his list. The last thing he needed was to be stuck in the middle of an international terrorism scandal.

"I don't like being tied to the word terrorism, though."

"I wouldn't either," Roarke agreed. "We Irish don't exactly relish the term. Quinn might be able to pull a few strings in Brussels. Get it classified as something else. My advice? Let it play out a bit first."

Matteo nodded. Roarke was good at reading people. If he said Matteo should let it ride, Matteo trusted him.

"I'm going to stick around to make sure you're in the clear and then head back to Dublin. Did you want me to reach out to Quinn's people while I'm here?"

"Maeve is already calling them."

Roarke was silent for a beat. "How is she?"

"Not looking forward to coming back to Ireland, but resigned to it."

"If she doesn't, she'll end up dragged by her hair kicking and screaming by the sounds of it. Quinn is very determined to get her wed."

"So I've heard," Matteo replied. "And you're okay with that?"

"It's none of my business what Quinn does with his own. I'm just here to close deals and break bones."

"Right. Keep me posted on any developments in Belgium. And Roarke? I owe you one."

"You owe me several. I'll put it on your tab."

Disconnecting the call, Matteo shoved his phone into his pocket. He wasn't out of the woods yet. But with the police in hand, he could zero in on who the fuck was involved. And once he found out, he was going to make them pay.

He was eager to get his hands dirty.

Chapter Twenty-Nine

Pulling the blanket tighter around her against the chill, Tessa stared into the unlit fireplace. She'd tried to ask the maid who'd brought her breakfast to bring in more firewood, but Giulia wouldn't even make eye contact, let alone have a conversation with her.

Matteo's orders, no doubt. He hadn't come to see her in the two days since he'd locked her in. Sometimes she thought she heard him coming and going from his room, but he never responded when she called his name through the door.

He well and truly hated her. And she couldn't say she blamed him. She wouldn't be likely to put much stock in what he had to say if the roles were reversed. But that didn't stop her from wanting to tell him the truth.

Worse than that, she missed him. Missed feeling his arms around her at night, missed the feel of his breath on her shoulder while she slept, missed the sound of his voice. It was downright pathetic how much she missed him. But she was no more able to stop it than she was to get him to come in here and talk to her.

Of all the things her father had taken from her already,

he'd succeeded in taking one more. A man who didn't view her as a piece of property or a wild thing to be beaten into submission.

But that look in Matteo's eyes when he put the pieces together, when he realized she'd been lying to him all this time. It cut deeper than she'd expected it to. The hurt, the betrayal, the anger. She might never be able to purge it from her mind. It bubbled up a guilt that squeezed until she could barely breathe.

She thought she'd braced herself for this part, for the distrust and the rejection, for the seething rage. But apparently she hadn't. She wasn't sure anything could have prepared her for the searing ache in her chest whenever she thought about him or heard him on the other side of the door.

It might have been easier for him to stomach if she'd been able to tell her side of it first. If she could have at least been the one to tell him before he found out from someone else. From Luca. The brother who hated her enough to look smug when Matteo dragged her from the study.

Now she was stuck in this room, scheduled to meet her father in a few hours, with no way to contact him, no way to get out of here. Her window of opportunity to make this right was slowly closing.

Matteo would kill her father eventually, that she was sure of. But he would never trust her again, and she had no way of redeeming herself if he wouldn't even sit down and listen for five minutes.

When the key shuffled in the lock again, Tessa didn't even bother getting up. Whoever it was, the butler, a maid, they would come in, set the tray on the little desk against the wall, and leave again.

They wouldn't look at her, wouldn't speak to her. It was as if she'd ceased to exist for everyone in this house. The only acknowledgment of her presence was making sure she didn't starve to death.

The door swung in, followed by the soft sound of footsteps, and the rattling of the metal tray when it met wood. She waited for the footsteps to recede, the door to close, the lock to slide back into place with a click that never failed to make her stomach tighten and her teeth clench.

"It's freezing in here."

Tessa went still at the sound of Carina's voice. The first voice she'd heard in two days, save for her own. Keeping the blanket wrapped tight around her body, she stood and turned.

"I ran out of firewood yesterday. None of the staff will speak to me."

"Yeah," Carina said with a frustrated sigh. "Matteo told them not to."

A bitter laugh escaped her. "What does he think I'm going to do? Encourage them to stage a coup?"

When Carina didn't immediately hurl back an angry retort, Tessa began to worry something might be wrong. No one else in the family had bothered to come see her since Matteo locked her in. Why would they start now unless there was bad news?

"Did something happen?" She took a step forward when Carina pursed her lips, refusing to answer. Or maybe debating whether she should. "Is Matteo okay? Just tell me that much if you can't tell me anything else."

Something in Carina's eyes shifted, softened, and she crossed her arms over her chest. "Matteo is fine. Just busy. We've all been busy cleaning up after your lies."

Tessa gripped the blanket in her fingers as the guilt punched through her again and dropped back into the chair with a heavy sigh.

"When my father first told me my mother was still alive, I

never even considered saying no to his plan. He knew Matteo might take me if he came back for Drago. I didn't know if it would work, but I had to try. You understand why I had to try, right?"

Carina shook her head, shoulders slumping, and blew out a breath. "Just because I understand why you did it doesn't mean I condone it. You put the people I love most in this world in danger."

"I know. I wish I could tell you I wouldn't do it again if presented with the same choice, but I can't." Tessa bit the inside of her cheek and blinked back tears. "I spent years wishing my mother would come back. Then years after that making peace with the fact that she never would."

She looked up at Carina with tears swimming in her eyes and blurring her vision. "But she's dead."

"How do you know that?" Carina asked softly.

"That's the reason you saw my number on my father's phone. I told him I wouldn't help him anymore if he didn't let me talk to my mother. If he couldn't prove to me she was alive. I guess when he had her call me, he slipped up and used his regular phone. But the woman I spoke to wasn't her."

"It's unlikely she left your father's house alive."

Mouth suddenly dry, Tessa rubbed sweaty palms on her thighs. She should have known better. Should have known her father was doing what he'd always done. Lying to get what he wanted no matter who he had to step on or hurt in the process.

"You really didn't know." Carina's voice was soft but thick with tears, and Tessa frowned, shaking her head.

"No. I might not have told the whole truth, but I never lied. I was here because I thought my mother was alive and I wanted to find her. By any means necessary. I just didn't know I'd fall in love with Matteo when I agreed to come here," she added, swiping at a tear that slipped down her cheek.

"If you could make it right, would you?"

"In a heartbeat." She pressed her fingertips to her eyelids. "But how am I supposed to do that when he won't even talk to me? And even if he did talk to me, he wouldn't believe me."

Carina didn't say anything else, didn't bother offering false words of hope that Matteo might come around. A kindness Tessa appreciated. She couldn't stomach any more hope.

"Is my father dead yet?" Tessa asked, stopping Carina at the door.

Carina hesitated, then shook her head. "Not yet. We're having some trouble pinning him down."

"You can't find him? Let me talk to Matteo. I can—"

"Don't worry about it, Tessa. We're handling it."

"But I know where he's going to be."

Carina paused in her reach for the knob, her mouth thinning into a hard line. "How?"

"When I talked to the woman who wasn't my mother, I set up a meeting with him. A lure. I was going to tell Matteo about it all before." She sighed. "Before everything happened."

The way Carina studied her made Tessa feel like a specimen under a microscope. But she supposed she deserved this level of suspicion. She had it coming.

"Where are you supposed to meet with him? And when?"

"At the grocery store where we first met. On Via Roma. Today. At two."

Carina's eyes flicked to the clock on the nightstand, and she nodded. "All right." Twisting the knob, she paused in the doorway. "I'll try to convince Matteo to come talk to you. At least hear your side of it."

"Carina. You have to tell him," Tessa replied, urgency in her voice.

The door closed and the lock reengaged, and Tessa dropped her head into her hands with a sigh. Maybe Carina could get Matteo to come around; maybe she couldn't. Tessa had little faith that she'd ever speak to Matteo again. At least not more than a few harsh words when her father was finally dead, and he kicked her out to fend for herself. Or worse, did exactly what his father would have done and killed her for the betrayal.

But more importantly than that, if they couldn't find her father on their own, then intercepting him today was their best option for a fast end to all of this. If only Carina had seemed the slightest bit interested in the information about the meeting.

She'd breezed out, her face giving nothing away. Maybe Carina saw it as just another lie, or worse, a trap being laid. And if they weren't going to do anything about it, what did that mean? Was Salvatore going to get away?

Tessa eyed the knife on the tray. She couldn't let that happen. If she could get out of this room and meet her father, she could just as easily be the one to end him once and for all as anyone else. She'd killed before. She could do it again.

And her father wouldn't expect her to be the one to attack him. He was only expecting information. She'd make sure he got something else entirely.

Because Tessa wanted her father to pay, and if no one would listen to her, then this was the only way to do it.

Stalking across the room, she grabbed the knife from the tray and carried it to the door. She'd read about this in a book once. She hoped it was art imitating life and not the other way around.

Wrapping her fingers around the knob, she twisted it as much as the lock would allow and wedged the knife in the gap between the frame and the door. Sliding it through, she felt something give, heard the scrape of metal as she pushed back the latch, but the door still wouldn't open.

Pulling the knife free, she took a deep breath and tried again. Angling the blade higher so she came down from the top instead of straight on, she again felt something give way and pressed back on the heavy spring latch.

When the door swung in, she swallowed a triumphant shout, mouth rounding into a silent O of surprise while she jumped up and down. Tossing the knife on the bed, she reached for the door and stopped herself. If anyone came to her room before she came back, she'd seal her fate where Matteo was concerned.

Pushing the door to but not latching it, she dug a pen and an old receipt out of her purse and scribbled a quick note along with the name and address of the store. She hoped it was enough to explain what she was doing and why. And that Matteo would believe her when she got back.

She anchored it under the knife in the middle of the bed and slipped quietly into the hallway. Looking left to make sure the coast was clear, she darted across the hall for Matteo's room.

If it was locked, she could try the knife trick from the outside, but the knob twisted easily in her hand. No need to be worried about her snooping while she was under lock and key.

The room was empty, and it smelled like him, like cedar and spices. She gave herself a minute to take a single deep breath, letting the scent of him wrap around her. She missed that too. Crossing to his nightstand, she crouched in front of it.

The top drawer was a normal one, but the bottom one was locked and required a numeric code to open it. She'd watched him secure a gun and extra magazines inside it right before they left for Paris, after the incident at the restaurant.

4-9-3-2-7 Enter

She held her breath while she waited for the light to go from green to blue, nearly sobbing with relief when it did. Sliding the drawer open, she lifted out the 9mm, hefting the unfamiliar weight of it in her hand.

It had been a long time since she'd fired a gun. Her mother was still alive, and her grandfather had been visiting and insisted on teaching her how to load and fire one. She hoped she remembered enough to make sure her father didn't walk away from this meeting today.

Tucking the gun into the waistband of her jeans, she moved toward the balcony doors, pulling them open and shivering against the blast of icy February air.

Her balcony was small and narrow, with just enough room for a table and two chairs. Matteo's balcony was wide and long, and it had a set of curved stairs leading down to the backyard. She didn't really understand their purpose, and she'd never seen Matteo use them, but she followed them down and crept along the back of the house to the garage.

She hadn't thought this part through. How to actually get into the garage to get the keys hanging on pegs along the back wall. She needed a code to access the automatic door from the outside and had no idea what it was.

Slipping along the perimeter of the garage, she found a door on the far side. Twisting the handle, she grunted when she found it locked. If only she had a knife out here. It was too risky to go all the way back upstairs to get it, and she was running out of time.

Toeing the grass around the edge of the building, she nudged a rock free, stooping to pick it up. She could do this. She could break into his garage and steal his car and kill her father in cold blood. What other choice did she have? Live as

Matteo's prisoner until he decided he was ready to deal with her?

Squaring her shoulders, she braced herself and launched the rock through the window. It slid across the floor a few feet, and she breathed a sigh of relief that it didn't hit the car closest to her and set off any alarms. Using a second rock to clear out the remaining shards of glass, she reached in and opened the lock.

Grabbing the first set of keys she touched, she hit the button on the remote and blew out a breath when the red Alfa Romeo gave a series of beeps. It was as good a car as any, even if it was a little bright, and she didn't have time to be picky. It wouldn't be long before someone noticed she was missing. And when they did, they'd call Matteo.

She climbed behind the wheel, set the gun on the passenger seat beside her, and stuffed the key into the ignition. As soon as she hit the button for the garage door, she started the engine, prepared to leave the second it opened wide enough to let her through.

All she had to do was convince her father she was still on his side, catch him by surprise long enough to kill him, and then plead her case to the only man who'd ever given a damn about her.

No big deal.

Chapter Thirty

"What I want is to know who the fuck cost me seven million in premium Columbian coke! Antonetti is smart, but he's not that smart. Are you really suggesting he covered his tracks so well on a last-minute op we can't find a single shred of proof it was him?"

"What I'm saying is I don't have anything concrete. Yet," Luca bit off.

"Or it wasn't Antonetti."

Luca scoffed. "Of course it was. Who the hell else could it be?"

Matteo had been asking himself that question for almost twenty-four hours. Every single angle they worked, every direction they looked, every contact they uncovered, none of it pointed back to Antonetti. They were running out of things to search and leads to tug.

As unflinchingly certain as Luca was that Antonetti had to be behind the attack in Bruges and Tessa was responsible for tipping him off, Maeve couldn't believe Tessa would do such a thing. Matteo was sure the truth lay somewhere in the gray area in between.

There was no denying Tessa had been in contact with her father. She herself admitted to it through all her tears and pleading. But it was becoming clear there was more to the story, and at some point, he was going to have to stop avoiding her and find out what the fuck it was.

"We could check the burner number we recovered from her phone records again."

"We've checked it a dozen times," Maeve said to Luca, sounding as annoyed as she looked. "Are you so intent on pinning it on her that you won't be satisfied until you find a way to make her guilty?"

"I haven't trusted her from the moment she crossed the threshold into my fucking house—and I was right, need I remind you."

"Oh, God forbid you forget to remind us you were right." Maeve rolled her eyes. "If she was feeding her father any kind of useful information, wouldn't he have held up better against us? The man's fallen like dominoes at every turn."

"Maybe," Luca snarled, "he was just luring us into a false sense of security. Trying to make us think we had the upper hand so we'd let our guard down. Or so Matteo would. Seems to me it worked."

"Enough, you two," Matteo said when Maeve scoffed. "I want to take a step back and make another pass at this. Remove Antonetti as the focus and use a broader net to search. See what we come up with."

"Sienna's working from home today, but I'll pull her in to help me."

The phone rang on Maeve's desk, and she jogged across Matteo's office to answer it, closing the door behind her and drowning out the sound of her voice.

"How's everything look for pushing the Antonetti sale through?"

"Good. We've got everything we need lined up and ready to go. Sienna suggested a paper trail that extended all the way back to before you came home."

"Makes sense."

"What are you going to do with her when this is all said and done?" Luca asked after a beat.

Matteo rubbed his eyes with his fingers and pinched the bridge of his nose. He'd been trying not to think about it. What he wanted to do was rewind his entire life and never agree to take her from her father's house. Better yet, to never have met her in the first damn place.

If he hadn't, he wouldn't want to both rage at and hold her every time he walked past the closed door to her room and heard her call his name. He wouldn't give a fuck what happened to her. But he had, and he did, and now he was stuck.

Because there was no good answer here. All roads ended with her gone. As much as he might love her, he didn't trust her. And he had no idea how to come back from that. Letting her go was the only option.

"I don't," Matteo said honestly. "First I want to deal with her father. Then I'll deal with her."

"You should—"

"I'm not in the mood for your opinion on this, Luca."

"If you'd listened to my opinion from the beginning, maybe we wouldn't be in this mess."

Matteo's lip curled back over his teeth. "I'm finished being lectured by you about this. You were right, brother. Is that what you want to hear? You were right, and I was wrong. Does that make you feel better?"

"That's not what I—"

"Don't bother. You and Dom both have been eager to take

me down a peg since I arrived. I guess you finally got your moment. Enjoy it. There won't be another one." Matteo swiveled back to his computer. "You can go."

Luca pushed to his feet at the same time Maeve poked her head back in. "Sorry for the interruption."

"We're finished," Matteo replied with a pointed look at Luca. He waited until Luca stormed out and motioned Maeve forward with a wave of his fingers. "Who was on the phone?"

"Belgian police. They wanted to speak with you, but I wasn't sure how you wanted to handle it, so I told them you were in a meeting."

"I spoke with Schmidt again this morning." Matteo tapped the end of his pen against the blotter on his desk. "He's not hearing any whispers that they think I'm involved. No blowback on your family either."

"Grandda's people in Brussels don't seem worried at all. I had a call from Callum yesterday and a text from Roarke. They're in agreement. Of all the problems this caused, it doesn't seem like the police will be one of them."

A relief. One less thing he needed to worry about. "I'll call the cops back when we're done here. What about the Spanish?"

Maeve cast her eyes to the ceiling, and Matteo swallowed a chuckle. "Sienna spoke to them, so if you want nuance, you should ask her, but they seemed stuck somewhere between not giving a shit because they'd already been paid and wanting to remind us they can choose to take their business elsewhere if their product isn't safe with us."

"Dramatic as always."

Maeve snorted her agreement. "Need some more time, or should I place a call to the Belgian police?"

Straightening, Matteo adjusted the cuffs of his shirt. "Might as well get it over with."

Maeve nodded, closing the door behind her again, and

within a few minutes, her voice came over the intercom to announce she had the officer on line two.

Taking a deep breath, he pressed the button to connect the call and put it on speaker. "This is Matteo Bianchi."

"Mr. Bianchi." A deep, gravelly voice filled the room. "My name is Oscar Mertens. I'm an officer with the General Directorate of the Judicial Police in Belgium. Do you have a minute to speak to me about the accident at your airport?"

"Of course. I'm just as eager as you are to find out who did this."

"I've spoken with a few of your associates. A man by the name of Roarke Kennedy who said he was a silent partner."

Matteo shook his head and bit off a wry chuckle. "Yes. We've worked together for years."

"He provided all the paperwork I need, and everything seems to check out. We have some preliminary thoughts on what happened, but I guess my big question for you is, do you know anyone who would do something like this to you? Any enemies, deals gone bad, disgruntled ex-employees. Things like that."

Shifting in his chair, Matteo leaned closer to the phone and wondered how much he might be able to get Mertens to divulge without being obvious about it.

"I suppose one is bound to make enemies at some point. But no one comes immediately to mind," he lied. "I've been trying to rack my brain on who in Sicily might want to hurt me like this, but I can't think of anyone."

"You think it might be someone local to you?"

The surprise was evident in the man's tone, and Matteo sat up straighter. "You don't think so?"

There was rustling on the other end of the line. "Does the name Clyde Stewart mean anything to you?"

Instantly Matteo snatched his phone off the desk and sent

Maeve a text asking her to listen in. He waited for the click that signaled her engaging the second line before speaking again.

"I sort of know a Clyde Stewart. We socialized in the same circles when I lived in Dublin for a few years."

"We have pretty solid evidence suggesting he's been casing the airport for a few weeks now. But nothing more concrete that would allow us to charge him with anything."

"I can't imagine what he would stand to gain from this."

That was a lie. Matteo could list three motives Stewart might have off the top of his head. And it wasn't trouble for him so much as the Quinns.

"Rest assured we're looking into this, and as soon as we know more, we'll be in touch."

"Thank you. I appreciate your hard work on this."

As soon as the call disconnected, his office door flew open so hard it bounced off the wall. "That son of a bitch! What the hell kind of game does Stewart think he's playing at?"

"He was pretty sour over the fact we cut him out of the last agreement."

"We cut him out because he was skimming off the top. Grandda isn't going to like this one bit."

"But you're going to enjoy telling him."

Maeve grinned, propping her hands on her hips. "Clyde Stewart and his smarmy sons have had it coming for a long time. Now they're going to finally get it, and I can't wait. You know what this really means, though."

"The Quinns are about to go on a rampage through Scotland?"

"Well, yes. They are that. But I meant about Tessa."

That dull ache whenever he thought about her seated itself back in his chest, and Matteo sat back in his chair with a huff. It was time he stopped avoiding the issue and actually spoke to her. See what she had to say for herself and if he could tell the lies from the truth this time.

"I'll speak to her tonight."

"Good," Maeve said with a decisive nod. "You should've done that two days ago."

Matteo's snarled response was cut short when Maeve disappeared from the doorway to answer the ringing phone. Everyone was a fucking critic. They wouldn't have to worry, though. Once he did whatever he ended up doing with Tessa, he would never let anyone get close enough to make him vulnerable to this kind of mistake ever again.

He would make the Mafia his sole focus. Eventually he'd arrange a marriage for himself, produce a couple of heirs. But he had time before he would be forced to do any of that. Time to close himself off the rest of the way and get Sicily and the Bianchi Corporation on its feet.

"Tessa's gone."

He glanced up at Maeve's wide eyes. "What do you mean, gone? Where the hell could she go?"

"That was Taglia on the phone. He went up to collect Tessa's lunch tray, and her room was empty. He said he can't find her anywhere."

Matteo shoved to his feet and grabbed his jacket, slipping it on as he headed for the elevator at a jog. Something foreboding slithered over him and wrapped around his throat, though he couldn't explain it. He should be pissed she'd figured out a way to outsmart his locked door, but the only emotion he could conjure up was worry.

Taglia was waiting for him at the courtyard gate when Matteo careened up the driveway and screeched to a halt.

"How the hell did she get out?"

"I'm not sure, *Il Signore*. But I think maybe with this." He held up a butter knife. "I found it on her bed with this note."

Matteo stopped short at the base of the stairs and snatched the note from Taglia's hand.

I'm supposed to meet with my father today. I'm going to prove to you I'm on your side. Or die trying.

Then there was an address on the bottom. Matteo crumpled the note in his fist and took the stairs two at a time, racing down the hall and around the corner to her room. It was empty, as Taglia said, her lunch tray untouched, the closet full of her clothes.

He crossed to her balcony doors and wrenched them open. It was too high up for her to jump, and there was nothing she could have used to climb down. There's no way she would have waltzed out the front door without being seen. If she had, everyone was getting fucking fired.

Turning to go back inside, he noticed his own balcony and the sweeping spiral stairs that led down to the grass. Cursing under his breath, he tore across the hall and into his own room. Sure enough, his balcony doors were unlatched, and the bottom drawer of his nightstand was open and empty. Clever.

"Are there any cars missing?"

Taglia looked at him with wide eyes. "I didn't… I haven't checked, *Il Signore*. I'm sorry."

Sprinting back down the stairs and out the door, Matteo was barely fighting his growing panic as he mashed the buttons on the garage's keypad. The door swung slowly open. Impatient, he dipped underneath it.

The Alfa Romeo was gone.

She'd snuck out of her room, taken his spare weapon, and stolen his car to go meet her father, but why? Luca would say it was to give him more information. But what else was there to give him? She'd been locked in her room without a way to communicate for two days.

Pulling his phone out of his pocket, he dialed Maeve. "Can you track the Alfa Romeo for me?"

"She took it? One second." The sound of tapping keys drifted over the line. "It's not far from the house. I'll ping the address to your phone. Matteo," she added before he could hang up, "I'm going send Luca to you as backup. Be careful, and don't do anything stupid."

Chapter Thirty-One

Tessa circled the block around the shop where she was supposed to meet her father for the fifth time. She didn't recognize any of the cars in the parking lot, didn't see her father waiting for her in the alley. He was late, and that wasn't like him.

Maybe Matteo had tipped him off, or her father knew she was compromised and decided not to show up. If that was the case, she was only making things worse with Matteo by sneaking out and going back with nothing to show for it.

Someone had probably realized she was missing by now, and the first thing they would have done was call Matteo. Matteo, who didn't trust her anymore, who had people like Luca whispering in his ear about how horrible she was. Luca might be right, but she was trying to make up for that now.

Assuming she got a chance to prove herself. It would be next to impossible if her father really wasn't coming.

On her next pass, she saw a familiar steel-gray sedan pull into the lot and park close to the mouth of the alley between the store and the restaurant next to it. Her father climbed out, a hat pulled low to hide his eyes, and hunched into his jacket to obscure more of his face.

Tessa frowned. Carina was right. Her father really was trying to lay low and avoid being recognized. Even on this side of the island, where people were less likely to be looking for him. She wasn't used to seeing him so cautious, his moves jerky while he scanned the parking lot.

Tomaso climbed out of the passenger side and moved to stand with their father, his blond hair dancing in the breeze. Tessa gritted her teeth at his presence. In eight years, she'd never once been able to get out from under his bastard shadow.

In another life, born to different parents, they might have had the opportunity to be as close as brother and sister. They were only two years apart. They could have had a relationship if her father would have allowed it, if Tessa didn't hold Tomaso's very existence at least partially to blame for her mother's disappearance.

Death. Her mother was dead. And now Tomaso was an added complication, the signature on her death warrant. There was no way she could walk away from this alive with Tomaso standing by her father's side.

Pulling the car around, she parked a few rows away from the sedan, securing the gun under her sweater. She willed her pounding heart to slow as she paced across the lot.

This would have been easier to manage if her father had come alone like she asked him to. She could have taken him by surprise then, put a bullet in him before he knew what was happening, and then take the proof of her loyalties back to Matteo.

Now she desperately needed a plan B.

Rubbing her sweating palms on the thighs of her jeans, she stepped into the alley's cavern and surveyed the narrow space blanketed entirely in shadows. A few paces away was a rusted dumpster, garbage bags piled as tall as the metal bin itself on one side. Rats scurried along the building's perimeter, and water dripped from a drainage pipe into a dirty puddle.

"You're late. I've been waiting almost twenty minutes," her father lied, making a show of checking his watch.

"It took me longer than I anticipated to get Matteo to agree to let me drive myself instead of being chauffeured. Sorry."

Well, at least they were both lying now.

"You said you had documents for me." He scanned her empty hands with a raised brow. "Where are they?"

Shit. In her mad rush to break out of her jail cell and sneak out, she'd totally forgotten she'd baited her father with documents that didn't exist. She didn't expect to ever actually need to produce any. If things hadn't gone so horribly wrong, it would be Matteo and his men confronting her father right now, taking him prisoner, killing him slowly.

"It was too much to carry. They're in the car."

Her father's eyes lit with greed, and he rubbed his hands together while Tomaso's gaze flicked to the parking lot at her back.

"And it's enough to end him?"

She shrugged. "In the right hands, I guess. His international contacts, some business deals, and a piece of property he owns in Belgium."

Waiting for some kind of recognition to spark in her father's eyes, Tessa cocked her head when there was nothing. So her father probably wasn't even the one who attacked Matteo in Belgium.

"Excellent. Let's get this over with then, I—"

"What happens to me once I give you Matteo?"

He sighed loudly, flicking an irritated glance at Tomaso, who wouldn't even make eye contact with her.

"You'll come home, of course. I've arranged some better matches for you this time around."

"That's it? After all this, my reward is to come back to the very life I was trying to escape from?"

"Don't be greedy, Tessa. I'll give you your mother back, as I said, but I need some stronger ties to an ally than money can buy after what Matteo has done to me. And this one will drag you kicking and screaming down the aisle if he has to."

She shoved down the rising anger when he mentioned her mother. That he would still use her as a bargaining chip when they both knew she was gone. Death really would be the only way to ever escape from him. His or hers, did it even make a difference who at this point?

Shaking her head, she took a step back, hands clenched into fists at her sides.

"I hate you." The words were a whisper almost lost on the wind, but there was no less venom in them.

His grin was sharp, and he took a step forward. "What would you prefer? I leave you with the Bianchis and let them kill you instead? Let you get caught in the crosshairs?" He dismissed the notion with a wave of his hand.

"At least Matteo would kill me quickly," she spat.

The idea of dying by Matteo's hand twisted sharply in her chest, but anything would be preferable to a slow wasting away over decades married to a man her father had chosen only because it afforded him the wealth and power he thought he deserved.

He leapt forward, gripping her by the throat and shoving her up against the wall of the alley, the gun digging into the small of her back.

"Is that what you want? A quick death?" He squeezed, satisfied when she coughed and sputtered.

"Fuck you," she said through clenched teeth.

His grip tightened painfully, cutting off her air, and he

leaned in until their noses were nearly touching. When her vision wavered, she dug her fingernails into the stone wall at her back. If he was going to kill her right now, at least it would all be over. At least she'd finally get to see her mother again.

A single tear slipped free, and her father grinned, releasing her and taking a step back.

"If you weren't worth something to me, you'd already be dead. You're mine until you cease to be useful. Until then, I need you very much alive. Now stop wasting my time and give me the documents," he demanded. "I have better things to do than stand here and listen to you whine."

She took a deep breath, swallowing around the rough ache in her throat. Sliding her hand around to the small of her back, she wrapped her fingers around the butt of the gun. This was as good a moment as any. Even if Tomaso killed her, at least her father would be dead too.

And Tomaso was no match for Matteo. The Bianchis would hunt him down and truly put an end to the Antonetti name forever.

Her heartbeat pounded through her ears, time slowing as she gripped the gun tighter in her fist. One shot in the center of his chest. That's all she needed, and then, whatever happened to her, her father would be dead and it would all be over for good.

"Father." Tomaso shifted on his feet, tilting his head as he studied the area behind them.

"What?" Salvatore snapped, looking from Tessa to his son.

"That's the tenth time the same black SUV has driven past us."

Tessa's head jerked up, eyes scanning the parking lot. She didn't see Matteo's car, but that didn't mean he wasn't doing another loop and looking for his best way in. Had he come for her? And if he had, who was he here to punish?

"You told Matteo you were coming?" Her father took a menacing step forward, and she shook her head.

"Of course not. Don't you think he'd have attacked long before now if I had? It's probably not even the same car. Lots of black SUVs on this island."

Tomaso's lip curled back over his teeth. "I know what I saw, bitch."

"Enough," her father barked when Tessa opened her mouth to reply. "Give him your keys, Tessa."

"What?"

He backhanded her across the face, and she stumbled into the wall, cupping her cheek and ringing ear. "Give your brother the goddamn car keys so he can get the information and I can get the fuck out of here."

Tessa let out a hissing breath through tight lips and dug the keys from her pocket, placing them in Tomaso's outstretched hand. She hoped it really was Matteo out there circling the lot. Because if not, she was cutting off her only means of escape once she shot her father.

"They're in the trunk. Under some blankets."

Tomaso turned and strode quickly from the alley, twirling the keys around his finger. And as soon as they were alone, Tessa kicked her foot into her father's kneecap. As he collapsed against the far wall, she pulled the gun from the waistband of her jeans and aimed it at his chest.

Chapter Thirty-Two

Matteo pulled into the parking lot in front of the address Maeve had sent him, the same one Tessa had left on the bottom of her note, and backed into the shade of a large tree. The Alfa was here but empty, and he hadn't spotted Tessa in any of his rotations.

Luca was on his way, but he was across town in the wrong direction. And he knew from Carina that Tessa had arranged to meet with her father. A lure, she'd called it. A lure for who was the question.

In the last forty-eight hours, pinning Antonetti down had been impossible. His behavior had become more frenzied and erratic. It had been harder to predict his movements and make sense of where he might go next.

They'd assumed he was laying low after the hit in Belgium, but now Matteo knew better. Antonetti was trying to shake any tails so no one would know he was planning on being in Palermo today. Close enough to take out. He'd succeeded.

That pissed him off almost as much as Tessa being here to meet with him. Her note insisted she was trying to prove her loyalty, but every word out of her mouth had been a lie since the first moment he met her. This could just as easily be a trap as it could be her attempt to help.

Still, there was a part of him that didn't want to take the chance that she might be on his side and willingly putting herself in danger. Even with the gun she'd taken from his room, she was hardly a match for her father and his callousness.

Climbing out of the vehicle, he crept along the low stone wall separating the lot from the road, ducking down behind a car when Tomaso appeared at the mouth of the alley and jogged toward the Alfa Romeo.

When Tomaso rounded the trunk of the car, his back to the rear of the parking lot, Matteo closed the distance between them in quick strides, unholstering the gun at his back and carrying it low against his thigh.

Tomaso wasn't paying attention as he unlocked the trunk of the car. Matteo had his arm around the kid's shoulders and the gun pressed to his temple before Tomaso even registered his presence.

"You're a long way from home," Matteo said, voice low.

"Just came here to get what was promised to us."

"Yeah? And what was that?"

"My sister isn't quite what she seems." Tomaso grinned. "Did you enjoy fucking a traitor, Bianchi?"

He pressed the gun harder into the kid's temple. "What did she bring you?"

"Documents. To end you."

Documents? Where the fuck would Tessa get hard copies of documents? He kept most of that shit at his office or locked in the study. Occasionally he'd bring work to bed, but he'd been doing that less and less since she stopped sleeping across the hall. And even when he did, it was financial reports and other boring shit for the clubs or casinos. There was no way she'd brought them anything of value.

"Then look for it." Matteo loosened his hold, gesturing with the muzzle of the gun but keeping it aimed at Tomaso. "Go on."

Tomaso tossed around blankets and tools for changing a tire and an emergency roadside kit from side to side. There was some trash. But no documents. Tessa had lured them here with the promise of a silver bullet, but she'd brought nothing. The perfect opportunity for her to betray him to her father, and she wasn't. Relief flooded him, and he wrapped his arm around Tomaso's shoulders again, yanking the boy back against his chest.

"Looks like I'm not the one being played here. Get in."

Tomaso scoffed in a way that sounded exactly like his father and jerked against Matteo's hold. "I'm not getting in the trunk of a fucking car. You'll have to kill me," he said with all the bravado of a kid who'd never faced down death before.

"I'd love to."

"Just know that as soon as my father hears the shot, your little whore is dead."

Holstering his weapon, Matteo leaned in to murmur against Tomaso's ear. "Unfortunately for you, I've learned a thing or two from my siblings. Like my brother's favorite way to kill. It's very personal. And very quiet."

Gripping Tomaso's jaw in his hands, Matteo quickly twisted at a sharp angle until he heard a faint pop, and Tomaso collapsed. He caught the boy under the arms and shoved him in the trunk to keep his body out of sight. He'd clean up that particular mess later.

Glancing up at the dark rectangle of the alley, he slammed the trunk closed and palmed his weapon, careful to give the alley a wide berth so they didn't see him coming. Eventually

Salvatore would put it together that Tomaso wasn't coming back, and Matteo needed to figure out a plan before that happened. A plan that didn't involve putting Tessa in the line of fire, if at all possible.

Pulling his phone out of his pocket, he sent Luca a quick text with instructions to advance from the street side of the alley. They could take Salvatore by surprise that way, and Matteo might still manage to salvage the accidental death he wanted. Luca responded with his ETA. Ten minutes.

Edging along the side of the building toward the mouth of the alley, Matteo froze when he heard voices. They sounded closer and clearer than he anticipated.

"What are you going to do, girl? Shoot me?" Salvatore chuckled. "You don't have the fucking nerve."

"Are you sure about that, Father?" Tessa asked, tone cold and mocking. "I've killed before. I think I'll especially enjoy watching you take your last breath."

He gave a derisive laugh. "Who could you possibly have killed?"

"You're always underestimating me. When your little hired hitman didn't come home, didn't you wonder what happened to him?"

"And you expect me to believe you're the one who killed him?" Salvatore scoffed.

"You don't have to believe me," she replied. "That doesn't make it any less true. I'm the one who stopped your plot to kill Sienna Gallo. I'm the one who gave Matteo your contact in Spain."

"You little cunt," Salvatore snarled.

"Don't move, you son of a bitch. Or I will shoot you."

"Please," her father said. "If you were going to shoot me, you would have done it already. But you can't, because you're weak like your mother was."

"Why did you kill her?"

Matteo's fingers tightened on the butt of his gun at the pain in her words.

"What? She's not dead," Salvatore insisted. "You demanded proof of life before you would give me anything else, and I gave it to you. You spoke to her."

"I spoke to someone. But it wasn't my mother."

"I don't have time for this, Tessa. You're trying my patience."

"I just want to know why."

Salvatore sighed like the entire conversation was boring him. "She didn't want my heir in the house. And I didn't have much use for a bitch who wouldn't follow orders. Satisfied now?"

"Go to hell."

At the sound of a shot, Matteo rounded the side of the building, weapon raised. Antonetti had blood dripping down his arm from a wound in his shoulder, and Tessa held the gun out in front of her with shaking fingers.

Her father lunged at her, noticing Matteo at the last moment and causing Tessa to look over, her eyes widening in surprise. It was enough of a distraction for her father to disarm her, grabbing her by the hair and yanking her back against his chest, gun pressed tight to her temple.

"Careful, boy. Or I'll blow her brains all over the wall."

"Do it then." She laughed, low and dark. "You've been threatening me for so long. Do it."

"Shut up," he barked, yanking her head back until she stopped struggling.

"I'm not afraid of death or of you. Not anymore. You've already taken everything from me. My mother, Matteo, any kind of chance at happiness I might have had. Might as well take my life too."

"I said shut up, you little fucking cunt."

"Hell of a way to talk to your own daughter." Matteo met

Tessa's resigned gaze, and it arrowed straight through him. She wasn't allowed to give up yet. He wasn't finished with her. "You went to a lot of trouble to slip a spy into my house to give her up so easily."

"It's not like she was very useful. Too busy on her knees for you to be much help to me. Apparently she didn't want her mother back bad enough." Antonetti pressed the gun harder against her head, and she shrank away from him.

"Her dead mother."

A tear slipped down Tessa's cheek, and her body jerked.

"Yes, yes. Her mother is dead. But *she* didn't know that." He gestured to Tessa. "In the end, though, she was just as big of a disappointment as I suspected. And after all the trouble I went to to find someone who sounded just like my Eliana."

"Next time find a better whore," Tessa spat, gasping when her father tightened his hold on her neck.

"You always were too much trouble." Salvatore tsked. "Couldn't pay men to marry you, couldn't get you to keep your mouth shut, couldn't bribe you to finally be useful for once in your life."

"My apologies for being such a burden to you. Why didn't you kill me when you killed my mother?"

"Because I wanted to sell you. I didn't realize you'd drive such a hard bargain with this fucking mouth." Salvatore gripped her chin in his hand and squeezed while she fought against his hold.

"You think he'd enjoy watching you die?" A wicked grin spread over Salvatore's face, and he looked between them. "You lied to him, after all. He's here to kill me, and since I suspect he's already killed your brother, he'll get his wish. But it might be fun for him to watch you die first."

Tessa blew out a shaky breath, her eyes meeting Matteo's and darting away. He hated that look in her eyes, like she was ready for death. Like she expected him to enjoy watching it.

He didn't care if she was ready or not; he wasn't prepared to let her go. They had too many things to discuss, to mend.

"The only person dying here today is you," Matteo said. "Because she's mine."

Salvatore barked out a laugh, pressing his cheek to Tessa's temple. "Oh, he wants you all to himself. Your blood on his hands only. Or maybe he'll pass you around to his men first, let his enforcer have you. Alexei's skills with a blade are legend on this island."

"Let her go, and I'll kill you quickly." Matteo's eyes darted over Salvatore's shoulder when he caught sight of a shadow moving along the wall, but Salvatore didn't seem to notice.

"Or"—Salvatore shifted Tessa in front of his body like a shield and tightened his grip on her neck until she clawed at his forearm, her lips turning blue—"I'll shoot her so you can't have her. Yeah. I might enjoy that more."

Luca raced forward in a blur, driving the butt of his gun against Antonetti's temple so hard his eyes rolled back in his head. When his grip loosened enough that Tessa could wrench herself free, she fell to the ground, crawling away on her hands and knees while she coughed and sobbed.

Antonetti spun to face Luca, but his steps faltered, and he swayed on his feet from the blow. Another hit and Antonetti fell to his knees before slumping forward onto his chest. Luca bent to retrieve the discarded gun and tucked it into his waistband.

"Why the fuck didn't you just shoot him?" Matteo demanded.

Luca shrugged. "You said you wanted it to look like an accident. I figured this gave us options. Alexei and Berto should be here any minute to help us take him back to the casino."

Nodding, Matteo crossed to where Tessa sat on the ground, staring at all three of them. When he crouched next to her, she immediately scrambled away from him, flinching when he reached out to wipe away the blood her father had smeared across her cheek.

"If you're going to kill me, I would prefer not to be tortured first. Just…" She cast a furtive glance at Luca. "As much as you might enjoy a slow death, just make it quick."

Another black SUV pulled up to the mouth of the alley, blocking out most of the sun and casting long shadows over them.

She scooted further away at the sight of Alexei, pressing her back against the cold stone wall. Matteo pushed to his feet and took several steps back, keeping a close eye on Tessa. She didn't look like she would bolt, with her arms wrapped tight around her legs, but he didn't want to take any chances.

"What did I miss?" Alexei wondered, eyeing Tessa while Berto bound Antonetti's wrists and ankles.

"I'll explain later," Matteo said. "Take him back to the casino and do whatever you want to him." Tessa grunted her approval, and his lips twitched into a grin. "Just remember it needs to look like an accident."

"Sure thing," Alexei agreed, eyes gleaming with anticipation as they shoved Antonetti's body into the waiting SUV and sped away.

"Luca, you can meet me back at the house. I'll deal with this." He gestured to Tessa.

Luca gave them both a long look before ultimately nodding and turning to head back toward the other end of the alley. When they were alone, Matteo reached down to help Tessa to her feet, sliding his arm around her waist when she tried to move away from him.

"You're safe, *piccola*," he assured her. "I'm not going to hurt you."

She studied him for a moment, eyes filling with tears while she sized him up. "I didn't tell him about the airport."

"I know," Matteo said softly. "Your father wasn't even the one who attacked me in Belgium. A different enemy with a different vendetta."

Tessa nodded slowly. "I was going to tell you everything. About my mother, the deal I made with him, all of it. I waited up for you to come back from Rome so I could tell you. And I…"

Her breath hitched, and she pressed her lips together. "I fell asleep. Then everything happened so fast and… I'm sorry, Matteo. When I said yes to him, I thought my mother was still alive. I wanted to believe she was. Whether you believe me or not, that's the truth," she added, staring at a point over his shoulder.

Matteo trailed his fingertip along the line of her jaw to her chin, tilting her head back until she made eye contact. "I believe you. What changed your mind? About helping him."

Tessa trembled in his grip, and he ran a soothing hand up and down her back. "I never wanted to help him. All I ever wanted was what I told you from the beginning."

"Your mother back."

She nodded. "I should have known he didn't have her."

"I should have let you explain."

"I understand why you didn't. I'm not sure I would have done much differently if I was in your shoes."

"You lured him here."

"I did. I didn't get a chance to tell you my master plan."

"You shouldn't have come today. He could have killed you." The idea constricted his throat and made it difficult to breathe.

"Did you get my note?"

He nodded, brushing her hair back from her face and cupping her jaw in his hands.

"Prove I'm on your side or die trying. That's what I was trying to do." She captured her bottom lip between her teeth and slowly released it. "You were the one thing I didn't count on when I said yes to my father."

"Me?"

Her arms circled his waist, fingers gripping the fabric of his suit jacket. "I never meant to fall in love with you. I'll understand if you're done with me. If you can never trust me after what happened. I'll leave, and you never have to see me again. But I had to—"

"Tessa." He ran a thumb over her lips to silence her. "You're not leaving, because I meant what I said too. You're mine." He brushed a kiss over her lips. "Forever."

Chapter Thirty-Three

Standing in front of the tall mirror in the corner of the large walk-in closet, Tessa smoothed a nervous hand over the skirt of her simple black dress. She'd pinned her hair up off her face but left most of it down as Carina suggested. She'd kept her makeup simple and understated, as Sienna suggested. And she'd worn black to strike the right somber and serious note, as Emilia suggested.

"We have to leave soon, *piccola*," Matteo called from the bedroom.

Tessa's eyes dropped to the pearls around her neck. In all the years she'd had her mother's pearls sitting in her closet, she'd never once actually put them on. Running her fingertips over the small orbs, the corner of her mouth ticked up in a sad smile. Having a little bit of her mother with her today would help just as much as having Matteo by her side.

They still hadn't found concrete proof her mother was dead. But her father's confession in the alley that he'd killed her, coupled with his desperate attempts to use the location of her mother's body as a bargaining chip while they tortured him, was enough. She didn't realize how much harder the grieving process would be the second time.

Matteo stepped into the doorway, leaning his shoulder against the frame as he watched her.

"You look perfect."

She took in the A-line dress with its modest neckline and long sleeves one more time. Slipping into a pair of black wedge pumps, she looked at him in the mirror.

"Are you sure you really want to do this?"

He moved to stand at her back, trailing his fingertips down her arm and lacing their fingers together. "I'm sure."

"What if no one believes me?"

Pressing a kiss to her shoulder and then to the side of her neck, he led her from the closet and turned off the light. "They believed you at the funeral. Your performance was excellent."

She hadn't asked for details about how her father died. She knew only what they printed in the paper about the acci-dent that was so horrible they needed to have a closed casket service. His suffering was all that mattered to her, and Alexei assured her Salvatore Antonetti died weeping and begging for mercy. Hopefully he was enjoying his time in hell.

Playing the part of the grieving daughter had been a struggle, but Carina's tips and the ability to hide behind a lace mourning veil helped. She would not feel sorry for her father's death or the part she played in it. No matter how many people apologized for the loss.

"The funeral was a little different," she reminded him, letting him take her hand and following him into the hall. "I just had to stand there and look sad. This is something else entirely."

"It's a small statement to the press about the sale, your father's wishes for the company's future. You'll be fine. And we'll be with you."

They stopped at the elevator, where the rest of the family already waited in their own somber black clothes. The men in suits, the women in dresses with high necklines and long hems.

Tessa had spent a lot of time in the month since her father's death earning their trust. Whatever hoops she had to jump through, whatever tests they wanted to dish out, she would do them all. Whatever it took to prove she was with them and not against.

They were slow to warm, but they seemed to be coming around. Just last week, Carina asked Tessa about her opinion on linens for the wedding. It was nice to be included among the Bianchi women to plan a celebration, even for something as small as the color of the napkins and size of the tablecloths.

The only one who seemed less than willing to give her a second chance was Luca. It didn't matter how hard she tried; the man wouldn't make eye contact with her, let alone have a conversation.

Sienna swore he'd come around eventually, but Tessa wasn't so sure. And she didn't want to think about what the future might be like if she'd irreparably damaged the relationship between Matteo and his brother.

Matteo gave her hand a squeeze and pushed the button to call the elevator. They'd flown into Rome the day before and stayed in her father's flagship hotel for this press conference Matteo had arranged. Camera crews and reporters gathered in the lobby's soaring atrium. A perfect backdrop for a grieving daughter to talk about the future.

Then Matteo and Laurent would sign some paperwork, shake hands, and Antonetti Hotel Group would belong to the Bianchi Corporation. Simple as that.

The elevator doors opened on a lobby already buzzing with noise and the whirring click of camera shutters. Tessa swallowed around the lump in her throat, fingers tight on the elevator's railing and Matteo's hand.

"Come on, *piccola*," Matteo murmured, peeling her fingers free from the metal bar. "You can do this. Just read the prepared remarks and take a few questions."

"You should do it," she said, hating the tremble in her voice.

Matteo chuckled in her ear and brushed his lips over her temple. "It'll make more sense coming from you."

Tessa peeked around the corner, her heart thundering in her chest. "I don't think I can go out there alone."

"You're not alone," Carina said from behind them. "We're all here standing with you."

"It'll be easier than you think," Sienna assured her. "And over before you know it."

With a nod and a fortifying breath, Tessa stepped around Matteo, grateful for his firm hand on the small of her back, and crossed the expanse of marble to the podium set up with microphones. Cameras flashed, and reporters mumbled into digital recorders.

"Thank you all for coming today. As many of you know, my father, Salvatore Antonetti, was killed in a terrible accident a few weeks ago. He died before he could finish a deal he was very excited about."

Catching Matteo's eye, she took a deep, steadying breath at his reassuring nod. "The Antonetti Hotel Group was my father's life's work, but he was ready to move on to other adventures in his retirement. Sadly, the adventures he shared with me will only live on in my memories, but I can honor his other wish. The sale of Antonetti Hotel Group to Matteo Bianchi and the Bianchi Corporation."

She waited for Matteo to step up next to her at the podium, smiling at Laurent, who also watched from the sidelines. "I am proud to place my father's legacy into such capable hands. And I'm excited to see the future of Antonetti Hotel Group take shape under new leadership."

Hands shot up, and she pointed to the people Matteo had strategically placed in the media pool to ask the questions he wanted asked and stay away from the ones he didn't. Like why Tomaso wasn't here.

They'd sent him to Canada for school. At least on paper. Tessa was worried someone would eventually ask the right questions or try to track him down, but Sienna, Matteo, and even Maeve assured her that because he had no living relatives, people would eventually forget he ever existed. It was best to let him fade into the background.

Once all the questions were answered, documents signed, and hands shaken, the press began to break down their big lights and pack up their cameras. Tessa sagged against Matteo's side, feeling like she'd just run two marathons back to back without water.

"You were wonderful," Carina said, giving Tessa's shoulder a squeeze.

"You really were," Emilia agreed. "I'd have been a nervous wreck."

"I only almost passed out the one time."

"Hungry?" Sienna wondered.

"I could use a glass of wine or five," Tessa admitted.

Sienna chuckled. "I made a reservation for lunch. I've heard their wine list is quite good, so I don't think you'll be disappointed."

"You made a reservation for lunch? Why?"

Luca's frown lightened when Sienna raised an unamused brow. "Because Carina asked me to, and because being seen as a family right now is a good idea."

"And I wanted to try their prawn risotto," Carina added, grinning when Alexei laughed.

"You can stay here and pout," Sienna said, turning for the lobby entrance.

"Sienna," Luca said, reaching for her hand.

"You will have to get past it eventually, *amore*." Sienna looked from Luca to Tessa and back again. "Lunch without you pouting the whole time will be a lovely start."

"I do not pout," Luca insisted, the rest of their conversation trailing off as he followed Sienna across the lobby and through the revolving door.

"Any other objections?" Carina met each person's gaze in turn. Satisfied, she looped her arm through Alexei's and skirted the dwindling crowd to the door.

They filed out to the sidewalk, waiting patiently by the valet stand as all the SUVs were brought around. Matteo waved them all into the cars until they were the only two left.

"Is walking to the restaurant another one of my punishments?"

"Punishments? Who's been punishing you?"

She sent him a pointed look. "All of Luca's little tests. It's like he's trying to constantly catch me in a lie."

"I'll talk to him," Matteo promised.

"You won't." Tessa shook her head. "You won't, Matteo. If this is the price I have to pay to earn his trust, I'll pay it. Promise me you won't say anything to him."

He looked as if he was about to argue with her, but he ultimately sighed and nodded. "I promise. For now. But if it's not better in two weeks, I'm saying something to him."

"Two months," she countered.

"One month."

"Deal." She grinned, pushing onto her tiptoes to brush a kiss over his lips. "Now. Why are we still standing here?"

"Because." A sleek black town car rolled to a stop in front of them, and the valet stepped forward to open the rear door. "I wanted a minute alone with you."

"You rented a car just so we could drive alone to lunch together?"

"Among other things," he said, helping her in and sliding in behind her, pressing the button for the intercom to speak to the driver. "Drive in circles until I tell you to stop."

"In circles?"

The door closed, plunging them into shadows, and Matteo wrapped an arm around her waist, hauling her up against his side. Cupping her face in his hand, he tilted her head back and claimed her lips, teasing his tongue and then his teeth over her lower lip until she groaned softly.

When his hand wandered to her breast, squeezing firmly and making her shudder, she leaned back, hands braced on his chest. "Matteo, I've never—"

He growled, yanking her into his lap and grinding his thigh against her core as he kissed her again. "I love it when you say that to me. I want all your firsts and your lasts to be mine, Tessa. And we're adding this to the list."

"Matteo." She held his hands against her thighs when he started to push her dress up to her hips. "I am not having sex with you in a car with someone in the front seat."

He sighed. Leaning forward to give her a quick kiss, he punched the button for the intercom again. "Pull over." His fingers toyed with the hem of her dress and the exposed skin of her knee as the car left asphalt for gravel and came to a stop. "Get out," he commanded.

Light briefly flooded the car, and then it went dark again. "Better?"

"How's that better? He's right outside and knows exactly what we're about to do!"

Matteo grinned, slipping his hand between her thighs and rubbing two fingers over her clit through her panties. "The clerks at the boutique knew what we were doing in the dressing room. So did the flight attendant on our way to and from Paris. And you didn't seem to care about that."

She rocked against his fingers, capturing her bottom lip between her teeth. "In my defense, you were very distracting."

"Allow me to distract you again."

Slipping her panties to the side, he slid his finger up the length of her slit, rubbing circles over her clit. Hips jerking, Tessa rocked against his hand, making him grin. Circling her entrance, he thrust a finger deep inside her, using his thumb to maintain pressure on her clit.

"Fuck."

"I will," he promised. "But I want you to come on my fingers first."

"We're going to be late," she panted as he added a second finger and pumped them in and out, faster and deeper each time she clenched around him.

"They can get started without us. You're not leaving this car until you come on my fingers and my cock."

Digging her nails into his neck, Tessa rocked her hips in time with the thrust of his fingers, shuddering each time he dragged his thumb roughly over her clit. The man was insatiable, incorrigible, and she would never get enough of him. Of the way he touched her, the way he wanted her, the way he loved her. Deeply, passionately, possessively.

She belonged to him and he belonged to her, and in moments like this one, nothing else mattered.

"Be a good girl and come for me, *piccola*," he murmured, working his fingers in and out faster, eyes locked on her face.

"Yes," she breathed, shuddering when he curled his fingers up and brushed against her G-spot.

Over and over until her thighs quivered and her heart raced. And when her orgasm washed over her, she sobbed his name.

"That's my good girl." He peppered kisses along her jaw and down the column of her throat. "So beautiful. So perfect." He undid the belt and zipper of his suit pants, freeing his cock and palming it roughly. "All mine."

"Matteo."

"Say it," he insisted, repositioning her on his lap so her back was to his chest and the head of his cock dragged along her slit.

"I'm all yours," she replied, gasping when he drove the full length of his cock inside her with one thrust.

"Forever," he growled in her ear, squeezing her breasts through her dress as he fucked her hard and fast.

"Matteo," Tessa whimpered, rocking her hips against each thrust, every inch of her skin on fire.

"Rub your clit, *piccola*. I want to feel you come hard all over me."

Releasing his forearm, she slid her hand down her stomach and under the hem of her dress, groaning when her fingertips grazed the sensitive bud.

"That's it. Make that pussy come while I fuck you. Faster."

She swiped her fingers over her clit in rough, quick circles, keeping time with his brutally deep thrusts. He pushed her closer and closer to the edge until she couldn't think about anything other than the way he touched her, the way he felt inside her, the sound of his breath in her ear.

And when her pussy contracted around him, he drove deep and emptied himself inside her.

Wrapping his arms around her waist, Matteo pressed his forehead against her shoulder. "Check the backseat of a car off the list."

She laughed softly, giving his arm a playful slap. "You're keeping a list?"

Pulling out, he adjusted her panties back into place and shifted her onto the seat beside him before tucking himself back into his pants. "Absolutely. I'll show it to you when we get home. Maybe you can add some suggestions."

Chuckling and shaking her head, Tessa righted her dress and ran a hand through her hair to smooth any tangles. Once she was situated, Matteo leaned across her and knocked on the window. The driver slid behind the wheel as if nothing had happened and pulled back onto the road.

"You know," she said, leaning against Matteo's side when he wrapped an arm around her shoulders. "I have always wanted to have sex in a pool."

"Have you?" He grinned down at her, a challenging glint in his eye.

Tessa shrugged. "I saw it in a movie once."

"That actually was not on my list. But as soon as the weather is warm enough and the pool is opened, we're checking that one off."

"What about the rest of them?"

"We've got a lifetime to get to all your firsts, *piccola*." He pressed a lingering kiss to her lips. "And I plan to savor every one."